PRAISE FOR HILARY DARTT

The Dating Intervention

"It was very hilarious, had loads of funny accidents and still had a way of being sincere and romantic … I also liked how much it was based around friendship, which added a nice, fresh take on a romance story. This is easily a five-star read."

NATURAL BRI BLOG

The Marriage Intervention

"This was a great sequel. I tend to like the first book the best of any trilogy but this second book was even better than the first! A feel-good read that actually had me crying at the end!"

KATY MESSARE

The Motherhood Intervention

"This book was a heart breaker but full of spirit. I loved it. I loved how the relationships evolved, fell apart, and came back stronger than ever. Pass me a vodka cranberry, please, and a box of tissue."

AMANDA THOMAS

ALSO BY HILARY DARTT

The Intervention Series

The Dating Intervention

The Motherhood Intervention

The Garden Club Series

Jasmine's Pact

Studying Sequoia

Just Holly

The Seedling Homestead Series

The Composition of Order

The Architecture of Vision

The Structure of Perfection

THE MARRIAGE INTERVENTION

BOOK TWO IN THE INTERVENTION SERIES

HILARY DARTT

ISBN: 978-1-950335-03-9

CHAPTER ONE

Sharing a secret can bind people together. Keeping one can tear people apart.

Josie Garcia had kept her own secret folded into the recesses of her memory for the past six years. But things change, and recent developments had forced her to begin unwrapping it, revealing it layer by layer until it stood directly in the spotlight.

Now, she turned her secret over and over in her mind as if it were a precious gem.

Rowdy's Saloon buzzed with activity on this Thursday night. College kids in trendy skinny jeans and beanie caps sipped beers with a practiced nonchalance while basketball games played on a half-dozen TV screens above the bar. The after-work crowd trickled in, and men and women in smart suits drank cocktails and ate pub mix, laughing loudly at jokes too inappropriate for water cooler conversation.

When Josie realized her two best friends, Summer Gray and Delaney Collins, were practically boring holes in her with their eyes from their respective spots at their usual high top table, she tucked that gem safely into the back of her mind and smiled, first at Summer and then at Delaney.

"What?" she said, going for casual.

Delaney picked up her beer, but instead of drinking it, she pointed it at Josie.

"What're you thinking about?"

Her offhand tone contrasted the intensity of her stare. Although Josie was tempted to look away, she gazed back at Delaney.

"Nothing," she answered in a tone she hoped matched her friend's.

"You're a terrible liar, Josie," Summer said.

This time, Josie looked down, into the depths of her vodka cranberry. The half-melted ice cubes shifted, catching the twinkling lights draped along the ceiling at Rowdy's. They reminded her of gems, of the secret she wasn't supposed to be thinking about. She sighed.

"I was thinking about Paul," she lied, knowing they'd believe her.

"What about him?" Summer asked.

"Oh, you know." They didn't, so she added, "Just hoping he stays safe tonight."

That, at least, was the truth. As an undercover cop, Paul's evenings often comprised drug deals and takedowns, shifty, knife-wielding felons and thousands of dollars in cash.

Summer reached across the table and put her hand on Josie's arm.

"You know I'm kind of psychic," she said. "My gut says he'll be fine."

Josie smiled at her, but it was half-hearted.

"This is our weekly Happy Hour," she said. "We should be talking about happy things. I know you quit working here, Delaney, but do you think you could go mix me another drink?"

Delaney laughed. "I'm pretty sure it's still against policy, but I'll go up and order you one."

Summer sighed with contentment as she and Josie watched Delaney approach the bar.

"She's so much happier now," she said. "I am so glad The Dating Intervention worked."

"That was a stroke of genius on our part," Josie said, nodding and raising her empty glass in a toast. "It really was."

Summer clinked her water glass against Delaney's. "We should have taken over her life years ago."

"Definitely," Josie said. "But it's all about timing, too. I don't think she was quite ready for a great job and a great guy before the Intervention."

Delaney returned, Josie's drink in hand. She set the glass on the table and Summer pinned Josie with The Look.

"All right, sister," she said. "You've got your refill. What's going on in that pretty head of yours?"

Josie thought of her secret. She thought of Delaney, still in that new-relationship dream state with Jake Rhoades. She thought of Summer, madly in love with her husband Derek, expecting their fifth child. How could they possibly understand?

"Okay. I'll spill," she said.

Instead of telling the truth, she decided, she would tell *a* truth. It wasn't like she was lying. She was simply keeping a secret. Even as these thoughts rushed through her mind, she chastised herself for finding a loophole. Summer and Delaney had been her best friends for more than twenty years. Since junior high, when they dubbed themselves The Milkshake Sisters. They were thirty-four now. Adults. Surely she could tell them. Again, she sighed. She'd promised to keep a secret, and she always kept her promises.

"It's Paul," she said.

The girls looked at her sympathetically. Summer, who had just popped another green olive into her mouth (she always ate them during pregnancy), nodded. Delaney's forehead crinkled in concern.

"I think we're on the brink of divorce."

It was almost comical the way both of her friends' mouths dropped open in surprise. They glanced quickly at each other, and then looked at Josie again.

"What?" Delaney said. "You're kidding, right?"

"I'm sure you can work it out," Summer said. "Right? I mean, can't you? What's going on?"

"Wait," Delaney said. "How did it get to this point without us knowing about it?"

"Well, admittedly, we've both been a bit distracted," Summer said to Delaney. "You with Jake and the new job, and me with the band and the pregnancy. I feel terrible about this, Josie. Really bad. What's going on?"

"The truth is," Josie began, pausing when she felt the unfamiliar pressure of tears in her throat and behind her eyes. "Things are really, really bad."

When neither Summer nor Delaney spoke, Josie continued. "I never see Paul anymore. I mean, hardly ever. We're never home at the same time, and when we are, he's distracted. Not just watching-basketball-and-eating-chips distracted, but, like, thinking about drug deals and drug dealers and answering calls from informants distracted. And he's so angry. He's angry all the time."

Summer put her hand on Josie's arm again. The gesture was supposed to be soothing, but Josie didn't miss the quick look Summer and Delaney exchanged—again.

Delaney licked her lips in that way she always did when she was nervous. She inhaled quickly, as if she wanted to say something, and then she pressed her lips together as if to hold the words in.

"Spill it, Collins," Josie said, knowing Delaney would cave if she put her on the spot.

Summer's hand slinked back to its own side of the table. She entwined it with the other hand. Josie had no idea what she was looking at. A spot on the table, maybe? A water droplet on her napkin?

"Well?" Josie said to Delaney.

"It's just that, well, you know, Josie, you've been kind of, um, a bit, you know … a little help, here, Summer?"

Summer's eyes met Josie's. "I'll give it to you straight, my sister. You've been pretty angry lately, too."

Well, that was definitely a truth.

Thursday night Happy Hour with Summer and Delaney ended just moments later. Summer's husband called to say one of the kids had stuck a pencil eraser up his nose and couldn't get it out, so the girls quickly packed up their purses.

"This will all turn out fine," Summer whispered to Josie as she wrapped her in a tight hug. Then, still gripping Josie's shoulders, she looked into her eyes with a thoughtful expression. "Hey, I have an idea. Why don't you try really laying on the romance? I mean, how long has it been since you and Paul had sex?"

How long *had* it been?

"I honestly couldn't say," Josie said.

"Well, if you couldn't say, then that means it's been way too long.

Go home and set the scene. When Paul comes home, ravish him like he's never been ravished before. It'll be fun. And sex always relieves the tension. Opens the doorway for conversation."

"Now we know the secret to Summer's ever-growing family," Delaney said.

Summer pressed a hand to her belly. "True. But everything I just said is true, too. Try it. Gotta go. As you know, Luke is my difficult child, and you know he won't let his dad get near him with a pair of tweezers."

It was good advice, Josie thought as she perused the meat section at the grocery store a few minutes later. She'd feed Paul a fat steak, a baked potato, and some salad. Add a little wine and music, maybe some candles.

Did they even own candles? Josie checked her watch. It was five-thirty. Paul had gone into work at nine that morning, which meant she had about an hour and a half until he got home. Presumably. Unless something came up, which seemed to happen a lot lately.

"Stay positive," she said to a potato she picked up to examine. "Negativity kills a relationship."

At least, that's what all the "experts" said. If you considered authors of online articles experts. Yes, she'd done a quick Google search in the store parking lot: *how to fix my marriage.*

Was she negative? As she pushed her cart through the store, she thought about some of her recent interactions with Paul. Shame crept in like a spider under a closed door, fast-moving and sneaky.

Just last week, she came home complaining about how the new teachers at her school would be starting at a higher salary than she had during her first year of teaching. The next day when Paul got home, she complained about the terrible driver she got stuck behind on her way to the district office. To her credit, the middle-aged, pot-bellied, mustached woman driver couldn't use a turn signal or go even remotely close to the speed limit to save her life. The next day (the very next day, she thought, wanting to kick herself) she spent some time—a long time, really—complaining about how the school parking lot was closed for resurfacing.

"It's so inconvenient," she said as he took off his gun holster and the bullet proof vest he wore under his T-shirt. "It's like they expect us be sherpas or something! We have to park on the street and carry our supplies all the way to the building!"

Never mind that parking on the street meant walking only a few extra yards.

Yikes. No wonder he wants to work all the time.

Now she was on a roll. She searched the internet for *relationship mistakes*, and found that she was committing quite a few of the "7 Most Common Relationship Mistakes" and "12 Mistakes Couples Make Without Realizing It": taking her partner for granted, complaining about her partner, being passive-aggressive (how many times was she going to "forget" to pick his uniform shirts up from the dry cleaners?), believing her partner should be able to read her mind.

She found some scented candles in the grocery store's home section. Another quick search on her phone turned up an article about the seven best scents to enhance your love life. The top two were cinnamon and vanilla, so she set one of each in her cart.

At home in her kitchen, she laid her purchases out on the counter. To give the candles time to work their magic, she set them on the dining room table and lit them. She popped the potatoes in the oven and went to work on the steaks, rubbing them with olive oil and steak seasoning so they could marinate. As she began chopping vegetables for the salad, inspiration hit and she dug out a love songs CD someone had given to her and Paul for their wedding.

Although she still had another forty minutes before Paul came home, she turned the music on as she finished chopping, just to get her in the mood. By six-thirty, everything was ready, and she figured she had time to take a quick shower.

It had been so long since she prepared for romance that she was giddy with excitement as she soaped up, shaved, and scrubbed her skin to unprecedented levels of softness.

She even found some vanilla-scented lotion in the cabinet under the sink, and rubbed it on, letting the anticipation build. Why had she let so much time pass since they were last intimate? This was going to be fun. And Summer was right. It would give them time to talk when they both had their guards down.

All of her sexy underwear was crammed into the farthest recesses of her underwear drawer. She dug out Paul's favorite pair, lacy white boy shorts he said showed off her perfectly shaped rear end, and slipped into them before pulling on a silky nightgown. The sexual energy could build over dinner, she thought with a little shiver.

She heard it while she was looking in the mirror, smoothing her hair: the sound of a text message coming in.

Paul: *I'll be late. Just got a tip on a meth dealer coming back from Phoenix with at least an ounce. We're hoping to knock him off at Sunset Point. I'll call you when we're done.*

For the second time that day, Josie felt like crying.

When she responded to Paul's text, she left out all the things she wanted to include—a sad-face emoji, something about her plans for the evening, a giant thumbs-down—and she typed: *Okay.*

Then she sent a text to Summer and Delaney: *No romance tonight. Paul is running late. Won't be home for several hours.*

She turned off her phone and changed out of her lacy white boy shorts and silky nightie into granny panties and an old t-shirt Paul brought home from one of his innumerable trainings. Then she downed half a bottle of wine while listening to the romantic music and went to bed, the steaks still marinating on the counter.

LAYING THERE, blinking into the dark, Josie Garcia reminded herself that she didn't believe in romance. For a few minutes, she tried staring at the ceiling, but it spun so quickly she had to shut her eyes. This proved equally dangerous. A kaleidoscope of color swirled behind her eyelids.

Her mother, a stern Mexican immigrant who taught herself English and put herself through accounting school, hammered practicality into Josie's head from the time she was an infant clutching a homemade rattle in her fist. Yes, even her first toy, a rattle made from a baby food jar filled with dried pinto beans, had been practical.

"Don't look for a man who speaks in poetry and brings you flowers, *mija*," Carla Garcia said. "Look for a man who gives you a good life. Stability. Poetry and roses don't put tortillas on the table. They're false currency."

But Josie's mother was gone. She'd died seven years ago of a ruptured brain aneurysm.

Almost in a dreamlike state, Josie let her mind rewind to that moment three days after Mama died … the moment when she met Scott Smith and the universe put her mother's theory to the test.

It made absolutely no sense that Scott's lyrical language and haphazard bouquets of wildflowers had her quivering in her three-inch heels. But they did.

Josie, an orphan at age twenty-seven, sat on a bench downtown, the scorching summer sun making her scalp prickle with sweat.

Standing steadfast in the denial stage, Josie expected her mother to walk around the corner any minute, making *tsk* noises about Josie wearing shorts to work.

"It's summer, Mama," Josie whispered. "I'm just setting up my classroom."

Tears made the scene before her shimmer. The glittering white courthouse, the leaves dancing in the breeze.

It seemed so unfair. Mama dropped dead at her kitchen counter. Why her? She was a good woman. A hard-working woman who raised two children into productive adults, one a teacher and the other a soldier.

She didn't even get to see her grandchildren (not that they were imminent or anything).

There must be some mistake, Josie found herself thinking over and over again when it first happened. Some other woman must have been standing in Mama's kitchen, helping her make tamales or brewing a pot of coffee. Some other woman wearing her ruffled apron, turquoise like the blue bowl she'd brought from Mexico to sit on the kitchen table, full of oranges.

Josie found her lying on the floor, hands covered in masa and a streak of it on her cheek. Her hair was wound in a tight, low bun. Her eyes were open, but Josie could tell she was already gone. A sense of calm came over Josie then, and she remembered the ABCs from her CPR class. Airway, breathing, circulation. Mama didn't seem to have anything in her mouth, and she wasn't breathing. Her skin was cold. She didn't have a pulse.

Still, Josie refused to believe this was permanent. Even when the ambulance came screeching into the driveway, when the paramedics loaded her mother onto a stretcher after performing CPR, or when they told her there was nothing she could have done.

Mama had to be coming back. This was all a terrible nightmare.

She kept picturing herself sitting at her mom's table drinking coffee, tying strings around the tamales after Mama formed them with her strong hands. Three days had passed, and Josie found herself sitting on that bench at the courthouse square, reliving the scene yet again. They were wrong. Her mother wasn't dead. It wasn't true that a blood vessel in Carla Garcia's brain had weakened, widened and then ruptured. Carla Garcia had veins of steel. She was tough.

Summer, of course, helped Josie make the funeral preparations. She put an announcement in the newspaper, chose a dress for Mama to wear and somehow found turquoise flowers for the church. Delaney would drive up from vet school this evening and spend the night with Josie in her childhood bedroom.

All Josie knew how to do to bury the hurt was to work. So she'd holed up in her classroom, scrubbing desks, vacuuming the carpet and color-coding folders for her students. Until today ... the day before her mother's funeral. She'd decided to take a break, and walked down to the square in hopes of finding some solace.

Heat waves radiated off the roads in downtown Juniper. The summer sun hung high above the carpet-like lawn. Josie, wearing khaki cargo shorts and a salmon-colored tank top that perfectly matched her pedicured toenails, treated herself to a huge lemonade from the stand on the corner.

That moment, the moment she sought refuge from the worst hurt she'd ever experienced, was the moment Scott Smith walked into her life.

Maybe that's why the romance worked.

Juniper's signature fountain bubbled nearby, and a group of kids sat on the low concrete bench surrounding it, their bare feet in the water. Josie smiled as a little boy splashed his older sister, who responded by filling her empty soda cup and dumping it on his head.

Her own little brother would have done that very thing, if they'd ever gotten to sit around the fountain on a summer day. The truth was, neither of them had had any free time on a summer day since they were old enough to work the fields with Mama. Sometimes, when no one was looking, Juan grabbed a handful of fat red strawberries and shoved them into her mouth. She'd do the same to him, and they'd giggle like fiends trying to swallow the sweet fruit and wipe its traces from their cheeks before their mother caught them and punished them for being silly.

"People watching, huh?" Josie jumped at the voice, which was deep and smooth like a vat of melted chocolate. She loved chocolate.

She looked up, and had to shade her eyes to look at this tall, lanky stranger who interrupted her impromptu break from grief disguised as work. When they made eye contact, the man stepped back.

"Wow," he said. "You're even more beautiful up close."

Despite the unexpected fluttery reaction in her stomach, and the involuntary flush that rose to her face, Josie's internal voice—which was actually her mother's voice—whispered, *Poetry. False currency.*

She smiled coolly. "I was just leaving, actually."

"And your voice," he said, apparently unaffected by what she thought was a clear shutdown. "It's like honey."

When she quirked an eyebrow at him, he lifted his hands in surrender and said, "No, seriously. It is."

"I've got to get back to work," she said. She stood up.

"That's too bad. I'm the new guy in town. I was hoping I'd come down here and meet a friendly face, get some recommendations, on, you know, restaurants, grocery stores, whatever. I never imagined I'd find such a beautiful friendly face."

Josie couldn't help it. She laughed. For the first time since her mama died, the tension her throat and her chest relaxed. "You're good. But I'm afraid you've got me pegged incorrectly. I'm not that friendly."

"Even so," he said, his eyes twinkling with humor and a genuine interest. "Where's the best place to grab lunch around here?"

"The Sand Witch is pretty good," she said, pointing across the street at the deli. "And if you want Chinese, the Red Lantern is just a couple of blocks from here. They have a decent lunch special. Their cashew chicken is to die for."

"If you had to choose one, right now, which would it be?" the stranger asked.

Josie sipped her lemonade and considered, relieved to think about something other than her loneliness and the huge empty spot her mother had left in her life.

"The Sand Witch," she decided after a moment. She took a couple of steps away from him, in the direction of her school, but the stranger didn't take the hint.

Instead, he looked her in the eyes and said, "You know what would really make my day? Lunch with a lovely lady on this lovely afternoon. My treat. Consider it my thanks for your advice."

"I've got to get back to work," she said again. "I'm setting up my classroom."

He stooped and picked a lone yellow dandelion out of the lawn. He held it out to her, and she noticed his eyes were the color of bourbon when sunlight shone through the glass. "Please. Help a guy out. Don't make me eat lunch alone on my first day in a new town."

First poetry, and now a flower. Hear the warning bells, Garcia? Ding ding ding. It wasn't even warning bells, actually. It was a buzzer, the kind they put on emergency exits. For some reason, though—probably because she needed something warm and melty and happy to sink into—she couldn't resist. That's how they ended up eating lunch together that first day ... and spending incalculable time together throughout the remainder of the summer despite the fact they both knew it could never work.

And wasn't that the story of their relationship? She couldn't resist him.

IS it bad juju to daydream about your ex-boyfriend while laying in the bed you share with your husband? Does it still count as daydreaming if you're half-asleep and completely drunk?

Hours had passed since Josie crawled between the sheets in her granny panties.

She'd spent a good deal of that time thinking about the great news she'd received recently: she'd been awarded a huge grant to open a new community center in town.

A few months ago, the idea of opening the center had dawned on her as she watched one of her students, Joshua Morton, struggle in school. He rarely did his homework and often came to school hungry. His parents both worked long hours, and, Josie suspected, held more than one job. So Joshua and his brother were on their own, most of the time. They weren't the only ones. As she talked with other teachers at Juniper Elementary School, she realized a significant number of kids were alone before and after school, and most of them were struggling.

The community center would be a safe, structured place for kids like Joshua to go, to get help with their homework, to hang out with friends, to eat a little something. As soon as the concept developed in her mind, she applied for the grant. She'd been almost positive she wouldn't get it.

But when the envelope came in the mail—a big manila envelope, not one of the small, white ones that always meant rejection—she cried actual tears of joy as she pictured Joshua at the center, fed and happy and getting his homework done. She cried even harder when she pictured him at school, confident and rested. Then, if it were possible, she cried even harder when she imagined the sign that would memorialize her mom: *The Carla M. Garcia Community Center*.

Unfortunately, in addition to thinking about the community center, Josie had also spent hours letting her mind wander to romance. Not romance with her husband of six years, but romance with the stranger from the downtown square, the slightly nerdy guy looking for a restaurant tour.

The conversation flowed so easily during that first meal, that impromptu trip to The Sand Witch.

"Now, because you're a teacher on summer break, I absolutely forbid you from talking about work while we're at lunch," he said as they approached the deli.

Josie wrinkled her nose.

"Then what on earth will we talk about?"

He opened the door for her, and she felt chills where she imagined he touched her lower back to guide her in.

Maybe it's the poetry. You're losing it, Garcia.

In reality, she knew she had fallen into this guy because it gave her the chance to step out of her current situation, to stop picturing the way Mama looked when she died and to stop wishing she'd hop back up and start making tamales again.

After ordering, they sat at a corner table with a window overlooking the square.

"So, let's pretend we're total strangers," he said.

She laughed. "And how shall we pretend we met?"

"Let's pretend I picked you up downtown. At random. Under the guise of being new in town and needing a tour guide. But in reality, wanting a delicious-looking woman with whom to eat lunch."

"And to think I don't even know the name of this man who is lavishing me with compliments."

Blake, the deli's owner, called out their order, and the stranger retrieved the sandwiches from the counter. Josie admired his long legs and his broad shoulders. She admired the way his fingers curved around the plastic baskets their sandwiches were served in.

She knew, at that very moment, that she'd sleep with him. And more importantly, she knew she'd like it.

"Josie," she said, extending her hand when he sat back down at the table.

He chuckled. "Scott."

They shook hands. Suddenly ravenous after not having eaten for three straight days, Josie tore into her turkey and avocado.

"Why don't you play hooky and show me around for the rest of the day?" he said as they finished up. "It's summer. Surely you have a few weeks more to finish up whatever classroom stuff you're working on today."

She needed to prepare for the funeral. She needed to finish hanging the Star Student display and setting up the reading corner. She needed to make up her old trundle bed for Delaney to sleep in.

She needed to mourn her mother.

When she didn't respond right away, he barked out a laugh. "I can practically see the internal debate! You must be a model employee. But come on. Live a little."

"This goes against my grain," she said. "I am a very conscientious person. I have a daily to-do list and I have a compulsion for checking off every item on it."

She never returned to her classroom that day. Instead, grateful for the distraction, she gave Scott a locals' walking tour of downtown Juniper. They went to the famous western history museum, the library with its exquisite sculpture garden, and the little-known bar where Josie had had her first drink with Summer and Delaney.

Probably because she had a specific mission, Josie found herself feeling chatty, and even caught herself saying to Scott, "I'm not normally like this. Trust me. You bring out the friendly in me."

They were sitting on the little brick wall that bordered the rose garden inside the museum, and Josie fanned herself with the brochure she picked up at the entrance.

"I don't believe it for a minute," he said. "You're the nicest person I've met so far in Juniper."

"Didn't you say I was the only person you've met so far in Juniper?"

When they made eye contact, she could practically see little cartoon hearts floating around in the air between them. She still remembered that moment as magical, even now, years later.

The magic lasted about a split second before her inner voice kicked in.

What are you doing? He just likes your curves, that's all. He doesn't even know you.

But Scott was different. He was different from the boys in junior high who faked liking her just so they could get their hands on her breasts or cup her ass while passing her in the hall.

Scott didn't know her, but he wanted to. She could tell. And she liked it. At the time, she relished his attention, bathed in it like a springtime blade of grass bathes in the warm sunlight.

And maybe that was the reason she didn't notice until much later that he had not revealed a single fact about himself over the course of that first afternoon they spent together, or that evening when they made love (actually, scratch that: "when they had frantic sexual intercourse" was a more accurate description) against the side of her car, just steps from Juniper Elementary School.

She asked him questions, but he deflected them like a magician, training her attention on precisely what he wanted her to see, putting the spotlight back on her. Despite spending several hours with him that day, Josie had no idea what he did for a living, why he moved to Juniper, or even what kind of car he drove.

Scott was the first secret-keeper, and because he was a balm to her pain that summer, Josie fell so hard—*too* hard—for him, and became the second.

Keeping secrets is a hard habit to break.

When Scott eventually revealed his secret, Josie realized he was the Romeo to her Juliet. Tragic, lovestruck young people destined to be apart.

He knew from the outset they wouldn't be together. When she casually mentioned teaching at Juniper Elementary School, he should have walked away. But, he said, because he loved the slow curve of her smile, the quick chime of her laugh, he waited until she had fallen for him to tell her, ensuring they'd have at least some time together before school started and their respective career aspirations kept them apart. Suddenly, he said, every moment felt precious, like a diamond hundreds of years in the making, deep underground, only now twinkling in the sunlight.

They saw each other daily. For the first few days, Josie let Scott dictate the direction of their conversations. He steered the vehicle to whichever destinations he chose, never once pulling to a stop in any area of his own life.

Then, curiosity overcame her.

"Scott, you know almost everything about me," she said to him one night while they sat on her porch swing, licking ice cream cones. "But I don't know so much about you. I mean, you said you moved here for your job, but you've never mentioned what that job is. And you're never working."

"Well, I've only been here for a few days," he said, his tone indicating a flicker of offense.

She nodded and laid a hand on his leg. "I know. I was just wondering, that's all. I'd really like to get to know you better."

He sighed then, a big sigh that made his chest rise and fall, and moved the swing so it creaked on its chains. "Josie, there's something I need to tell you."

Uh oh. He's married, with kids. He's a spy and he's not allowed to date people. He's an assassin and I'm his next target. Mission: Kill Josie Garcia.

"I'm the new principal at Juniper Elementary School."

She sat there so long without responding that the ice cream started to melt, running down over her thumb. After a long moment during which the only sound was that of crickets chirping, she cleared her throat. The ice cream dripped onto her leg.

"Wait. So you're, like, my boss?"

He shrugged, nodding. "Well, yeah."

Their relationship could never work. She couldn't date her boss. Imagine what it would do to her reputation. Imagine how it could ruin her career.

Now, she nodded too.

"This can't work," they both said at the same time. Then they laughed.

It was a split-second, knee-jerk decision, and she knew it was the right one. They agreed to date, to enjoy each other's company, for the rest of summer, and not for a moment beyond that.

CHAPTER TWO

THE FINAL NIGHT OF SUMMER BREAK, SCOTT INSISTED THE TWO OF THEM do something fun, something, he said, "where we won't even have a chance to notice how sad we are."

That was Scott, always running away from serious topics, always hiding from feelings any deeper than a dirty puddle in the parking lot.

So they went to Orbit Golf. Josie hated that place. She'd gone there junior year on her first-ever date with Alejo Gomez, whom she'd pined after for months. He was the perfect gentleman until they came across some of his friends. It was Hole Twelve, and she was just getting ready to take her first shot. She tossed her hair over her shoulder, hoping Alejo would find the move sexy. Just as she swung her club, she heard the cat calls and teenage snickers. Alejo, embarrassed, insisted very loudly that she meant nothing to him, while her face burned with embarrassment. He told his friends she'd begged him to take her golfing as soon as she found out he got a new car. "Just like a woman," he sneered. His friends laughed. She missed the shot. They finished the golf course and never spoke again.

The grown-up Josie could never share this story with Scott, though. Even now, it made her feel vulnerable, and she was already feeling vulnerable enough knowing tonight was the last night they'd spend together. So she pasted on a smile and went to Orbit Golf to lay their relationship to rest among fluorescent lighting and glow-in-the-dark paintings of misshapen aliens.

Of course, they went back to her place afterwards.

That night and every night thereafter for a few weeks, she cried herself to sleep.

She always wondered, what if? What if they had met under different circumstances? What if one of them worked at a different school? What if she wasn't a teacher?

The answers didn't matter. Josie Garcia and Scott Smith were destined for tragedy.

Once the school year started, they split up. But there was something so painfully satisfying about pining for each other, sneaking kisses in the hallway, casting long looks across the table during staff meetings.

When she and Paul made their relationship official about a month later, though, she told Scott it was over. Really over.

PAUL COMSTOCK WAS EXACTLY the opposite of Scott, and maybe that's why she fell for him so quickly.

They met the second week of that same school year, when she saw him in the classroom next door. He was talking to the second-grade teacher, Susie Lockhart, and Josie snapped a mental photo. Artists dreamed of profiles like Paul's: all clean lines and perfect angles.

He stood with his thumbs hooked into his gun belt and his head cocked a tiny bit to one side as he listened to Susie's questions.

The moment he smiled, Josie knew she was hooked (although she should have known she was hooked the moment she realized she was totally and completely frozen in place, leaning against the doorjamb, her mouth hanging open as she watched him speak).

He had deep, striking crows feet at the corners of his eyes, and rather than making him look old, they made him look fun and kind and downright sexy.

She imagined him directing that smile at her, then wrapping those big, sculpted superhero arms around her waist right here in the doorway of Susie Lockhart's classroom.

When he did, she would put her arms up around his neck and pull his face to hers. What would he smell like?

Probably leather and cologne, soap and coffee. Don't all cops drink coffee?

Susie Lockhart cleared her throat, and Josie jumped, snapping her mouth closed.

"Did you hear me, Josie? This is Paul Comstock, with the Juniper Police Department. He's coming in next week to give a presentation to my kids."

"Paul," Josie said. "Paul Comstock. Nice to meet you. I'm Josie Garcia."

He took her hand to shake it and looked directly at her. So directly, it almost made her uncomfortable. It should have made her uncomfortable.

Only, it didn't. It made her all fizzy inside, like champagne. Little bubbles kept rising to the surface, bursting gently on her skin and making her shiver.

"Nice to meet you, Josie," Paul said. "Very nice to meet you."

No poetry, just straight talk.

He would later admit he experienced that same fizzy feeling during the handshake and had been rendered idiotic for the rest of the day, misplacing his handcuffs and leaving his gun in the bathroom stall at the police station.

The moment was fleeting though, because Paul's phone vibrated on his belt and he answered it right away in a tone so serious Josie smiled.

Susie wiggled her eyebrows up and down behind his back as he walked into the hallway. Josie shook her head and took that opportunity to slink back to her own classroom, her reason for visiting Susie's forgotten.

The following Thursday, Delaney came up from vet school for a weekend visit. The three girls went to Rowdy's for Happy Hour, and Josie confessed: "I'm not usually one to go for men in uniform, but wowza! I mean, he was hot."

"So did you get his number?" Summer asked.

"I'm working on it. You know, police officers' phone numbers are top secret. Classified."

"Delaney," Summer said. "Look at the way she's grinning right now. When's the last time you saw Josie grin like that? I sense some-thing special about this one."

Delaney nodded sagely. "Yes," she said. "I haven't seen her smile like that since freshman year of high school when Davey Richmond taught her what second base is."

"I'm scandalized," Josie said, but deep down, she knew it was true. She didn't often let guys get to her. Well, not usually.

Scott had gotten to her. And look what had happened there.

"Whoa, that was weird," Summer said. "The grin disappeared. What's up with that?"

"Oh, nothing," Josie said brightly. "Just need a refill, that's all."

The conversation moved on then, to Delaney's final exams at vet school and how Summer's daughter Sarah had started preschool. Even as they laughed at Sarah's insistence on wearing all purple - socks, pants, shirt, a sweater, and boots, Josie felt a tiny bit … nostal-gic, maybe? Sad? She couldn't quite put her finger on it.

And worse, she couldn't hash it out with the girls. Because she'd been in the middle of grieving for her mother, Josie hadn't mentioned Scott when they first met. Then he'd sworn her to secrecy, so solemnly she'd joked they should take a blood oath.

"I can't have anyone knowing we had a relationship," he said to her one night as he stood in her doorway on the way out. "You understand. It just wouldn't be … proper."

Of course, Josie nodded. She understood. She planned to ascend the career ladder, too, and didn't want scandal coloring her resume.

So instead of telling the girls about Scott, she told them she was going through the isolation phase of grief and needed time alone. In reality, she spent every spare moment with Scott. She told the girls she was getting ready for the school year. In reality, she and Scott were having steamy sex on her classroom floor.

It was easy to fool them. Summer was about to give birth to Nate and Delaney was finishing up school. The secret went completely undetected, and it stood sacred, even until present day.

Josie's relationship with Paul erased her feelings for Scott with the efficiency of a chalkboard eraser. The solid lines disappeared, but that fine white dust, made of memories and possibility, always remained.

The following summer, Josie married Paul in a wedding that

blended romance and practicality. She carried a bouquet of orchids (romance) and wore her mother's wedding gown (practicality). She and the girls transformed one of Juniper's lakeside parks into a wonderland by draping twinkling lights in the trees and setting potted trees and flowers on almost every flat surface.

As the Comstock-Garcias—she chose to keep her mother's last name—walked back down the aisle after the minister pronounced them husband and wife, Josie felt like she was flying, soaring with happiness. She looked into Paul's eyes and thought nothing could ever take him away from her.

BACK IN REAL TIME, Josie's eyes snapped open when the front door finally clicked open. It was twelve minutes after two in the morning. Although she and Paul both knew she only half-slept when he worked late, Paul tried to be quiet. She could picture him now, pulling his gun and holster out of his waistband and putting them in the safe in the coat closet. He would take off his shoes next, stepping on the heel of one with the toe of the other. He'd set them next to the front door and then go to the kitchen to make himself a drink.

Whiskey on the rocks.

The sounds seemed amplified in the house: the cabinet closing, Paul setting the glass on the counter, opening and closing the freezer and then dropping ice cubes into the glass. *Clink, clink.* Next he'd drop one cube. It clattered to the floor. "Shit," he muttered. Josie knew he was bending down to pick it up, and then she heard it land in the sink. The liquor cabinet closed next, and she heard the whiskey glugging out of the bottle.

Now he would sit on the couch, feet on the coffee table, and wind down.

And she would pounce. Not in the way she hoped to pounce earlier. She felt her body sway, side to side, as she walked through the bedroom to the living room.

He didn't hear her behind him. With a mix of nostalgia and irritation, she thought about the conversations they had when he couldn't find a specific shoe, or the scissors, or the sharp cheddar.

"The man can find a gram of meth behind the headlight of a nineteen-eighty-five Mustang," she'd say, "but he can't find a pound of sharp cheddar in the fridge."

"I'm off-duty," he'd say, putting both hands up in a "what-can-I-say" gesture.

Now, he sat on the couch exactly as she pictured, reading something on his tablet. As she always did (it had become automatic after all this time), she admired the way the muscles in his shoulders bulged just enough as to be visible underneath his shirt.

"Hi, Paul," she said.

He jumped and the tablet tumbled off his lap and onto the floor. She noticed he managed to keep his drink from spilling.

"Geez, Josie! You startled me! Don't do that!"

"Since when is it a crime to say hello to my husband when he gets home from work?"

He picked up his tablet and set it on the table, then turned around to face her. "I thought you'd be sleeping."

"I was."

"Why is there steak on the counter? Did you forget to put it away? It'll go bad."

She didn't answer, and he said, "I put it in the fridge for you."

"For me? You put it in the fridge for me? Why, thank you, Paul. Thank you so much."

Confusion made his eyebrows draw together and his mouth form a tiny o.

"What are you talking about?" he said.

"God, I feel so stupid!" she said. Then, Josie Garcia did something she had vowed after Scott that she would never do again. She cried. Over a guy. This guy happened to be her husband, but still. The sensation was so unfamiliar she didn't realize it was happening until she felt the moisture on her face.

"Are you crying?"

Again, she refrained from answering.

"Josie. What's wrong?"

He stood up and came around the back of the couch. He lifted his arms as if he wanted to hug her, but he dropped them back at his sides like he was afraid she'd explode at his touch. A small laugh made its way to the surface. Paul had entered full panic mode.

"I feel so stupid," she repeated.

"Is it the steaks? It's okay, I've left meat out before. They'll be fine."

"It's not the steaks," she snapped. "Actually, it kind of *is* the steaks. I've been feeling so, I don't know, so disconnected from you lately, and I thought I'd make a nice meal and, you know, seduce you, and have a romantic evening. I went to the store, bought some steaks. I even looked up which scents are best for romance and bought candles. Candles! I put on those lacy undies you like. I shaved my legs!"

"It does smell really good in here," Paul said. In nervous gesture, he rubbed his nose with the knuckle of his pointer finger.

"But you didn't eat the steak."

"I can eat it now," he said, shrugging.

He was trying, she'd give him that. He didn't like to see her cry.

"You're missing the point," she said.

"Oh. Ah… what is the point?"

"I just told you! Weren't you listening?"

"I *was* listening! You wanted me to eat the steak," he said.

Okay, maybe he wasn't trying as hard as she thought.

"You shaved your legs?" he tried.

Josie sighed, and pressed her fists against her eyelids. When she looked at him again, she saw realization dawning on his face. If it had happened at any other moment, she would have found the transformation comical. His shoulders drooped and he looked down at the floor.

"Now do you get it?"

"You planned a romantic evening, and I ruined it," he said.

"Yes! Yes. Or, your job ruined it. What makes it so bad, to me, is that it's not the first time. Lately, you're barely home. Instead of spending your time with me, you spend it with tweakers and drug dealers. And you know what's really sad? I've come to expect the late nights, the never seeing you, the lack of sex because you're always too tired or too wired or whatever. I've come to expect it. It doesn't even surprise me anymore."

Paul shrugged. Not in a way that signified he didn't care, but in a way that signified he didn't know what to do or what to say. Josie waited.

"It's the nature of the job, Josie," he said. "And I didn't know you were feeling this way."

"That's the problem," she said. "Exactly. If you didn't realize I was feeling this way, and you think this situation is a given, then we have worse problems than I thought."

She spun around and stomped back into the bedroom. She shut the door quietly and leaned against it.

In her imagination, she heard a tongue clucking, and her mother's voice saying, "See, *mija*? You married for practicality and yet you want romance. Romance lets you down. He's a hard-working man, providing for you. Cut him some slack, eh?"

Josie knew she should cut him some slack. But she wanted romance, at least a little. And was there anything wrong with that?

CHAPTER THREE

"So what happened last Thursday with the romance? Did you wait up for Paul?" Summer chewed an olive, slowly, while waiting for Josie's answer.

Josie had been tempted to skip out on Thursday Happy Hour at Rowdy's, but knew she'd have to face her friends eventually. So she showed up. She did pause in the doorway to let her eyes adjust to the dim lighting and to give herself an extra minute before the inevitable inquisition began. But, here she was.

Josie crossed her arms on the table and rested her head on them.

"That good, huh?" Delaney said. "I'll order another round."

Out of the corner of her eye, Josie saw her raise her hand to signal Benjamin.

"Dish, sister," Summer said. "What happened? I thought you'd just delay the … gratification until he got home."

Summer snickered. Josie groaned.

"You're not getting out of this, Josie," Delaney said. "If I had to endure the two of you intruding on my life for your so-called 'Dating Intervention,' then you can at least open up about how your night of romance went once Paul got home."

"Or didn't go," Josie said. Her voice was muffled, but she couldn't bring herself upright—to make eye contact with her friends —just yet. "Nothing happened. I bought some steaks and wine and scented candles and I even shaved my legs. Seriously. I shaved my legs and put on his favorite underwear and this stupid, impractical silky nightie thing, and he didn't even come home until after two. I mean, it's not like he knew about it. I wanted to surprise him. But he got stuck at work. Again."

When she lifted her head off the table, she remembered Delaney doing something similar just a few months ago when Josie and Summer had insisted on making all the decisions in her love life and a few in her regular life. They'd required her to learn how to cook, and to get a new job, swapping out bar tending for veterinary medicine.

The result: she was now in a serious, sappy relationship with Jake Rhoades, a sexy Roman god of a man who brought Delaney coffee and sometimes flowers. She could cook a mean roasted chicken and a better-than-decent spaghetti. Recently, she'd solved several complicated veterinary cases. Josie's thoughts wandered to her own professional predicament.

Delaney interrupted her. "See? You're thinking about it right now, aren't you?" she said. "You're thinking about how much better off I am, and you want the same for yourself."

Josie opened her mouth to answer. Yes, she was thinking about Delaney's life. But she was no stranger to her friends' interference: she had also been thinking about how the girls had hacked into her human resources file and applied for the Juniper Elementary School principal position on her behalf. Before she could speak, Benjamin returned with their drinks.

Summer held up her water glass and said, "I'd like to make a toast. "To Josie's marriage. More importantly, to our help fixing it. Cheers."

"Cheers!" Delaney said, with a little too much enthusiasm.

Even as Josie giggled, she felt the emotion well up in her chest. She loved these girls. Feeling more stirred up than hopeful, Josie clinked her glass to each of her friends'.

Then Delaney became businesslike. She pulled out a notebook and set it on the table, aligning its corners with some invisible guidelines. Josie immediately became tense. Yes, the three of them had been friends (best friends!) for the past twenty years, and they knew almost every detail of her life ... but not *every* detail. Some things were meant to remain private.

"Okay. So. I have some questions for you," Delaney said. She opened the notebook to a fresh page.

"Okay," Josie said, drawing out the word and taking a big gulp of her drink.

Delaney was silent for a moment, writing something down. "How often do you guys have sex?" she asked then, looking up at Josie.

"Delaney!" Summer said quickly. "Don't start with that one! Derek and I have sex like, once a decade."

"Well, we know that's not true," Josie said to her drink.

Delaney added, "You're pregnant. And you have four kids. Typically, frequency of sex is a good marker of any romantic relationship." She blushed. "Fine, I'll start with a different one."

"She and Jake are doing it, like, three times a day," Summer stage-whispered to Josie.

Delaney, now bright red in the face, went to cross out what she'd written. Josie stopped her by putting a hand on her arm.

"No. Don't cross it out. It's fine. If I can't tell you two everything, what kind of friendship is this?"

Well, not everything.

She pushed the little voice to the back of her mind and answered Delaney's question: "Once a month."

Delaney couldn't hide her shocked expression, but she managed to bring it back to neutral pretty quickly when Summer elbowed her.

"I saw that," Josie said. "Not all of us are in the throes of fresh, new love like you and Jake are."

Delaney grinned.

"Yes, I have you two to thank for my stellar sex life, that's for sure," Delaney said.

"Let's move on before she starts regaling us with stories of Jake's between-the-sheets prowess," Summer said to Josie.

"He is pretty amazing. He does this thing where he—"

Summer cut her off. "Next question, please."

Still smiling, Delaney asked: "How often do you hug?"

"'How often do you hug?' What kind of question is that? I'm going to need sustenance for this." Josie waved to Benjamin, held up her drink, pointed at it and held up two fingers.

"So?" Summer said. "How often do you guys hug, Josie?"

"Like, I don't know, every few days or something?"

"Wait. So how do you say good-bye when he leaves for work or whatever?" Delaney wanted to know.

"He's sleeping when I leave for work. I'm sleeping when he gets home. I'm telling you, ships passing in the night and all that."

"Yikes," Summer said to Delaney. "This is worse than we thought."

Delaney nodded. "I think it's time to lay out The Rules."

Josie sighed. "Fine. But I'm not promising anything."

"Geez, Josie, it's your *marriage*. It's not like we're going to make you go out with guys who feed you ham sandwiches while wiping hog's blood off their boots from that morning's butcher."

"That was only one date, Delaney," Josie said. "And how could we have known that Jesse the Rancher would be obsessed with hogs?"

"Didn't he have, like, a pig as his online dating profile picture?"

"He was very good-looking, if I recall," Summer said, and Josie added, "And he had exceptional manners."

"That's true," Delaney said. "But still. Be patient, Josie. Give us a chance, here. I followed your rules."

"Kind of!" Josie said. "You used loopholes. Like when you went shopping for office supplies when you were supposed to be writing your resumé."

"I needed a good atmosphere for working."

"Whatever. Fine," Josie said. They all laughed. Their use of "fine" had become a running joke since Delaney started using it every time Summer and Josie coaxed her into following their rules during The Dating Intervention.

"All right," Delaney said. She turned to a fresh page in her notebook and wrote *The Marriage Intervention* at the top. "Let's get started."

"First of all," Summer said to Delaney, "she's got to start initiating sex."

"Who says I don't?"

"Whether you do or not, once a month just isn't going to cut it," Summer said. "Research has proven that sex makes you feel closer to your partner. So even if you initiate it now, you've got to initiate it more."

"What if I never see my partner?"

"Write it down, Delaney," Summer said, pointing to the notebook. "Rule One. Initiate sex with Paul at least once per week."

Josie thought, *What if he rejects me?* but she remained silent.

"Rule Two," Delaney said. "Date nights. Once every two weeks."

"How is going out to dinner and a movie any different from staying home and watching a movie while eating dinner?" Josie said.

"Oh my God," Summer said to Delaney. "She really is clueless."

"I know," Delaney said. "She's all practicality, no romance."

"That's not true!" Josie said. "I can be romantic."

"Give me one example," Summer said.

Dozens of images flashed through Josie's mind. Images of her and Scott together. Him feeding her grapes at the top of Granite Mountain as they both gazed over the twinkling lights of Juniper. Her surprising him on July Fourth with a home-baked apple pie and homemade ice cream. Him braiding her hair in a horribly messy braid, and both of them cracking up as he stood behind her at the bathroom mirror.

Of course, she'd promised Scott she'd always keep their relationship a secret, so it was impossible to use these moments with him as proof of her romantic capabilities. Plus, how would it look if all of her examples came from a previous relationship? And furthermore, if she told the girls about Scott, she'd feel obligated to tell Paul. If she didn't, he'd be the only one who didn't know.

She shifted her attention to Paul, searching her memory for examples of romance, but she came up dry.

"See?" Summer said, her voice self-satisfied and cheerful.

"Well, don't look so smug about it."

"Wow, you're a bit prickly about this, Josie," Delaney said.

"What's Rule Three?"

"Rule Three," Summer said. "Hug at least twice a day, for at least twenty seconds each time."

"Wait. You're going to help me restore my marriage through hugging? I think it's you guys who are clueless, not me."

"After twenty seconds of hugging, your body produces oxytocin," Summer said. "It's a feel-good hormone."

"Oh my God," Josie said. "I cannot believe you two think you're taking over my marriage. And secondly, where are you coming up with these statistics?"

"FriendZoo," Summer said, raising an eyebrow at Josie. "Aren't all those articles accurate?"

Josie shook her head. Delaney continued: "Rule Four. Go to marriage counseling."

"I will not get through this with my dignity in tact," Josie said. "I guarantee it."

"Rule Five," Summer said. "Participate in an adventure date every month."

"What does that even mean?"

"It means rock climbing or water skiing or sledding," Delaney said. "Or something like that. Something new. An experience you and Paul can share."

"How about bringing Paul to our next Happy Hour?" Josie said. "That's an experience everyone should have."

Delaney shook her head. "Rule Six. Enter a race."

"A race? Like a running race? Or, like, a political race?"

"Yeah," Summer said. "Like a running race."

"I don't run," Josie said. "You guys know that. I walk."

"I don't run unless I'm being chased by coyotes," Delaney said. "Don't mock me."

"It can be, like, a five k or something," Summer said. "Three miles. That'll take you like a half-hour."

"Fine," Josie said.

"Fine," Summer and Delaney echoed.

The three of them dissolved into giggles, although Josie was thinking, *Yeah, right. I'll be lucky to get three yards.*

WHAT WOULD Mama say about The Marriage Intervention?

Josie couldn't be sure. Although their mother had always taught Josie and Juan they could support themselves, no spouse necessary, Josie also knew she often felt lonely and missed her husband, Ricardo, who left when Josie was four and Juan was two.

"He was a dreamer," Mama said. "He lured me away from Mexico with the promise of a new life, and I believed him. Our time together was short, but it was big. Big and bright as the full moon.

But just like the moon, he couldn't be tied down. We were living what he told me was the dream, but he was dreaming of another life, and couldn't resist it. Mind you, I wouldn't have gotten you two if I hadn't followed him to the States. But I want more for you, Josie. I want you to share a long life with the man you marry."

Josie remembered nodding thoughtfully, believing with every atom of her being that she would be a dreamer, too. After all, her father was three states away in Texas, enjoying himself on some fishing boat while she and Juan and Mama worked the fields, all of them sweating in the heat.

Then she'd grown up. Mama moved them to Arizona, where she got a job as a translator for the government and began attending college to get her accounting degree.

That same year, they learned that Ricardo died in an accident just a few hours away. He'd taken yet another new job, probably following another new dream, and the train he was conducting derailed, killing him.

As Josie began to understand how the world worked, she learned to respect her mother's determination. She began to emulate it. She worked hard in her classes, joined the speech and debate team and took college courses in high school so she could start her career as soon as possible.

The Marriage Intervention was practical, and Mama would love it. But was Mama right about practicality?

She died just short of her fiftieth birthday. Yes, she was making tamales, doing something she loved. But how much of her life had she really enjoyed? How much had she worked away? And how much would she miss?

Practicality paid off: Josie had earned herself her dream job—the principal position at Juniper Elementary School—and would start next year. But still, right now, she found herself craving romance.

CHAPTER FOUR

IF PAUL WAS SCOTT'S OPPOSITE, JOSIE'S FIRST DATE WITH PAUL WAS equally different from her first date with Scott. She still felt heartbroken over the dissolution of her relationship with Scott. But in his absence, she stopped bargaining for her mom's life. She moved beyond depression and embraced acceptance. In acceptance, she found she wanted to follow her mother's advice and give up romance in favor of practicality.

Josie tracked down Paul's number and called to ask him out within seven days after she first saw him in Susie Lockhart's classroom. By pursuing him, Josie was following one of her mother's best tips: "Don't wait around for Prince Charming, *mija*. If you find him, snap him right up and show him where to sit. On the throne right beside you."

"I'll pick you up at six," Paul said after recovering from his surprise that she'd taken the lead.

"I'll be ready," she said.

"Actually, I'll probably be sitting in your driveway at three minutes 'til, waiting for six o'clock to roll around."

That Saturday she looked out her front window at five fifty-seven to see his truck parked on the street. He knocked just as the big hand on her clock reached the twelve, and they were both smiling when she opened the door.

Josie couldn't help herself: she compared Paul to Scott at every stage of the date.

Scott was always a minute or two late, rushing in with some excuse designed to make him sound important or chivalrous. ("Sorry 'bout that, they really needed me at work," or, "I stopped to help a little kid get his basketball out of the street without getting run over.") For some reason, although Carla had taught Josie to value punctuality, she found this quirk charming.

Paul was three minutes early every time they met, without exception.

Despite the poetry and flowers, Scott said he was a feminist. He believed in equal rights for women. So he never hurried to open doors for her. On the other hand, Paul opened every door they encountered, including the passenger door of his truck. This was real gallantry, she thought, not the fabricated kind. Scott avoided all the serious topics, and Paul dove right in. Scott seemed to want to skim the surface, while Paul wanted to know everything. Every why, every how, and every what. Once Scott learned his way around Juniper's restaurant industry, he always chose the most romantic restaurants and insisted they take turns paying (another indicator of his feminism, he said). He chose tables on the outskirts of the room, so no one they knew would notice them together.

On their first date, Paul chose a casual, cozy diner where they sat right in the middle of the room. Josie felt a higher level of intimacy with him than she had on any of her dates with Scott. The server never delivered the bill, and when they walked out, Paul revealed he'd paid it when Josie was in the bathroom.

During that first dinner, Paul quizzed Josie on her reasons for becoming a teacher, her motivations for buying a historic house downtown rather than a new house in a subdivision, and why she hated working out.

And when she asked him questions, he answered them carefully, as if he wanted her to know him.

He told her he decided to become a cop when he was ten, after a burglar broke into the house where he lived with his mother. One of the police officers who responded to the midnight call sat with him until morning while a team of detectives and evidence technicians scoured the house and interviewed his mom.

"He even ran to the store to grab me some Doritos," Paul said, laughing. "And when he found out the burglar had stolen some of the gifts my mom planned to give me for Christmas, including my first brand new bike, he got together with a bunch of the other guys and bought me another one."

Once they finished dinner, they went for drinks at a little Irish pub just around the corner from the diner. The Blarney Stone. It had since closed, but Josie had fond memories of sitting in the crowded room at a high top table, feeling like she and Paul were the only people there, maybe the only people in the world.

At one point, he reached across the table and took her hand.

"I'm having a really great time," he said.

"I bet you say that on all your dates," she answered, although somehow, she knew there weren't that many.

"The truth is," he said, still serious, "I don't date very often. I put it all out there, no secrets, and I guess I'm a take-me-or-leave-me kind of guy. You either love me or you hate me."

Yes, this was only their first date, and she wouldn't call it love just yet, but judging by the way she felt whenever they made eye contact—as if he'd never laid eyes on another woman and never would again—she had a really good feeling about Paul Comstock.

And judging by the way he kissed her when he walked her to her door that evening, he had a good feeling about her, too.

AFTER SIGNING The Marriage Intervention's Rules document during Happy Hour Thursday night, Josie went home, heated up some leftovers for dinner and ate them while watching a rerun of *Friends*.

Then she went to bed. Alone.

She was too exhausted to think about The Marriage Intervention, The Rules, or Paul and she slept a deep, dreamless sleep.

The next morning, though, as she slipped out of bed before her alarm went off, she thought about the questions Summer and Delaney asked her the night before. How often did they have sex? She said once a month, but even that was generous. How often did they even have eye contact? Once a month? Maybe. Things hadn't always been this way. It took several years for their relationship to evolve into its current state.

In the early days, she felt giddy just thinking about him. She'd wait up for him to get home from work, just so she could hear about his day and tell him about hers. They'd sit at the kitchen counter, her in a robe and him in his uniform pants and an undershirt, and talk half the night.

She survived on barely any sleep and lots and lots of sex.

During this period of time, she missed her mother with a fierce longing. Josie could imagine Mama examining her face with her shrewd eyes, and saying things like, "You see, *mija*? You are happy. You have *el pasión*. Real passion. Because you married for practicality and not for romance."

Just after their first anniversary, Paul went undercover. That was the first curve of the downward spiral. His facial hair got longer, and so did his hours, she thought now as she got into the shower while the water was still cold. He pulled all-nighters waiting for Phoenix drug dealers to make deliveries to Juniper. He contracted with sleazy informants, took calls at all hours of the day and night, and several times had to leave family functions to take someone down.

Not that it was all his fault, Josie thought now.

After drying off, she began dressing in the outfit she had hung in the bathroom the night before. She tried to be understanding. She tried to embrace Paul's new position. He was good at it, he enjoyed it and the overtime checks were a nice bonus. She learned to appreciate her nights alone watching girly TV shows and reading cheesy romance novels.

Over time, though, she began to resent his frequent absences. And one night, while they were making what she thought was really passionate love, he froze.

"What's wrong?" Josie said.

"Nothing. Just hold on a minute."

He leapt out of bed, grabbed a notepad and a pen, and began scribbling away like a madman.

"What are you doing?" she asked.

"I just thought of something. This could be a major breakthrough. Vasquez couldn't have seen Davis at the bowling alley. He was being questioned that same night by the guys from Phoenix Metro. It just came to me."

He looked up at her then, excitement shining in his eyes. "Hold on, okay, baby? Hold on just one minute. I've got to make a call."

He left her there, laying on her back on their messy bed.

"Oh, Mama," she said to the ceiling. "I didn't marry for romance, but I didn't marry for this, either."

That was the first time, but it wasn't the last. Not that he interrupted their lovemaking again, but he did disconnect, emotionally, over and over. So she followed suit. She made herself the unavailable one, staying late at school, running unnecessary errands, shopping for new shoes she didn't need.

When they were together, she was short with him. Snippy. She picked at him for leaving his dishes in the sink rather than putting them in the dishwasher. She criticized the TV shows he watched and the amount of beer he drank. He switched to whiskey. Of course, he came back at her, his own criticisms sharp and observant. She never squeegeed the shower door. She always left her wet towel on the bathroom counter. When she got home from work she took her shoes off at the front door and left them in the walkway.

And now here they were: adversaries living together in a constant state of discord, each of them always looking to strike before the other could get in a good hit.

On the short drive to Juniper Elementary that morning, Josie made a decision. She decided to begin again with Paul. She decided she would repair their marriage, not because Summer and Delaney insisted, but because she wanted to. She wanted her marriage to get back to where it was before that downward spiral. Or maybe not where it was exactly, but somewhere close.

The parking lot was still empty except for one other car. Dread, cold and clingy, crawled up the back of Josie's neck at the thought of running into that car's owner inside. Her classroom was on the third floor, and for the briefest moment she imagined climbing up the fire escape rather than walking in through the front entrance. She chuckled when she remembered Summer and Delaney doing just that a few months before, to ensure she'd go to the interview for the principal position after they submitted her application.

But she didn't need to sneak around.

Why did she still feel the need to steel herself, even after seven years? In the fresh, purple light of the sunrise, Josie approached the wide wooden doors at the front of the century-old schoolhouse. She walked in, and he was standing in the doorway of his office. Scott Smith, as tall and handsome as ever. Scott Smith, the almost-perfect man with whom it would never, could never work.

"Josie," he said.

"Scott."

"You look nice."

She probably did. Fashion was one of her strong points. Because she couldn't remember the outfit she'd chosen the night before and she'd gotten dressed in a haze this morning, she looked down at herself: dark blue slacks that did make her legs look damned sexy, if she said so herself, and a white blouse with navy blue polka dots, tucked in neatly.

She nodded. "Thank you."

"It's been a long time since we had a chance to talk, just the two of us," he said. "Why don't you join me for a cup of coffee?"

Over the course of the past seven years, Josie often caught Scott looking at her during meetings, standing a little too close at staff parties and laughing a little too loudly at her jokes. Even after she married Paul. Even after her flame for Scott died. Well, almost died. And most importantly, even after she discovered his secrets.

Since her flame for him was long dead, or almost dead, what could it hurt to have coffee with him? He was leaving after this year, anyway. She already knew she'd be taking over his position. Besides, her fellow teachers would start trickling in within thirty minutes. How much could happen in thirty minutes?

"Two creams and two sugars?" Scott asked, although he was already stirring them into the *Recipe For A Human: Just Add Coffee* mug. She nodded, trying not to be just the tiniest bit charmed that he remembered how she took her coffee. She thanked him and he sat down behind his desk.

"You know, I've been thinking," he said.

"Yeah?"

"I've missed that slow smile, Josie. You don't even realize how sensual it is, do you?"

"Mr. Smith, that's hardly an appropriate way to speak to one of your employees."

"That's what I've been thinking about. You realize, don't you, that as soon as this school year is over, you won't be my employee any longer?"

Josie nodded. "I do realize that, yes."

Scott stood up, and Josie took in all the features that had become so familiar to her during that intense (okay, *very* intense) summer years ago: the long muscles in his thighs, the soft dark hair on his forearms and the star-shaped mole on his left cheek.

A tiny flutter rose in her belly, and she hated herself for the reaction. *You're married, Garcia.*

He sat down in the chair next to hers and grinned at her. She couldn't help it. She grinned back.

"You realize, don't you," she said, "that I'm married now? And not to you?"

"I do realize that, yes," Scott said. "But I'm not saying we have to be an item. I'm just saying we can go out for drinks now and then."

Josie considered. He was smooth. But was he right? Could they go out and have drinks, as friends?

"I'm not sure that's appropriate. With our ... history."

Scott let his gaze travel down Josie's face, her neck, her torso and back up. She shivered.

"It's probably not appropriate," he said.

She laughed, but for some reason she felt uneasy. He reached over and took her hand. Her skin tingled. His thumb caressed her fingers. She bit her lip.

She withdrew her hand, remembering The Marriage Intervention and picturing Summer and Delaney's reactions if she told them about this finger caressing.

"So? What do you think? Can we go for drinks as soon as I retire from Juniper Elementary?"

Bad idea. Of course you can't go for drinks with him. You really should just steer clear.

She shrugged a shoulder, going for aloof, blasé. Inside, her blood thrummed along in her veins like a symphony.

Scott reached for her hand a second time. When he touched her, two things happened. First, her attention-starved body reacted involuntarily, waking up from a deep sleep. Second, memories of all of Paul's infractions against her, against their marriage, paraded through her mind.

Last year, he completely forgot her birthday. They'd planned to go to dinner at Evan's Steakhouse and spent ten minutes laying in bed the night before, salivating over the fresh baked rolls, the juicy steaks, and the house steak sauce. But at three a.m., just a few hours later, Paul's phone rang. Another load of drugs was making its way up Interstate Seventeen, and he had to sit on the highway and wait for it.

The bust turned into a huge search warrant, and Paul and his team spent her entire birthday at a seedy apartment complex. He never even checked in, and didn't answer his phone when Josie called to see whether he'd be home in time for their reservation at Evan's. Needless to say, she canceled it and sat at home alone that night eating birthday cake.

On one of their rare date nights just a few months ago, Paul's work phone vibrated during the movie. She hissed at him to turn it off, and made an ugly angry face at him when she saw his sergeant's name on the screen. He went outside to answer and returned a few seconds later whispering that he had to go. Like any normal married couple, they'd come to the theater together, which meant she had to leave the movie halfway through to drive him home so he could get his work car. She spent the drive complaining about missing the rest of the movie, but in truth, she was upset because they had to cut their time together short.

Just last month, one of Paul's partners, Michael, confessed to the guys that he was having an affair. He said that ever since the birth of his first child, his wife, Jennifer, ignored him, gave him the cold shoulder. When Paul told Josie the story, she found herself enraged on Jennifer's behalf, and even more enraged when Paul defended Michael, explaining that he was just really lonely. They hadn't spoken for the entire week following that fight, but she couldn't be sure whether it's because they were fighting or because he was gone. Working.

Josie dragged herself back to the present moment and looked at Scott, whose worst fault was that he wanted something he couldn't have.

"Well, I'm not saying no," she said.

The words dangled in the air between them, stretching the moment taut.

They both jumped when they heard the building's front door open. Purposeful clicks echoed off the polished wood floor, and Josie held her breath.

"Blair Upton," Scott said as the steps approached his office. "What a pleasure so early in the morning."

Ah, my arch rival.

Blair arched a penciled-on eyebrow at Josie, and in that glance, Josie saw so many things. She saw Blair questioning what she was doing here, in Scott's office. She saw her remembering the one mistake Scott and Josie made: the time they shared a kiss just outside the auditorium and Blair came around the corner and caught them touching only at the lips but so tangled up. Josie saw Blair wishing Josie hadn't landed the principal position and taking note of the distance (the very short distance) between Scott Smith's hand and Josie's on the desk at this very moment. Finally, she saw Blair calculating exactly what this moment meant, for the two of them.

It meant nothing for Scott. He was moving on, to a new position at the school district, one where the school-level politics wouldn't touch him.

But it means everything for Blair and me. If Blair could prove Scott and Josie had a relationship, she could bring Josie down. *The lights would be out on my own role as principal of Juniper Elementary before the curtain even went up.*

Worse, the community center project, which depended on so much support from members of the community, would be a lost cause.

"It's nice to see you, as always," Josie said to Blair.

She stood up, thanked Scott for the coffee and walked out, leaving Blair and her eyebrows in the doorway, Scott and her veiled acceptance of his invitation behind the desk.

Josie ascended the stairs to the third floor, turning the lights on as she went.

Blair Upton had wanted Scott's principal position. She'd wanted it badly. So had Josie. And Josie had gotten it. But still. If Blair saw an opportunity to move in and snatch Josie's career out of the air, especially as it related to the community center, she would seize it in one of her taloned claws. Josie had to be careful.

She turned on the lights in her classroom, and just as she did every morning, she took a deep breath and surveyed her surroundings. Everything neat and organized, just as she liked it.

The desks were grouped into tidy tables, each with a colored bin atop it. The students' art, drawings of the life cycle of trees, hung on one wall in perfect rows. Vocabulary words—absorb, average, brilliant, clever—lined another wall. In one corner, fluffy pillows sat on the floor in front of book cases packed so full the kids had to pry books out of them.

Josie nodded. She was good. She had built her career from scratch to become the lead third grade teacher in just eleven years. Other teachers sought her out for advice on curriculum, discipline and wardrobe. She was indispensable. She'd be perfect as the principal.

And no one, not Scott Smith and his charming smile, nor Blair Upton and her fake eyebrows, would stand in her way.

CHAPTER FIVE

For once, Paul arrived home early that evening. Josie took it as a positive sign. He texted her at six to let her know he'd be home at seven. She normally ate dinner at six, but she decided to wait for him. They could talk over dinner, just like old times.

Josie had learned, though. Just before seven, she dished leftovers onto plates and set them on the counter. She would heat them up when he was actually sitting at the table. To her great surprise, Paul walked in the door at seven sharp.

"Wow, you got dinner all ready for me? I feel loved."

His movements seemed at once so foreign and so familiar. She walked toward him and put her arms around his waist. He froze, just for a split second, and then put his arms around her shoulders.

"Everything okay?"

I cannot believe he's asking if everything is okay just because I hugged him. Wow. We really do have problems.

"Fine," she said, her voice a little too bright. "I'm just glad to see you."

He put a hand to her forehead, pretending to check her for a fever.

"Are you all right? Lately every time I see you you're bitching me out about something."

She flinched, but forced herself to brush off his dig.

Truth hurts, Garcia.

Instead of responding with a snide remark about his work, Josie patted Paul's butt and headed to the kitchen. She waited until they were both seated at the bar and had gone through the usual how-was-your-day pleasantries before setting down her silverware and launching into her speech.

"Paul."

"Josie."

She giggled. "I need to talk to you."

"Ah. I knew it. This isn't just a regular, innocent dinner together. Tell me Summer hasn't talked you into starting our own little football team."

It was a running joke. Paul didn't understand how anyone could raise more than two children. Summer and Derek, their fifth on the way, astounded him.

"No, no. It's nothing like that. It's just, I mean, I wanted to talk about us."

Why was she nervous? Paul took a bite of spaghetti.

"Okay," he said. "What about us?"

"Well," she said, "things haven't been very, you know, very intimate lately."

"Like, we haven't been doing it very often? I agree with you there."

"No, although that's true too." She picked up her fork and twirled some noodles onto it. "I guess what I mean is that I feel like we never talk anymore. I know I blame you most of the time, but I could do more to fix things."

"What do you mean you blame me?" he asked. Now he set down his silverware. Josie felt even more nervous than she had a minute ago. She took a sip of wine.

"I mean, I complain about how you're always working," she said. "And you're always getting called out during family functions. You're thinking about drug deals when we're supposed to be having sex."

"Oh, right." Paul rubbed his forehead. "And you're constantly bitching at me about everything, just like you're doing right now. This is actually a bitching session disguised as a talk."

Shit. That's exactly what it sounds like.

Josie took a deep breath. She wiped her palms on her legs. "I didn't mean it like that. I meant, we agreed you should pursue the undercover position. Living it is different than I expected, but I agreed to it. I need to accept it."

Paul sighed. "It always comes back to me going undercover."

Josie groaned. "This isn't coming out how I wanted it to.

"I'll say," Paul said.

"Look. I just wanted you to know that I know this … distance is partly my fault."

"But mostly my fault?"

"Don't do this, Paul. I'm trying to fix things, here."

"Sorry. I didn't know things were broken."

"They're not broken, Paul. But remember how things used to be? Remember how much fun we had? We did so much fun stuff together. Remember that time we sneaked into that outdoor mini golf place and played a round at midnight? Or that time we were both wide awake at two a.m. so we went to the grocery store and bought ice cream and made sundaes and then had sexy ice cream sundae topping sex? We ate dinner together every night. We were so nice to each other."

He nodded. "You were lots nicer to me."

"At least I admit it. Isn't that the first step toward recovery?"

"Yep. You're on the road to recovery. Bitchy Wives Anonymous will be glad to have you."

She slapped his arm and returned his smile.

"Seriously, though," she said. "I want you to know that I want to make this right. I want to get back to how we used to be."

"To tell you the truth," Paul said, "I didn't realize anything was wrong. I mean, I definitely noticed the constant nit-picking. But I guess I assumed that's how wives are supposed to act. All the guys say the same thing. I'm kind of offended that you're sitting me down for this big talk about a problem I didn't even realize we have. You're blindsiding me, here."

Josie was the one who felt blindsided. She felt her face fall and her appetite disappear. Unsure of what to do or how to proceed, she stood up and cleared her plate. Paul's phone chirped. A text. Probably a drug deal needed tending.

With more force than necessary, Josie put her plate in the sink and stalked into the bedroom.

Alone again, Josie shot Summer and Delaney a text: *This Marriage Intervention thing isn't going to work.*

Summer: *What? Why not?*

Delaney: *Sheesh. Way to be a pessimist. We're just getting started, here. Give it a chance.*

Josie flopped down on her stomach on the bed, and growled into a pillow before responding.

Josie: *Paul doesn't even realize we have a problem.*

Summer: *Of course he doesn't. He probably just thinks you're being bitchy.*

Why did everyone feel like they could say that so freely? Was it common knowledge?

Delaney: *Did you tell him there's a problem? Wait. Who am I kidding? Of course you did. I don't think you were supposed to reveal that to him just yet.*

Summer: *She's right, Josie. You weren't. He probably thought you were blaming him.*

Josie: *Wait. What was I supposed to do? I was just telling him I wanted things back to the way they used to be.*

Delaney: *You should have started with the sex. Always have important conversations right after sex. You know this, Josie. We should have covered this at our initial meeting.*

"Are you kidding me?" Josie said to the empty bedroom. "I can barely get the man to sit down to dinner with me. Much less get naked with me."

Josie: *That would have been really awesome.*

Summer: *So what did he say?*

Josie: *He was offended I was sitting him down to talk about a problem he didn't even know we had. He felt blindsided.*

Summer: *Oh for goodness' sake. He had to have known something was off. Men! Seriously.*

Josie: *He probably does. Just doesn't want to talk about it.*

Delaney: *Hang in there. He'll come around.*

Josie: *I hate The Marriage Intervention. I quit.*

Summer: *Go initiate some hot Latin sex.*

Josie didn't respond. Instead, she rolled over and tried to find shapes in the texture on the ceiling. Her phone chirped.

Summer: *Stop procrastinating. Do it. Haha. Dooo it.*

Josie knew they were right. She dragged herself to a standing position and walked to the bedroom door. She took a deep breath and opened it.

But when she got into the kitchen, Paul was gone. A note sat on the counter, in the spot where his plate had been. His messy, all-caps handwriting read: *GOT CALLED OUT. DON'T WAIT UP.*

Worse than anything—Paul getting called out in the middle of dinner, him not realizing their marriage was in trouble, everyone saying Josie was bitchy—was the fact that Paul apparently didn't even realize Josie hadn't waited up for him in years.

CHAPTER SIX

A wobbly line exists between secrets and lies, Josie thought as she prepared for work the next morning. Paul still wasn't home, and she found herself thinking about Scott Smith. Again. Especially as she applied a little extra eyeliner. His drinks invitation and his renewed interest in spending time with her had brought up all kinds of feelings she shouldn't be having.

Stop it, Garcia. You're just sexually deprived. Jump your husband tonight and all will be well.

It turned out Scott was full of secrets, and just as Mama had warned, he covered them up with romance. When they first met, Josie didn't want to consider them lies, but now she wondered whether she should have. It would have saved her a lot of heartache.

For starters, he was not a newcomer to Juniper. He grew up in Juniper, but moved to Phoenix to teach, always fully intending to come back and become principal at Juniper Elementary School.

"And I always get what I intend to get," he told her after revealing he'd be her boss.

The day they met at the downtown square, he had just moved back to town. But it's not like the place was unfamiliar to him. Yes, some new restaurants had popped up and some old ones had shut down. But still.

"I played up the whole 'stranger in a strange land' angle so you'd take pity on me that first day," he said later.

"So you lied to me?" She said it playfully, but he must have seen she was a little serious.

"No, I just kept it a bit of a secret," he said. "I mean, things change so quickly, here, I *felt* like I was new to town."

At the time, she found it charming that he wanted her so much he put off dropping the bombshell that would keep them apart long-term. Now, as she pulled on a very serious, practical dress that did absolutely nothing for her figure (okay, who was she kidding? She rocked it in this dress!), she wondered if she should have backed off right then.

Or maybe she should have stopped seeing him when he told her he had a secret FriendZoo profile, so he could "lurk" (he actually used the word lurk!) on his friends' and colleagues' profiles without them seeing his.

Just like the other secrets, though, he explained it away.

"It's just that I'm a very private person," he said.

"Don't you feel kind of like a stalker, though? Like they don't even know you're looking at their profiles?"

He shrugged.

"They accept my friend requests, so they know I can see what they're posting."

"But you're making a friend request from a fake profile."

"True. But it's not like I'm a creepy bad guy or anything. I just want to see what people are up to."

"Without them seeing what you're up to."

"I'm not up to anything interesting, anyway," he said.

That was probably true. And anyway, it wasn't *that* creepy. She might do the same thing. Of course, she wouldn't do the same thing, but she was crazy in infatuation with this guy.

As she did with so many things, she laughed it off: "You could start posting post-coital selfies of the two of us."

The modern-day Josie knew what she had to do: she had to turn her sexy dress into a power outfit, and there was only one way to do that. She went to the back of her closet and dug out the highest heels she owned. She stepped carefully into them before checking herself out in the mirror.

"Oh yeah," she said aloud.

As she ate breakfast, she thought about The Biggest Secret Of All, the one where he was set to become her boss in a few weeks. She definitely should have stopped seeing him after he revealed that one.

But his lavish attention was like a balm after losing her mom. She needed the distraction. A child is always the most important thing in her mother's life, and when Mama was gone, Josie felt a burning solitude. Scott soothed that. So she continued to see him, think about him, and daydream about him like a stupid junior high girl. Even after he said he couldn't possibly date one of his employees. She may have even doodled his name on her classroom whiteboard, but just his first name.

The week before school started, they lay together in her bed, their sweaty limbs tangled and heavy with relaxation and bliss. He rolled toward her and brushed her bangs back from her forehead with a tenderness that made her insides vibrate.

"You know this can't last, right?" he said, not for the first time.

Although the vibrating stopped and her body welled up with dread, she nodded as if it were no big deal. As if she didn't feel like bawling.

"I know."

"I mean, we both want the same thing, right? We both want to focus on our careers. And we can't do that, working together at the same place and, well"—he motioned to their naked bodies—"sleeping together."

"You call this sleeping?" she teased, running a finger up his arm.

Even though she knew he was right and that it was impossible for them to stay together once the school year started, the sound of his sleepy chuckle made her want to do it all over again, and she turned toward him.

"Well, I guess we'd better sneak in as much of this sleeping together as we can."

They had, but only for a few more hot, passionate weeks before school started. They tried to quit each other cold turkey, but more than once that first couple of weeks, they ended up in some tiny secret place, putting their hands all over each other like hormone-crazed teenagers.

Now, nearly a decade later, Josie strode out to her car to drive to work and face the music. Yesterday's coffee with Scott had been a come-on. But if she was serious about fixing her marriage, she needed to stop it in its tracks.

"WOW. I get to see you first thing, two mornings in a row."

As usual, Scott was in his office when Josie arrived in her power (a.k.a. power sexy) outfit well before the start of the school day.

"Coffee?" he said.

"Not today," she said. "Look, Scott, I need to talk to you."

"Over coffee?" He gestured to the chair in front of his desk.

She didn't move. "No, not over coffee. Or drinks. Or lunch. Or anything else. Look, I'll be honest—"

"Are you ever anything other than honest?"

She allowed a tiny smile, but continued as if he hadn't spoken. "The time we spent together—years ago—was magical. And I admit, I thought we were a really good fit. There have even been times when I thought we might have been—never mind, actually." She shook her head. "Anyway. I thought we were a really good fit. At the time, the only reason we couldn't be together was—"

"Wait. You thought we might have what? What were you going to say?"

"Nothing," Josie said. "The point is that our work was keeping us apart. And with you leaving, that's not the case anymore."

When she paused, he jumped right in. "Which is why I asked you to go for drinks with me."

She held up a finger.

"I no longer think we're a good match," she said. "And as you know, I'm married now. So even if work wasn't standing between us, my marriage would be. I can't go to drinks with you. Not now and not in the future."

Scott was silent for a moment, and Josie leaned against the door-jamb waiting for him to respond. Suddenly, he smiled, a quick flash that still sent a shock of heat to her lady parts.

"So are you saying you no longer consider me a friend?"

Uncomfortable, Josie shifted her weight and switched her bag to the other shoulder. "It's not that. I do consider you a friend, but I also consider our history."

"Which no one knows about. Or needs to know about. I'm just asking you to go for drinks. As friends."

"Somehow I don't think the two of us going for drinks is quite the same as me going to Rowdy's with Summer and Delaney."

"It could be somewhere more intimate, like Rosa's," he said.

"Somehow I don't think you're getting this," Josie said. "Intimacy is the exact opposite of what we need."

"Fine," Scott said. "Let's go for beers at The Pennant. As friends. No strings."

"You're insufferable."

"I know. That's part of my charm, right?"

Josie simply shook her head and walked out of his office and up the stairs to her classroom. As she neared the first landing, she heard Scott call from below, "Love you in that dress, by the way."

Even though she had renewed her commitment to her marriage, even though she had sworn off Scott and had come here this morning to tell him just that, even though she wanted to seduce her husband into the sack this very night, she warmed at the remark.

Yes, partly because she was an absolute expert at choosing the right outfit. But also because he still knew exactly what to say. And damned if it didn't affect her.

Josie's cell phone rang at precisely eight o'clock, just as the school's first bell tolled.

"Oops," she said to herself. "Forgot to put it on silent."

She didn't recognize the number but picked up anyway, a reflex to stop the ringing.

"This is Melody from Doctor Strasser's office, calling to confirm yours and Paul's appointment with Doctor Strasser on Monday afternoon at four p.m."

"Oh. Um. Okay. Thanks. See you there."

The call caught her off guard, but not so much that she didn't know who to blame. She'd recognized the name Dr. Strasser the moment his secretary had said it in her perfectly musical voice. Summer and Derek had gone to him a while back, and over the course of a few months, Summer talked about him like he was a new BFF. "Dr. Strasser this," and, "Dr. Strasser that." Josie wouldn't be surprised if he showed up at Happy Hour one day.

Students started trickling in, so between greetings, her fingers flew over the texting keyboard as she composed a message to Delaney and Summer.

I'll kill you for this, ladies.

Summer: *Oh, good. Dr. Strasser's office must have confirmed. You won't kill us. You'll thank us. You'll worship us. Remember when we said that to Delaney during The Dating Intervention? Haha. Anyway, I thought Monday afternoon should work since it's Paul's day off.*

Delaney: *Remember how much Summer loved him?*

Josie: *How could I forget?*

Summer: *We knew you wouldn't go if we didn't schedule it for you. Just show up, okay?*

Josie: *Fine.*

Summer: *PS. I saw you looking sexy in your power sexy dress this morning. What is the meaning of that?*

"How did she—"

Josie realized her entire class was seated now, and twenty-four little faces looked at her expectantly.

"Never mind," she said.

She turned off her phone, slid it into her purse, and smiled at her kids.

"It's time to begin bell work, please. Today's question is: If you had to choose between excitement and stability, which one would you choose and why?"

After a moment of stunned silence, Joshua Morton—the student who'd inspired the community center—raised his hand. "Um, Mrs. Garcia? What does this question even *mean*?"

CARLA GARCIA WAS AN OLD-FASHIONED WOMAN. She didn't believe in "any of this woo-woo stuff," like marriage counseling or antidepressants. If she knew Josie was planning to go to marriage counseling, she would flap her hand dismissively, and say, "Nothing a little hanky panky won't fix, *mija*. You're paying thousands of dollars to a head doctor to tell you what I already know. Just get in his pants. All you've got to do to keep a man happy is feed him and make sure he's getting enough sleep and enough sex. Food, sleep, sex. That's it."

It was lunch recess and Josie sat alone in the teachers' lounge. She laughed to herself and took another bite of the turkey wrap she'd made this morning.

"What's so funny?"

Josie felt her body go rigid at the sound of Blair Upton's voice. That woman's way of speaking was grating. Forget nails on a chalkboard. It was ten times worse.

"Nothing," she said when she swallowed the bite she'd just taken. "Just thinking."

Blair slid into a chair across the table from Josie, and Josie put her wrap down. When she noticed Blair didn't have any food, she looked pointedly at the empty tabletop and said, "What's up?"

"I know the truth about how you got the principal position," she said.

Josie almost laughed again, but managed to hold it in by biting the inside of her cheek. Blair couldn't possibly know Summer and Delaney had hacked into her human resources account, used her password (bigpenis, all one word) and submitted her almost-complete application after she chickened out.

Working to keep her expression as serious as possible, she said, "How? Applied for it? Aced the interview process?"

Blair smiled as if she knew something Josie didn't. Something really good and juicy.

"No. How you slept with Scott Smith. Nothing feels as rewarding as sleeping your way to the top, does it?"

Josie sensed Blair was bluffing, feeling out the situation. Blair had a thing for Scott. Josie had seen her batting her eyelashes at him all over the place.

The temptation was strong to admit that she had, in fact, had a relationship with Scott—but that it was years ago and had nothing to do with her earning the principal position. However, it wouldn't look good for either her or Scott, even though they were long over by the time she applied.

"I don't know where you get your info," Josie said. "But it's inaccurate. Maybe you should try checking your sources before you make veiled threats."

Josie stood up, put her half-eaten turkey wrap back in its plastic bag and pushed in her chair.

"Oh, they're not veiled," Blair said. "I'm going to the school board with this information. You'll never become principal. And as you know, I came up second on the list. You'll be answering to me next year."

Whether the anger resulted from Blair's old-fashioned nastiness, or from the fact that she couldn't tell her the truth about how long gone her relationship with Scott was, or from the fact that her marriage was falling apart, Josie felt the blood rush to her face.

"I'm afraid you're quite wrong," she said to Blair, whose eyebrows arched at her maliciously like they had minds of their own. "Whether I ever slept with Scott is irrelevant because I'm the best qualified for the principal position. That's why I got it, and that's why you'll be answering to me. Until I find a reason to fire you."

"We'll see," said Blair, unaffected. "We'll see."

Josie walked back to her classroom, conscious of keeping her pace normal and even.

Threatening Blair with being fired was probably a bit over the top, but it sure felt good to say it. And who would Blair report the threat to? Scott? Even if Blair did bat her eyelashes at him, he wouldn't give her the time of day on this one.

And if Blair went to the school board, her eyebrows would gravely diminish her credibility. At least, Josie hoped so.

CHAPTER SEVEN

If Paul thought Josie had blindsided him with the whole "I want to work on our marriage" thing, he had another thing coming. That thing was marriage counseling, prescribed by Summer and Delaney.

Monday morning, as Josie dressed in a decidedly non-sexy outfit of khaki pants and a demure pink button-up blouse, she told Paul about their appointment. Having gotten home late Sunday night—yes, he'd worked late on one of his days off—he was still in bed.

"You've got to be kidding me," he moaned into his pillow.

"Don't blame me. Summer and Delaney made the appointment."

He groaned.

"You know we have to go. We can't cancel now or we'll still have to pay for the appointment. And it would really offend Summer and Delaney if we didn't take their advice."

"I have so many issues with this, it's not even funny," Paul said. "We don't need counseling. If you have a problem, let's talk about it."

Tried that. It didn't work.

He rolled onto his back and put his hands over his face, then continued speaking. "Second, why are you talking to Summer and Delaney about our so-called problems? Wait. Don't answer. It's because you're women and that's what women do. Right?"

She opened her mouth to speak, but Paul interrupted her, again. "Don't answer. Third, why do they think it's okay to just make an appointment for us with some quack we don't even know? Don't answer. They think it's okay because aside from being women, the three of you are perfectly comfortable interfering in each other's lives. Like when Delaney and a pregnant Summer climbed up the ancient fire escape at your school to make sure you went to your interview. I can't believe Derek let that fly."

"See? We have lots to talk about with Dr. Strasser," she said, purposely omitting Derek's reaction which had been to say he wanted to forbid Summer from spending time with Josie and Delaney (only, he hadn't, because he knew she'd get into even more dangerous shenanigans sneaking out to see them).

Josie had put on her shoes and jewelry by this time, and she bent down to give him a quick kiss on the cheek.

"I'll see you at four."

As she walked out the front door, she could have sworn she heard him muttering, "Your mother would think we're crazy."

She pretended not to notice, because she knew he was right.

Josie was habitually late to everything except work, so she didn't understand why Dr. Strasser took such offense to her being late to the first counseling appointment. It was only ten minutes.

Of course, Paul showed up five minutes early.

"I'm a cop," he often reminded her. "On time is late. Early is on time."

When she finally rushed into the office, Paul looked bored and the illustrious Dr. Strasser looked irritated.

I thought psychologists weren't supposed to look irritated.

"Sorry I'm late," she said. "I got caught up in something at work."

"Ms. Garcia," Dr. Strasser said. "I value my own time. I value your time. And I value your marriage as I hope you do. Please arrive at the scheduled appointment time in the future."

Josie looked at Paul, hoping for some kind of silent moral support, some there-won't-be-a-next-time shrug or eyebrow raise, but he continued to stare straight ahead as if she hadn't entered the room.

"I apologize," she said in a voice that sounded stiff and huffy even to her own ears.

She sat down in the chair next to her husband and put her purse on her lap. Dr. Strasser's eyes flicked to her purse and then back to her face.

"As you know, I'm Dr. Strasser," he said. "You may call me Dr. Strasser, Dr. S., or John. Let's jump right in. Why are you here?"

Josie realized she was clutching her purse like a life preserver and forced her hands to relax. Her eyes snapped over to Paul, but he continued staring straight ahead.

"Um, okay," Josie said. "We're here because I feel like we've drifted apart. We rarely see each other anymore, and when we do, Paul is distracted with work. His work is way more important to him than our marriage is."

Out of the corner of her eye, she saw Paul flinch. She hadn't meant to say that, but realized right away that she meant it.

Dr. John Strasser nodded.

"Paul, why don't you give me your reason for being here."

Her husband smirked at her, and for that split second, she recognized the old Paul. She wanted nothing more than to reach out and take his hand. But the expression was gone as quickly as it had appeared.

"Josie made me come," he said.

Dr. Strasser smiled, but it was a thin, almost condescending smile and instead of answering, he continued looking at Paul, forcing him to provide a better answer.

"Geez, this is worse than being on the stand in a courtroom," Paul said. He shifted in his chair. "The truth is, I thought things were fine until Josie said she wanted to work on our marriage. I admit she's been a little, um, critical lately, and I'm often relieved when I get called into work on my days off. But I just thought it was, you know, that time of the month or she was stressed out with applying for the principal position and this big grant to open a community center for kids. It's a passion project for her—they both are, actually. She seems happy at work. I mean, I didn't really think anything was wrong with our marriage. All relationships have their ups and downs, right?"

"Yes, they do," Dr. Strasser said. "But that doesn't mean we can't decrease the frequency and severity of those down cycles. Now. I don't want to make any assumptions here, so let me ask each of you a question. At this point do you want to remain together, to stay married?"

Josie laughed, an ugly, barking sound, and looked at Paul.

"Of course," she said. "We both do."

A tiny flame of fear flickered somewhere between her chest and her throat. Did Paul want to stay together? He hadn't said anything to indicate otherwise. He thought their marriage was fine. Fine! But who wanted fine? Who wanted mediocre? Shouldn't their marriage be good, or even great?

Not even a second had passed, but Dr. Strasser was looking expectantly at Paul. Josie's stomach fluttered wildly.

To her immense relief, Paul nodded. "Of course," he said.

"Good. Okay. Let's begin with what *is* working. What's good about your marriage?"

"He's my best friend," Josie said.

Paul looked sideways at her. "I am pretty sure—positive, actually —that Summer and Delaney are your best friends."

Yikes.

"We tell each other everything," Josie said.

"You didn't even tell me we were having problems," Paul said.

"I'd think you would have noticed on your own."

"Let's not turn this into an argument," Dr. Strasser cut in. "I just want each of you to share a few things that are working for you. Josie's given us one. It's your turn, Paul. What is working right now?"

Paul shrugged.

"Well, I feel kind of stupid saying this now, but I always thought Josie was supportive of my career. We both have big aspirations and I thought it was something we had in common. I've been supportive as she's applied to become principal. I helped her with statistics and ideas for her grant application. And I thought the support went both ways."

"I *am* supportive of your career!"

Both Paul and Dr. Strasser looked surprised at Josie's outburst, which exited her mouth in a shriek. "I am supportive," she said in a calmer voice. "But not when it completely ruins any time we have together."

"Perhaps I should have done this at the beginning, but I wanted to jump right in since you were a bit late," Dr. Strasser said. Josie closed her eyes to keep from rolling them and Dr. Strasser went on, "Let's lay a few ground rules. During every appointment, I will ask questions that I want each of you to answer without interference from the other. I promise you, you'll get a chance to respond. In fact —" he paused and opened a desk drawer, producing two pads of lined paper and two pens, which he handed to Josie and Paul— "Here. Take notes. This way you won't forget what you want to say."

The rest of their appointment was fairly amicable, if a little uncomfortable. And very revealing.

Apparently, Paul felt like their sex life had gone downhill to the point of being completely nonexistent. He felt like Josie was a hypocrite for talking about how his work had taken over his life. He even said she had evolved into a cold, closed-off stranger with a propensity for angry outbursts.

"So you said you thought everything was fine, but it didn't take much prodding from Dr. Strasser here to bring all of this to light," Josie said after he poured his heart out, and all his other organs, too.

He just shrugged.

"I want to give you some homework," Dr. Strasser said. "In your notebooks, I want you to describe the best time in your marriage, and the time when you've felt like it was at its weakest. For each entry, write down how you felt during those times. Bring your notes to the next appointment."

"And don't worry," he added when they both remained silent. "The end of the first appointment always feels a bit … well, a bit depressing. I have a feeling with you two that things will get better from here. Chins up."

THE BEST TIMES

Josie underlined the three words, then sighed and set down her pencil.

"Nothing, huh?" Paul looked at her from the opposite end of the couch.

He was so handsome, she thought, with his dark hair and five o'clock shadow. His eyes twinkled at her.

Maybe sharing a nemesis will be good for us. Stop it. Dr. Strasser isn't a nemesis. We're paying him to help us.

She felt like crying and laughing. Summer's kids had a name for that. Craughing. It wasn't that she didn't have anything to write down on her "The Best Times" homework assignment. It was just that she missed those times.

Because she felt herself bordering on hysteria, Josie stood up.

"I have lots of things, actually," she said. "But I think it's better if I do this alone."

Rather than responding, Paul looked back down at his own notepad.

Josie could see his writing already scrawled over half a page. She sighed and wondered whether he had written about the New Year's Eve when they were both so sick with a stomach virus they fell asleep on the couch watching TV, waiting for the ball to drop in New York City. They woke up drenched in sweat at two a.m., their fevers broken, and hobbled to bed where they fell asleep in each other's arms. It wasn't the most celebratory New Year's Eve, but for some strange reason it was one of their mutual favorites. Maybe he wrote about the time they went horseback riding and she fell off within a few feet of the trailhead. She refused to get back on, and they both ended up walking the horses back to the stable. They went for a beer at a new pub, joking that trying out a new brew was just as adventurous as going for a trail ride.

Locked in their bedroom, Josie was able to concentrate. She found that once she began writing, the words flowed effortlessly.

I guess what initially attracted me to Paul was that what you see is what you get. No secrets, no pre-planned stories, no contrived situations.

His marriage proposal is a perfect example.

He took me out for a hike on Granite Mountain. The lookout at the peak is nothing short of incredible. How could it not be romantic?

So we're standing there, and Paul is taking in the views, I mean just soaking them up like he's never seen anything so beautiful. And I'm behind him, huffing and puffing with my hands on my knees like I've never hiked up such a high mountain. At that time, I hadn't.

After the next few minutes, which I spent getting my breathing and heart rate almost back to normal, I finally brought myself to a standing position and took a few wobbly steps toward Paul. He turned to face me, and we were both grinning like idiots.

It seemed natural to put our arms around each other, and we stood there looking out over Juniper for a few minutes in silence.

I remember these moments so clearly. "It's pretty awesome, right?" he asked me. "It's awesome, but I'm not sure it's worth the hike," I said.

He said, "I wasn't talking about the view, Josie. Being together is awesome. Whether we're hiking or… shopping."

We both laughed, but then he turned me toward him, his hands on my shoulders. He looked so intense all of a sudden.

"I want to marry you," he said, still looking straight into my eyes. "I want to be with you forever. Will you marry me?"

"Yes" came right out of my mouth. I didn't even have to think about it. I wasn't even surprised or shocked. I think I somehow knew our relationship would come to this. I knew we were meant to be together. I knew I wanted to marry him. Even if he'd tried to kill me by dragging me on that hike.

We were giddy all the way down that mountainside.

He later told me he hadn't planned to propose that day. He had decided to ask me, but wanted to do something more romantic. Something with candles and flowers and a fancy dinner. But the moment was so perfect, he asked me right then.

And you know what? I wouldn't have had it any other way.

How did I feel at that moment? I felt happy. Over-the-top happy. I felt surprised. I felt out of breath. Not only because I'd hiked up that mountain, but also because I was so in love with this man and I couldn't wait to begin our life together.

CHAPTER EIGHT

Josie couldn't believe she'd almost slipped and told Scott Smith she once believed they were soul mates. The Romeo and Juliet of Juniper. Each of them should want to die rather than be apart (yes, Mama would be turning over in her proverbial grave).

Surely Scott would have latched onto that, begged her to reexamine the possibility over drinks, to consider being with him now.

How could she be so stupid?

Of course they weren't star-crossed lovers. Scott Smith was a secretive man (a charming man, too, she'd give him that), and she never knew what he was really thinking. For all she knew, his whispered proclamations of never-ending love were simply pre-planned steps to make his contrived story of heartbreak more realistic.

She didn't know why she hadn't given him a firm "no" to the drinks invitation. Upon reflection, and after the appointment with Dr. Strasser, she realized she had to tell him their personal relationship was completely over, that she couldn't and wouldn't talk to him about anything unrelated to Juniper Elementary School.

It was Thursday morning, and she put on a crisp, light blue button-up shirt, a black pencil skirt, high black heels and a string of pearls. She knew she looked as serious and determined as she felt, and she strode into Scott Smith's office ten minutes before school with her heart pounding in her throat.

He looked up, surprised, and she couldn't help but smile. When he smiled back at her, she felt like she was the only woman in the world.

Well, you are *the only woman in Scott's office, Josie. So it's nothing special. Don't let that one smile blow up your skirt.*

"I need to talk to you," she said.

"Coffee?"

Josie glanced quickly around her. The front office ladies, Cheryl and Tammy, made a big show of not listening, but she knew their ears were pricked by the way their hands were poised over their keyboards and their backs were razor-straight.

"Um, no. But can I shut the door?" Josie said.

He inclined his head toward the door, and she shut it behind her. For some reason, being this close to him still made her nervous. Scott motioned to one of the chairs in front of his desk, but Josie shook her head. He looked at her as if she were a tiger who might attack at any moment.

Not in a sexy, I'm-wearing-silk-boxers way, but in an I'm-slightly-scared-you-might-kill-me way.

Josie blew out the breath she was holding and said, "I just came to tell you that I can't talk to you anymore. About personal things. I can't have drinks with you. I can't have coffee with you in the morning when the moon is still up. My marriage is very important to me, and I don't want to do anything to threaten it."

When he didn't answer, and instead continued to stare at her with his eyebrows raised, she said, "Okay?"

He nodded. "I understand."

A few seconds ticked by. At first, Scott looked shocked and maybe even hurt. Then his expression became unreadable. Blank.

Again, she felt vaguely uncomfortable.

"Okay then," she said. "I guess that's it."

She turned around to open the door. Through the pane window, she could see Cheryl and Tammy in the front office, still holding suspiciously still.

"Josie," he said.

She turned toward him, her hand still on the doorknob.

"I want you to know that my invitation to drinks was purely professional."

Josie nodded—an automatic response. But inside, she actually felt stupid. Of course his invitation was purely professional. They had been over for a long time. For the past seven years, their relationship remained purely professional. The steam started rising only recently, because Scott was leaving Juniper Elementary. Belatedly, she realized maybe there *was* no steam. She probably just imagined he was looking at her in that sexual way.

On-the-spot, her ego stinging, she imagined—but didn't verbalize—a response: *You know, Scott, I want to believe you. And I would believe you if you weren't so … so … slick. Everything is part of your master plan. You wouldn't have asked me for drinks if you didn't plan on getting something out of it.*

As she strode out of Scott's office, she pretended not to notice Cheryl and Tammy, their identical expressions of surprise, mouths hanging open and eyes following her quick exit.

How could I have been so stupid? Of course he meant the invitation in a professional way. He doesn't even think of me that way anymore.

Even while her less-than-sane inner voice chastised her for her foolish behavior, Josie's practical voice piped up with its own message: *He's lying. He just had to cover his tracks. He thought you'd come running into his arms now that he's leaving Juniper Elementary, and he's probably just as embarrassed as you are.*

Which one was the truth?

Josie couldn't be sure. But she did know she was proud of herself for standing her ground and choosing her marriage. She felt a whole lot lighter.

On the second-floor landing she saw Blair Upton standing in her classroom doorway, glaring at Josie. She almost certainly would mistake Josie's carefree attitude for post-coital bliss, or something like it. But Josie didn't care.

She pushed the niggling sadness out of her mind, and wrote the morning bell work on the board: *Explain the term, "mixed feelings." What does it mean? Have you ever experienced it?*

JOSIE WAS DREADING—OR, more accurately, *really* dreading—tonight's weekly Rowdy's Happy Hour with Summer and Delaney.

The girls would expect a report on her first marriage counseling appointment, and she didn't want to reveal that Paul had a list of complaints as long as hers, if not longer.

But they were her best friends, they meant well and more importantly, she and Summer had absolutely dissolved any semblance of privacy when they stalked Delaney during The Dating Intervention.

She looked at her watch. Five minutes after four.

Josie pushed open both of Rowdy's swinging doors and paused in the doorway. She took a deep breath and gathered her confidence, then walked toward their table as if she wasn't about to be forced to reveal every weakness she brought to her marriage.

"Whoa, you just looked like the cover of a romance novel, silhouetted in the doorway like that, the sun shining in behind your sexy body," Summer said as Josie slid onto her barstool. "I'm starting to look like a puff pastry over here and there you are, as curvy and hot as ever."

"Oh, Summer. You're the most beautiful pregnant lady we know," Delaney said.

Glad for the distraction, Josie beamed at both of them.

"How are you feeling, anyway? You *are* starting to show a little. It's so cute."

"I still feel horrible," Summer said. "These olives help. Thinking about it doesn't, though, so let's talk about something else."

Shit. Let's not talk about me.

"Delaney, has Jake proposed yet?" Josie asked.

"Josie, we've only been dating for, like, a few months. Of course he hasn't proposed yet. I haven't even seen his feet yet."

"What are you talking about?" Josie said. "And of course you've seen his feet by now. Right?"

"Remember your rubric during The Dating Intervention? 'Have you seen his feet?' was one of your questions. 'It's an intimacy thing,' you guys said. Remember?"

"Oh, yeah," Josie said. "But you've seen his feet, right?"

"Of course," Delaney said. "I was kidding. But that doesn't mean a proposal is imminent."

"Yeah, it is," Summer said. "Has he started talking about how many kids he wants? What kind of architecture he likes?"

"Ooh," Josie said. "Or his favorite sexual positions? You know, like, kinky stuff?"

"You guys," Delaney said. She dipped her head.

"She's blushing!" Josie said, possibly a little overzealous with relief that they were talking about Delaney and not her own marriage. "He's kinky!"

Summer laughed, but only for a second. Only for long enough for Delaney to switch gears.

"So, Josie. How was your appointment with Dr. Strasser?" she said.

Shit. Two can play at this game, I guess. I shouldn't have gotten so excited about Jake and his sexual positions.

Josie sighed. "We don't have to talk about it, do we?"

Summer, reading her reluctance correctly, as always, reached out and took her hand. "What happened?"

Josie felt her eyes fill. She blinked to clear them and a tear rolled down her cheek. She brushed it away, impatient.

"What happened?" Delaney repeated.

"I guess I should have expected it," Josie said. "I thought I was the only one who was unhappy. But it turns out, Paul has his own complaints, too. Plenty of them."

She ticked Paul's grievances off on her fingers: she was cold, she constantly criticized him, she hated his job, she no longer supported his career. She was a hypocrite who valued her career as much as he did his, if not more.

"I mean," Josie said, "Is it all true? I've always kind of blamed him for the distance between us, but to hear him tell it, I'm just as bad. Worse."

Delaney and Summer looked at each other and Summer stirred her olives with her pointer finger.

"What? What, you guys?"

Summer licked her finger and looked at the top of the table as if she were studying it for a calculus exam. Delaney elbowed her.

"Josie," Summer said, scratching at the table with her thumbnail. "You have been a bit, well, a bit ..."

"A bit grumpy lately," Delaney said. "You always seem unhappy."

"And no offense," Summer said. "But I'm sure it's not that fun for Paul to be around you. He might have a point."

Josie's mom had always said, "Happy wife, happy life," as if that one statement could solve all marriage problems and prevent any new ones from developing.

What resulted from an unhappy wife, though? And was she really unhappy? She hadn't thought so, but maybe Paul did. And if so, then he was probably equally unhappy.

IS IT TRUE?

At home, eating dinner solo at the kitchen counter, Josie asked herself over and over whether Summer and Delaney—and Paul—were right. This wasn't the first time in recent history the girls had pointed out her bad moods. While mixing her meatloaf with her mashed potatoes, Josie thought about the last couple of interactions she and Paul shared.

Be subjective, she told herself. *Pretend you're a fly on the wall. Or a spider. A black freakin' widow.*

Just a couple of weeks ago, Paul texted her at five one evening to say he was coming home early. Because Josie was still at school, working on lesson plans for the following week, she didn't even think to check her phone. Needless to say, she didn't get his text until she left school at nine p.m. By the time she got home, Paul was in bed. What if he had planned a nice dinner for the two of them, just as she had with the steaks? It never even crossed her mind.

A week or so before that, Paul came into the bathroom while she was in the shower. He worked late the night before, and he must have gotten up early just to spend time with her. He slid the shower curtain back, peeked his head in, and ran a hand from her shoulder to her ass, where he stopped for a little squeeze.

"Can I join you?"

And what did she do? Instead of welcoming a connection, she pushed him away. "I'm in a hurry. I've got to get to work."

Without another word, he pulled his arm back, closed the shower curtain, and went back to bed.

Being subjective, she thought, she *was* cold.

"Ugh," she said to herself as she put her dishes in the dishwasher. "You've got a lot of work to do, woman."

Friday morning, Josie awoke with a renewed sense of purpose. She'd seen the light and she knew she had to change.

She could do it.

All along, she told herself she was just reacting to Paul's bad behavior. Even when she committed to fixing their marriage, she'd done so thinking she had to show Paul the errors of his ways. But now she realized she played as much of a role in the decline of their marriage as he did.

Today's outfit: skinny black pants with a bright pink sweater set. Cute, for sure, but still sexy, showing off the curves Summer so loved. She was thinking so hard about Paul and how she could fix things that she didn't even see Scott standing in the doorway of his office, waiting for her to enter the building.

"Good morning," he said.

She jumped.

"Good morning."

Despite her intentions to continue walking straight up the stairs to her classroom, Scott walked toward her, stopping on the bottom step. Impatient, Josie paused just long enough to say, "I've got to get to my classroom. I have lots to do before school starts."

"I just wanted to tell you something," he said. His tone was so overtly gentle that she expected him to ask her to sit down.

"Well, tell me." She placed a foot on the step next to him, making it clear she didn't mean to spend much time here.

"I'm moving. To Phoenix."

Josie didn't know what to make of this revelation. What Scott did shouldn't matter to her. "I thought you were taking that curriculum position at the district here, in Juniper."

He sighed and rubbed his eyes with one hand.

"I was. But the truth is, it's just too hard for me to be here. In Juniper, with you. I'd still see you at all the districtwide administrative meetings. And even now, I see you everywhere I go. I drive past the square and remember that first time we met. I walk past the pub and remember how you convinced me to try their fried crickets that night. I see a kid on a red bike and think about young Josie, pedaling up the hill on her first bike, losing momentum and tipping over just before the crest."

Josie tried for a smile. Even with her renewed introspection and her dedication to her marriage, Scott's words soothed the part of her that had felt so lonely lately. Something about him leaving Juniper made her inexplicably sad.

She wasn't sure what to say, so she wished him the best of luck and then she walked up the stairs, leaving him standing there. She imagined there was some invisible string that held them together. She imagined it stretching as she ascended the stairs. Then she imagined it breaking. When she passed the second landing, though, her mind flashed to the time they had stood in that same spot, just after breaking up, the tension between them like the buzz of a neon sign. She wanted so badly to reach out to him, to run a finger along the line of his chin. She wanted so badly for him to put a hand on her shoulder. Just one little touch. But before they wound up intertwined on that second-floor landing, they walked away from one another. He went down, and she went up.

CHAPTER NINE

Surprising Statistic #8. Marriage counseling may lead to divorce.

Josie had done a quick Internet search, "Does marriage counseling work," just before leaving her classroom, and she wasn't all that pleased with what she found.

The surprising statistics the article's headline promised were actually wishy washy, super-obvious discussion points disguised as answers. Basically, they all said, "It depends." On whether both people show up, how much you want to repair the marriage, how your marriage is faring, whether you go to a licensed counselor or a psychologist. "Of course it depends," she said to her computer before shutting it down and heading out to her car.

Nevertheless, Josie figured she could improve their chances if she made a point of arriving on time to the second appointment with Dr. Strasser. She felt smug as she walked into the reception area five minutes early.

A year ago, Josie would have sat down in the chair next to Paul's and leaned over for a kiss. Now, for some reason, with the spotlight on their relationship, she felt awkward, unsure of what to do.

"Hey," she said from the doorway.

"Hey," he said. He put down the magazine he was holding and stood up. At first she thought it was just his old-fashioned manners making an appearance, but then he walked toward her and put his arms around her waist.

"I miss you, baby," he said. "I know I said I wasn't aware we were having problems, or whatever, but the truth is that I just couldn't put my finger on what's wrong, and I don't know how to fix it."

Her body went from rigid to supple, and for the first time in as long as she could remember, she let him hold her. They stood there for a full minute before she spoke.

"We can fix it," she said. "Remember the first time we cooked for your parents? We decided we would make that fancy roast thing, only, I'd never made a roast before. I was in charge of browning it while you made the salad. I still don't know why you put me in charge of browning it. But anyway, I burned the crap out of it. Remember?"

"How could I forget?" he said. Although he didn't laugh out loud, she could feel his amusement.

"Remember what you said to me, then? You said, 'We can fix this. We can still get this dinner back on track.' You cut off all the burned bits and browned it yourself while I chopped vegetables for the salad. Your parents loved it. Afterwards, you said, 'If we can fix that roast, we can fix anything. That's how we know this marriage is solid.'"

He laughed.

"You know, you're right," he said. "And I still believe it, too. Trust me, fixing that roast was hard work. But we did it, right? I think that ended up being the best roast I've ever had. Even to this day."

The door to Dr. Strasser's office opened, and he smiled when Josie and Paul turned to look at him.

"Making progress already, I see," he said. He gestured to the open door, and followed them in.

"So, did each of you do your homework?" Dr. Strasser wanted to know when they were settled in their chairs.

Josie and Paul nodded, and each of them held up a sheet of paper, covered in notes.

"Good," Dr. Strasser said. "Now, I'm not going to make you read it aloud or anything, but I do want to talk about the feelings portion. I want to know how each of you felt during those best times and worst times. Let's start with the best times. Josie?"

Okay, I can do this. This isn't so bad.

"Okay," she said. She remembered from her speech and debate days that she wasn't supposed to start any speech with "Okay," so she cleared her throat and began again. "I felt happy, connected, loved and cared for."

"Paul?"

"I felt connected, too," he said. "And important. You know, important to Josie. I felt like part of a family."

Dr. Strasser nodded. He sat back in his chair and steepled his fingers.

"Now let's talk about those times when you experienced negative emotions. Paul, you go first."

"All right." He cleared his throat. Josie realized he was nervous, too. She gave him an encouraging smile, but he was staring at the paper in his lap.

"I felt alone," he said. "Like, lonely. And I felt angry. Sad. Disappointed."

Josie sat up a little straighter. Paul went on, "I felt exhausted. Like things were out of my control. Like I was trying so hard, but I was failing."

"You sure have a lot of negatives compared to your very short list of positives." The words escaped from Josie like a bull coming out of a chute. She clapped a hand over her mouth, but she could tell from Paul's expression (and even from Dr. Strasser's carefully blank one) that the damage was already done. "I'm sorry. I didn't mean to say that. I'm really sorry."

"Josie, why don't you go ahead and tell us about your emotions during the tougher times."

She nodded, eager to put that outburst behind her. Paul's ears turned red, which meant he was either angry or embarrassed. Probably both.

"I felt lonely, too," she said. "I felt angry and sad."

The three of them sat in silence for a few beats.

"Take a minute and sit with those feelings," Dr. Strasser said. "Just sit with them."

Josie didn't know why, but she felt surprised that Paul had experienced feelings similar to hers. Lonely? Paul felt lonely? It always seemed like his work fulfilled him so much he didn't even need her. She suspected that's where a lot of her resentment came from.

This was very unexpected.

"Good," said Dr. Strasser, as if he could hear her thoughts. "Now, I want each of you to talk about your reaction to your partner's feelings." Paul shifted in his chair. Dr. Strasser must have taken that as willingness to go first. "What are you thinking, now that you know how Josie feels, Paul?"

Paul nodded.

When she was teaching, Josie always thought it was cute when a student nodded after she asked him a question, as if he was verifying he understood it.

"I guess I feel kind of guilty, knowing Josie's been feeling lonely. She seems so self-sufficient all the time. And when I do try to help her or just keep her company or whatever, she blows me off."

Was it possible they were feeling the exact same way?

"Josie, I want you to think about Paul's comment—that he feels like you blow off his efforts to help you or keep you company. Before you respond to that, I'd like you to talk about your reaction to the homework assignment."

"Well. First, I'm surprised and hurt to hear how many negative emotions Paul is experiencing with regard to our marriage. That being said, it's interesting to hear that we're both feeling similarly. I had no idea Paul felt lonely. He is so wrapped up in his job. Even when he's home with me, he's on his phone, texting some informant, texting his partner, whatever."

Then something dawned on her.

"I was going to say, 'How could he possibly be lonely? He's never actually alone?' but I'm wondering now if he buries himself in his work because he feels distant from me."

If they were in a game show, a bell would be ringing: *Ding, ding, ding! And Josie has just stated the correct answer!*

It was actually comical. Relief-related humor. Maybe they shared more similarities than she realized. Instead of laughing (because she knew Paul and Dr. Strasser would mistake her laughter for a lack of seriousness), she reached across the space between their chairs and squeezed his arm. When he glanced at her, looking a bit panicked, she smiled at him.

Relief washed over her when she saw his answering smile.

"Yes," Dr Strasser said. "I think we're making some progress here."

When the session was over, Paul had to go back to work to finish some reports. Josie decided it had gone so well she would treat herself to a cocktail at Juniper's swankiest restaurant, Juniper Station. Sitting on a tall stool at the modern stainless steel bar, she savored her vodka cranberry.

As she drove, she replayed the remainder of the appointment in her mind. After Paul's heart-stopping smile, Dr. Strasser asked her to really think about why she reacted the way she did when Paul offered help or company. She asked Paul for examples, and he actually had a couple to offer.

Once, he was running just a few minutes late after work, he came home to find her in the middle of decluttering the linen closet. He offered to help, but she basically told him to go away.

She remembered the day clearly. She expected him home at seven. When he didn't walk through the door by seven minutes after, she ditched the dinner idea she had planned and got elbow-deep in the decluttering project she'd been considering for quite some time. Still steaming when he did get home at seven-fifteen, she gave him the cold shoulder. She didn't even give him a chance to explain the reason he was late: he stopped on the highway to help a woman his grandmother's age put the spare tire on her car after she had a blowout.

When she finally heard him out, it was such a classic story she chose not to believe him, instead concocting some wild tale in her imagination about how Paul had probably gotten stuck talking to that one tweaker all the guys joked about, the girl who was smokin' hot except for her horrible teeth. "She's fine—I mean, fiii-iiiine—as long as she keeps her mouth shut," they all said. But what reason did he have to lie?

He wasn't the secret-keeper, after all, Josie thought as she parked and got out of the car.

This wasn't about placing blame, Dr. Strasser pointed out. It was about identifying the reasons for their own behaviors and then resolving the issues there. Treating the cause rather than the symptoms.

She opened the door of Juniper Station and scanned the bar for an empty stool. Spotting one, she made a beeline and sat down. Speaking of secret-keepers, was that Scott Smith right here in Juniper Station, sliding his lanky body onto a stool a few seats over? Carefully, trying not to let him see that she noticed him, Josie looked at him through her lowered eyelashes.

It is him. *Why does he keep popping up?*

The teeny tiny part of Josie that had always thought Scott might be her soul mate raised her arms in victory. *Maybe he keeps popping up because you're meant to talk to him. Possibly even have drinks with him.*

The rest of her, the sensible part of her, smacked the other part of her on the forehead. *Shut up, dummy. He's probably here meeting someone for drinks. You're the one in a completely different place than you'd usually be.*

Josie angled her body away from Scott, placing her elbow on the bar so her back was to him. She heard him order. Scotch on the rocks with an extra ice cube, as always.

See? People don't change, Josie.

Within a minute, she heard his voice close to her ear.

"So, I guess we're going to have drinks together after all."

She sighed in response, and didn't turn around.

"What's the matter? I thought you'd be happy to see me."

"I was just here for some alone time," she said. "Some thinking time. I didn't expect to run into anyone."

He didn't get the message, despite what Josie thought was sparkling clarity. He slid onto the stool right next to hers.

"Can we talk for a few minutes? For old times' sake?"

Finally, Josie turned to face him. "The old times are over."

"But don't you like to remember them fondly?"

"I remember them fondly, when I do think about them, but to tell you the truth, I try not to think about them."

"You know, you broke my heart when you married Paul."

You broke my heart when you said we couldn't be together. And again when you told Blair Upton I meant nothing to you, that our kissing that day outside the auditorium was a fluke.

Wow, she hadn't recalled that part of the memory until just now. After whichever assembly they had been headed to that day Blair caught them kissing, she overheard Scott and Blair talking in the office during recess. Yelling, actually. It was quite heated, if she remembered correctly.

Blair said something about how unprofessional it was of Josie and Scott to be romantically involved, and that she should report his behavior to the school board. Scott responded that they weren't romantically involved. He said the kiss was a fluke, that they were talking and it just happened. He went so far as to say Josie rubbed him the wrong way. She was brash and harsh and not even that good-looking.

For a moment, standing outside the office, Josie felt steam coming out of her ears. How dare he say something like that, when they were so in love? Yes, they had agreed they couldn't continue a relationship once school started, but it had all been so tragic. Because they *cared* about each other. Josie had spent every evening since their split watching *Titanic* just so she could have a good cry.

When she heard Scott tell Blair she meant nothing to him, she wanted more than anything to knock on the office door and give both of them a big piece of her mind.

But something stopped her.

It was probably that stupid voice in her head, the one that thought they were soul mates.

It said, *He's just saying these things to protect both of you. He knows you want to be a principal someday, and he wants to move into district administration. Of course he is saying these things. You'd be offended if he wasn't. He doesn't mean them.*

But a pattern was emerging, and Josie was starting to see it clearly. Scott Smith said whatever he needed to, whenever he needed to. He was a chameleon. As an audience to his carefully-crafted monologues, you never knew when he was telling the truth and when he wasn't.

As Josie turned off of Memory Lane, she almost felt surprised to find herself looking into Scott's eyes.

What did he just say? "You broke my heart when you married Paul."

That's right.

I broke his heart.

"I actually don't believe that," she said, although she did kind of enjoy thinking it was true. What woman doesn't like the thought of someone holding up the pieces of his heart in her wake? And not just someone, but someone for whom she holds a flame, herself? She shook her head. *Held a flame, Garcia. Past tense.* "You always made it clear we couldn't be together long-term. I thought you preferred to think of it as a tragic love story."

He ran a fingertip up and down the side of his glass. She shivered. Those fingertips.

Stop it. Don't even think about those fingertips.

"It *was* a tragic love story. If you had waited, we could have been together now."

"If I had waited?"

His audacity shouldn't have shocked her, but it did. She would have been waiting a long time. Too long.

"I know what you're thinking," Scott said. "That would have been a long wait. A man can wish, though, right?"

"You're right," Josie said. "It would have been a long time to wait. Especially for someone who made it clear we couldn't work."

Scott shrugged. "But still. You're having a drink with me."

Exasperated, Josie sighed. "By chance."

"By Fate," Scott said.

Josie shook her head. "You're relentless."

He held up his glass as if to make a toast. She wasn't sure whether he was toasting Fate or his relentlessness. "You know it," he said.

"So why did you invite me to have drinks with you, a couple of days ago?"

"For old times' sake. Because I miss you. Because I realized now that I'm moving on, I won't be seeing you anymore. I know we haven't been together, together. But at least I've been able to see you every day. Your perfect eyelids, that face you make when you concentrate, the way you look absolutely sexy, I mean, mouthwatering, even when you're going for professional. We haven't been together, but at least you've been in my world. I can't imagine my life without you."

"You really feel that way?"

"I do."

For the fourth time in as many days, memories flooded in. How could she possibly have so many memories of their relationship when they'd been together for only a few weeks?

She remembered a walk they'd taken around the historic district, sipping iced teas she picked up at Umbrella Coffee, talking about which houses they liked, which they'd move into, and which they'd remodel. The trees that lined the street were leafed out and the warm summer breeze stirred them overhead so the light sparkled. Hand in hand, they walked along, and Josie felt more content than she could put into words.

Another time they went to a performing arts festival, and a group of kids from a circus camp put on a very cute, if a little clumsy, circus act, some of them teetering on stilts and others tumbling wildly across the stage. Josie spent the entire nine-minute spectacle imagining what hers and Scott's children would look like. Would they have his deep, round eyes, or her cat-like ones? Would their skin be that perfect mix of dark and light, the color of coffee with creamer? Would their children be the ones walking on stilts, or the ones performing cartwheels and flips? Yes, their lovemaking had been a little more passionate than usual that night, and she imagined he was picturing their potential children as well.

They truly had shared some good times.

An hour together to commemorate those times couldn't hurt, could it?

"All right," she finally said. "Let's have a couple of drinks. As a send-off. But that's it."

He grinned and they clinked glasses. Josie could practically feel her mother, a little angel hovering over her shoulder, clucking her tongue and frowning. Josie hoped she wasn't making a mistake.

Bottoms up, Garcia.

"LOOK AT THAT GLOW," DELANEY SAID WHEN JOSIE WALKED INTO Rowdy's for Happy Hour.

"Somebody finally got between the sheets with her husband," Summer said.

"Well, not exactly," Josie said, feeling guilty that the glow didn't result from sex with Paul. "But things are a lot better."

She quickly recapped the second counseling appointment, and Summer shone with excitement.

"I knew it! I knew Dr. Strasser could work his magic on the two of you!"

"Speaking of magic," Josie said, eager, once again, to shift the attention away from herself. "Any word on a proposal from Jake, Dee?"

"No word, but I did find some evidence," Delaney said.

Summer sat up a little straighter. "Evidence?"

Delaney nodded. "Last night I was helping with the dishes at Jake's place, and I accidentally opened the junk drawer when I went to put the ladle away. I saw a brochure in there. From a jewelry store. There were a bunch of rings on the cover. It looked like he shoved it in there, like maybe he had it on the counter before I got off work and wanted to hide it when I knocked on the door."

"So what did you do?" Josie said. "Did you confront him?"

"Well, I know *you* would have!" Delaney said to Josie. "But I just quickly shut the drawer and pretended I hadn't seen it. I don't think he even noticed I went to the wrong drawer."

"Probably not," Summer said. "And that's promising news."

Delaney looked dreamy, and Josie squeezed her arm.

"Speaking of news," Josie said. "When do you find out whether Baby Number Five is a girl or a boy?"

"I think we might be surprised this time," Summer said. "I mean, we already have two of each, so either one will tip the scales."

"I can't take the suspense!" Josie said. "How will I find the baby the perfect coming-home outfit if I don't know whether it's a boy or a girl?"

"Your newest fashion challenge," Delaney said. "A gender-neutral coming-home outfit."

Summer laughed, but her expression turned serious within a couple of seconds. "Okay, Josie. We've let you get away with misdirection, but time's up. Why the glow?"

Shit.

Of course Josie couldn't tell them about her conversation with Scott. Although she knew their romantic relationship was over, and their reminiscing over drinks didn't mean anything beyond drinks as friends, it felt so good to hear someone talk about her the way Scott had.

He talked about her like she was a princess. No, a goddess. A sexy vixen. He talked about her like she was an invaluable part of his life. Even now.

"Where *are* you right now?" Summer said. "Geez, you look exactly like Sarah does when she's daydreaming about a boy in her class. I love Dr. Strasser but even I'm impressed that he could help you turn things around this quickly!"

Josie nodded and with some reluctance shoved Scott to the back of her mind.

"I found a location for the community center," Josie said.

"Tell us about it!" Delaney said.

She'd spent the past several evenings online, searching for a property she could lease. The criteria were many: it had to be within walking distance of Juniper Elementary School. It had to have lots of windows, and if it didn't have an actual kitchen, it had to have the space for one.

She'd learned enough about plumbing and square footage and zoning to make her head spin. She'd toured spaces in strip malls, historic areas, and new commercial zones.

Finally, she'd found it: a little cottage in the neighborhood around Juniper Elementary School. It was yellow with white trim, flower boxes under the front windows, and a wide open main floor with plenty of room for tables and computer desks and the ping pong table she'd found at a garage sale. The kitchen, with its generous countertops, sat in the back corner, which allowed for that ever-important "flow" her real estate agent kept talking about.

She told the girls all of this, and then she felt herself on the verge of tears (again) as she told them, "The moment I walked in, I could see it. I could visualize everything: kids sitting at the tables, doing homework. Kids playing ping pong. Teenagers helping the little ones with reading. I thought, 'I could put a reading corner there, with a little bookshelf, and I could put the music player over there, and the kids could take turns choosing the music.' I just felt it. I just knew it was the right place. So I put in an application. Now it's a waiting game, to see if the owners accept it."

Summer squeezed Josie's hand. "I'm so proud of you, Josie," she said. "Your mom would be so proud, too, I just know it."

"Thanks," Josie said. "She'd love it. She'd be baking cookies every day. Or making tamales."

"Eat!" Delaney said, mimicking Josie's mom. "You girls must eat!"

"Exactly," Josie said.

"And then I'd be there every day, eating, too," Delaney said.

"Actually," Josie said. "I was kind of hoping you'd be there often."

"Me?" Delaney said. "Why?"

"I don't know. Have you ever thought about getting your counselor certification again? You have the degree. I'd love to have you on staff to counsel these kids."

Delaney looked thoughtful and Josie couldn't tell whether she liked the idea—which made her panic. "You don't have to tell me now. Just promise me you'll think about it."

"Okay," Delaney said. "I'll think about it. I'll admit, I am intrigued."

"That sounds great," Summer said. "You'd be great at it, Dee."

"You're not off the hook," Josie said to Summer. "I'm going to hire you to do all the marketing materials. I'm going to need a logo, a letterhead, signage … the list goes on and on. I wouldn't want anyone but you to design it."

Now Summer looked like she might cry.

"You don't have to," Josie said. "I just thought, you know, you understand me. You understand my vision. It would mean a lot to me to have you design all the images for the center. But you can say no. Just think about it."

"Oh, Josie!" Summer said. She jumped down from her stool and wrapped her arms around Josie's neck. "I'll do it. You had me at, 'I'm going to hire you.' I would love to!"

"Thank you," Josie said. "Thank you so much. I'm so excited. I can't believe this is all coming together."

"When do you hear about the application?" Summer said.

"Hopefully within a week. So fingers crossed." Josie knew she was going to have to tell the girls about her appointment with Paul and Dr. Strasser. Better to get it over with.

She said, "But anyway. Yes, Dr. Strasser is pretty amazing. In fact, Paul is supposed to get home early tonight, so we'll see if all his talk carries over to the bedroom. Finally."

If nothing else, maybe sex with her husband would get her mind off Scott.

After leaving Rowdy's, Josie stopped by the grocery store to pick up dinner, which, Josie reminded herself, didn't have to be anything fancy. It was really just the appetizer, anyway.

She opted for fresh sushi from the sushi bar. Early in their relationship, she and Paul bought entire meals following a theme, and she was tempted to buy sake and Japanese wine for tonight. When the words, *For old times' sake*—an echo of Scott's words—crossed her mind, she flashed to an image of sitting next to him at Juniper Station. She decided on white wine from the chilled section.

Paul promised to come home early tonight, for once leaving off the caveat, "unless something comes up."

Josie's first reaction was to wonder why, if he he could arbitrarily drop those four words because they were working on their relationship, he never did.

Variations of "unless something comes up" had become the soundtrack for their marriage since he went undercover.

But when her mind started traveling this path, Josie thought of how Dr. Strasser had told her negativity was like a cancer.

"Stop," she said aloud, just as Dr. Strasser had told her to do. "Paul's making an effort."

This new positive thinking thing was going to take some practice. Music would help. At home, Josie dug through their massive CD collection until she found the love songs CD she made for Paul a few years back. It was upbeat and romantic, and when she turned it way up, its beat blocked concrete thoughts from forming.

For the first time in a long time, Josie found herself dancing at the kitchen counter as she laid the sushi out on plates and wiped down the dusty wine glasses.

It felt good to be in such a good mood. Foreign, but good. She swayed her hips to "Sexual Healing" and to her own surprise, picked up a wooden spoon to use as a microphone.

"Aaaand, she's back." Paul's voice startled Josie, and she jumped. The wooden spoon clattered to the floor.

Her husband stood in the doorway of the kitchen, smiling at her in a way he hadn't done in months.

He is so sexy. How could I have forgotten that?

The sunset's pink light slanted in through the kitchen window, and the shadows illuminated his biceps and the stubble that ran along his jawbone. His eyes glinted in a way that was at once affectionate and completely toe-curling.

She shrugged, then bent to pick up the spoon. When she returned to a standing position, Paul's smile had shifted to purely predatory.

Had she just deliberately angled her backside toward him? She had. Josie laughed, and Paul shook his head.

"You're pulling out all the stops, woman," he said.

The sexual tension built over dinner, as they sat at the counter chatting about their day. Several times between bites of sushi and sips of wine, Paul reached out to run a hand down Josie's arm or brush her hair away from her face. She got up to get them napkins and brushed the front of her body against the back of his.

When he finished eating, he ran a finger down the side of her neck, giving her chills.

Josie could practically feel sex in the air. Warm and luscious, soothing and promising.

"Do you know how long it's been since we, you know, did it?" he asked.

"I can't even recall," she said.

She actually could recall. It was several months ago, on a sizzling hot fall night. Heat waves always bring the crime rate up (thanks to the event in question, she'd never forget that). Josie was flat on her back on the bed, hands gripping the pillows and legs splayed, and Paul was doing something amazing to her breasts with his mouth.

Oh, this is going to be so good, she was thinking.

Then his phone rang. Of course, it was on the bedside table and it vibrated wickedly, completely destroying the moment. Paul groaned, then got up to answer it.

He was out the door three minutes later, Josie's entire body coming down off this ledge of incredible anticipation.

"Stop," she said out loud.

"Huh?"

Josie shook her head. "It has been a long time," she said.

"Let's not let that happen again."

They left their sushi on the counter and carried their wine with them. Paul linked his fingers with Josie's and led her to the bedroom. Neither of them spoke.

They'd left the bed unmade that morning, and the duvet was rumpled on top of the sheets. Josie felt a little thrill when Paul grabbed it and swept it to the floor.

He took Josie's wine from her and set their glasses on the nightstand.

"I've missed this," Paul said, pulling her towards him. "I've missed you."

Josie wrapped her arms around his neck and kissed him lightly on the nose.

"I've missed you, too," she said.

Paul put his hands on her hips, and pulled her even closer. For the first time in … well, in what felt like forever, the two of them looked at each other without any traces of anger or resentment, without cold politeness, and instead with passion and a knowing.

He pushed her away, gently, and said, "Undress. I want to watch you."

Josie turned around, hooked her thumbs in the waistband of her pants, and slowly slid them over her hips, arching her back before letting her pants slide down to the floor.

She looked back over her shoulder as she stepped out of them.

Paul's intense gaze traveled the length of her body.

"Lay down," he said.

Josie giggled. Paul stepped forward and gave her a nudge.

Once she was laying on her stomach on the bed, he began kissing her. He started with the back of her neck, then worked his way to her shoulder blades and then made a trail down her spine.

"Relax," he whispered, sliding his hands down her butt.

She realized she was tense, and began consciously relaxing her muscles, one at a time. He continued kissing her back, her shoulders and her neck.

"I feel like a stick of melting butter," she said.

"Well, you don't look like one." He flipped her over brought himself up so they were face to face. "You're so hot. Remind me why we haven't done this in so long."

She felt him between her legs and arched up to meet him. "I have no idea."

He slid into her and the sensation felt exactly like home.

"Well," he said, his lips moving against hers, "we should do it more often."

She groaned. "We totally should."

As they moved together, she brought her hands up to cup his face. She made him a silent promise that she would work harder to make things right between them.

Laying in bed afterwards, Josie no longer felt like a melting stick of butter. She felt like a rag doll, devoid of bones. Her entire body was limp.

"I may never move again," she said.

Paul laughed. "I feel energized. I could go for a run right now."

"It's time to turn over a new leaf," Josie said. "Sex every night. Or at least every week."

"I like the sound of that. I'm going to get us some water."

When he was gone, Josie stretched out, and for some reason

thought of the first time she had sex with Scott Smith. Her initial reaction was to douse the memory completely. She giggled a little when she thought of those signs at campsites: "Drown Your Campfire: Every Spark." After all, she had just had amazing sex with her amazing husband and she should be thinking of no one else. Especially Scott Smith.

But for some reason, it made her feel good to think about the experience. Maybe because it hadn't been very good. And it hadn't been very good, most likely, because it had been on the evening they first met at the square downtown.

It's not like the attraction was crackling all afternoon or anything, she thought. They had clearly had decent chemistry, but there was no melting butter.

After she gave him the mini-tour of Juniper, he insisted on walking her back to her car. He said it was because a lady shouldn't walk through town alone in the dark, but she suspected it was actually because he wanted to steal a kiss or something more.

He confirmed her suspicions after she unlocked the driver side door. She turned around to say goodnight and he had both hands on the roof of the car, trapping her between his body and the door.

"Do you kiss on the first date?" he asked.

"No," she said, drawing the word out for suspense. "But you're in luck. This was a tour, not a date."

He was on her then, his strong, wiry body pressed against hers. Now, Josie remembered thinking it didn't feel quite right, but she attributed that feeling to the fact that they were strangers. At the time she told herself sex with some men was similar to wine tasting. Just like you weren't supposed to judge a wine by the first sip, you couldn't really judge a man by the first round of lovemaking. Was that true? In Scott's case, he did show marked improvement in that department during the next couple of weeks.

Suddenly, Josie felt cold. She pulled the sheet up over her body. What was taking Paul so long?

That first time, Scott didn't bother with the pleasantries of foreplay. Josie found this irritating, but she pushed her irritation out of her mind, telling herself it was because he was so turned on, so anxious to take her, so ready for her. The next time they got to this point, she was sure he would slow down. Well, that didn't happen.

Scott Smith was intimate at all the wrong times, running a fingertip up her thigh in a crowded room or sliding his tongue along her ear during a meeting when he pretended to whisper something to her. He was only intimate when intimacy was nearly impossible. When they couldn't actually share the moment. She always had to pretend it wasn't happening. And when they were in bed, when she wanted to enjoy it, he rushed through it, crushing those moments like a little kid tromping through a garden of seedlings.

After they had sex a couple of times, she managed to get Scott to slow down, but she could tell it took a real effort. He was a skilled lover, always knowing exactly which buttons to push. He could bring her to climax in three seconds flat, yet it seemed more automatic than personal.

Interesting.

On the other hand, Paul was always careful. He took his time. He craved intimacy whether they were alone or together. Not sneaky groping disguised as intimacy, but quick moments where Josie felt like they communicated in some secret language no one else could hear or understand. They hadn't shared many of those moments lately, though.

She sighed as Paul walked back into the bedroom carrying two glasses of water.

"What's wrong?"

That was another thing about Paul. He was a damn mind-reader. She could never brush him off with a casual "nothing," because he always knew when some deep thought lurked beneath the surface.

So she didn't bother lying now.

"I was just thinking about how I miss those little intimate moments we used to have."

There. It was half of the truth, anyway. She could never tell him about her relationship with Scott. Especially now. Maybe if she had told him when they first met ("Hey, I had a fling with my principal before I met you. Yep, the guy I see every single weekday of my life. I thought we were soul mates, but it didn't work out. And now he's my boss. Nah, it's no big deal."). But now the secret had grown so big and Paul would make it even bigger by pointing out that it was weird and suspicious she hadn't mentioned it before.

Paul sat on the edge of the bed and handed her a glass.

"Like that time we made out all the way across the sky ride in California at that boardwalk?"

"Yes. Or that time we went to a dinner party at Susie and Rick's and we were going through the buffet line and you kissed the back of my neck while I was scooping scalloped potatoes onto your plate."

"Oh yeah. I'd forgotten about that. You looked really sexy that night. Remember what we did after? How was that for intimate?"

"Ah, yes. The night of the new vibrator. How could I forget?"

At the mention of that magical little toy (why were they called sex toys, anyway? Those things were capable of some serious business!) Josie felt herself becoming aroused again.

"I know what you're thinking," Paul said, setting his water on the nightstand and taking hers, too. "I think it's time that bad boy makes a reappearance."

"We're going to need new batteries," Josie said. "Those ones have probably died from lack of use."

Paul smiled. "I've got lots of batteries. Wait here."

CHAPTER ELEVEN

JOSIE WALKED INTO WORK MONDAY MORNING WITH A BIT OF A SPRING IN her step. The April air felt fresh and clean and the leaves on the trees were unfurling just enough to brighten up the branches overhead and contrast the fluffy white clouds floating in the pristine blue sky.

"What a beautiful day," she said to the trees, the sky, the clouds.

Yikes. I feel like a lovestruck woman in a romance novel.

She laughed out loud as she pulled open the school's big wooden door.

"What's so funny?" Scott stood just inside the building, obviously on his way out.

She held the door open for him, hoping it would accelerate this conversation.

"Oh, nothing. Just laughing at myself, that's all. Have a great day!"

Okay, maybe you're a little too perky, Garcia. This is so not you.

"Um, okay." He looked bewildered. "I need to see you in my office today at lunch recess."

"But I've got lunch duty."

"I swapped you out with Caroline Lewis. I need to talk to you."

Her arm was getting tired.

"Is that code for something we didn't finish talking about over cocktails?"

He laughed, and stepped partway out the door, taking its weight off her arm.

"No, Josie. It really is important. Just some things to help you transition next year."

"Oh. Okay. See you at lunch recess."

Maybe she took a little longer than necessary to get from her classroom to Scott's office when the bell rang for lunch recess. She was still basking in the memories of her steamy love session with Paul the night before. Her limbs felt relaxed and loose as she walked down the stairs.

"Hey," Scott said.

All business.

"Hey," she said back.

"We don't have much time." He looked at the clock, and then back at her. "So I'll get right to it."

Still standing, he began shuffling through a stack of papers on his desk.

"Okay," she said, purposely deepening her voice so it conveyed the same somber tone his did.

He froze and looked up at her again. "Are you mocking me?"

"A little?" She smiled at him.

Finally, the tension in his shoulders dissipated and his movements slowed. "Are you stressed?" Josie said. "Sorry, I wouldn't have mocked you if I knew you were stressed. What's up?"

Scott sighed. "You know that position I applied for in Phoenix? Well, that position I accepted, I should say?"

Josie nodded.

"It's not turning out to be exactly what I expected," he said. "I've already signed the contract, but the district down there is reorganizing and I'm going to be taking on some additional supervisory duties I wasn't aware of. It's not that I don't like supervising people, especially good people. It's just that I really wanted to focus on curriculum."

"I'm sure you'll make it work," Josie said. "Once you get down there and get into a routine I think you'll find it's just fine."

"I hope so. Thanks. Anyway, that's not what I called you here for. I wanted to talk to you about some of the after school programs, but I can't find the list I need."

"We can talk tomorrow," Josie said.

"I have back to back meetings tomorrow," he said. A growing sense of urgency radiated off him. "And the next day. This week is just nuts. I wanted to go over this stuff with you before spring break. Get it off my plate."

Josie nodded, even though he wasn't looking at her.

He looked at his watch and winced. "How about after school?" he said. "I didn't realize recess is almost over. It'll just take twenty minutes or so. Is that all right? Will Paul mind if you're home a bit late?"

Before she could stop herself, her auto-answer spilled out of her mouth: "I doubt he'd even notice."

Which, especially after last night, probably wasn't true. She wanted to kick herself.

"If you were my wife," Scott said, "I'd notice. Believe me." He finally stopped moving and rubbed his hands over his face. "Anyway. There's the bell. I'll see you later."

Now that Josie knew Scott's intentions were work-related, she hurried down to his office when the final bell rang. He held up a bright orange folder. "Right here under my trusty apple paperweight," he said. He shrugged. They both laughed.

"Want to discuss this over drinks?" he asked.

Josie felt her back go up, just a little. "Discussing it here is fine."

Was the lunch recess debacle really just a ploy to get me to have drinks again?

"I could really use a drink. The Pennant? Do you mind?"

She checked her watch, even though she knew it was five minutes after three.

"Okay. I guess that's fine. I need to be home by five, though."

"Twenty minutes," he said. "I promise."

It'll take twenty minutes from now just to get our drinks.

"Okay. Meet you there."

"I can drive us, if you want," Scott said.

"Nah. It's fine. I'll meet you."

Josie got there before Scott did, and, as she'd calculated, it was three twenty-five by the time they both sat down and the bartender slid their drinks across the bar. And they hadn't even started discussing whatever was in the mysterious orange folder. Speaking of which …

"Did you bring the folder?" Josie said.

"Oh, shit. I forgot the folder." He put his forehead down on the shiny bar.

Now this is getting really suspicious.

"After all that? You really forgot it? Is it in your car?"

He sat up. "No, I can picture it sitting right on my desk chair. I left it there so I wouldn't forget it."

Josie took a big gulp of her drink, hoping the vodka would calm her. She felt tricked.

"Well, why don't you tell me what you wanted to talk about," she said, determined to stick to the topic.

"Oh, great idea," he said.

Scott described the scheduling for the extracurricular activities, including the dog grooming club Blair Upton started. He explained how the custodian was responsible for making sure the classrooms, cafeteria and meeting rooms were unlocked before each club meeting, and locked up after each meeting, every day. By the time he finished speaking, he had already signaled for another round.

When Josie shook her head, Scott put a hand over hers and said, "No, I insist. My treat."

But the minutes were ticking by. Paul was supposed to be home at five. If she had two drinks, she couldn't leave The Pennant until five-thirty.

Is it worse to be home late when my husband is expecting me, or run late and risk being that cop's wife who gets a DUI? Probably the latter.

She decided to sip the second drink slowly, so as not to feed the little buzz she'd developed as she matched Scott's quickening drinking pace.

"I really can't stay," she said. "Paul's coming home early tonight and we're supposed to have dinner."

Scott looked crestfallen, and she remembered with mixed emotions that he said she broke his heart when she married Paul.

"I'm having a nice time, though," she added.

He smirked, and yet again she remembered why she found him so attractive before. And yet again, she mentally kicked herself and pushed the thoughts out of her mind.

Josie checked her watch almost obsessively as five o'clock neared. Why had he slowed down now? He guzzled his first drink and now nursed the second.

"What time did you say Paul was expecting you?" he said.

"Five."

"It's five now. You'd better get going."

Don't I know it.

Josie gathered her purse and stood up. She put a hand on Scott's shoulder.

"What, no hug?" he said.

She obliged, only to hasten her exit. His breath smelled sour from the Scotch. Finally, she made her way through the crowded bar and out into the spring night, where she inhaled deeply and checked her watch again. Five ten.

As she walked down the sidewalk toward her car, she passed Scott's, which was parallel parked a few yards down from The Pennant. What she saw on the passenger seat made her freeze in her tracks.

The folder Scott claimed to have left at the office—orange with a piece of masking tape peeling off its front—sat on the passenger seat. In plain view. Scott not knowing he had it seemed impossible.

Had he left it in the car on purpose? Was he really that manipulative?

Even as she got into her own car a few moments later, she could hear a tiny voice answering, *Yes. He really is that manipulative. Always has been.* For some strange, twisted reason she couldn't define, though, she kind of liked the fact that he wanted to manipulate her into spending time with him.

It just meant he really liked her, right?

Right? she thought again when her wise inner voice didn't answer.

CHAPTER TWELVE

One step forward, two steps back.

Josie turned the phrase into a little song and her mind put it on repeat. Why did she let Scott talk her into drinks? Why did she not insist on being home by five, when she knew Paul expected her? She drove home from The Pennant very carefully, going exactly the speed limit and using her blinker for every turn and lane change. The ten-minute trip felt like an eternity. By the time she walked through her front door, the living room clock read five twenty-seven. Reminding Paul it ran five minutes fast proved futile and maybe even counterproductive, especially when he smelled the vodka cranberry on her breath.

"Wow," he said. "A half-hour later than you said you'd be, having obviously stopped for drinks on the way home. I mean, it'd be different if you'd been working hard and lost track of time, but this? I thought we were supposed to be working on our marriage."

Josie hated seeing him angry like this. The air felt thick and difficult to breathe.

"We are," she said. "It's just that Scott wanted to talk to me about extracurriculars for next year."

"I cannot believe you just said that to me. *Extracurriculars*? Seriously, Josie? He wanted to talk to you about extracurricular activities? Like drinking vodka cranberry after school when your husband made a real effort to be home early?"

For once, she didn't have an excuse, or an angry comeback to put the fault on him. She could try to explain, to tell him Scott talked her into going to The Pennant and then talked nonstop even though he knew she wanted to leave at quarter 'til. But she knew that would only make things worse. So she didn't say anything. She lifted one hand in an I-don't-know gesture.

"Wow. She's speechless, folks. For once, she sees reason."

"Why do you always do that?"

"Do what? Point out that you're speechless because I'm right?"

"No! Talk like you're in front of an audience. Why do you do that? Why can't you just communicate with me?"

"There she goes, folks. Changing the subject. Using criticism to put the spotlight on Yours Truly."

Although she could see a spark of humor in his eyes, she knew he didn't find the situation funny. Not even a tiny bit. He was probably getting a kick out of his weird broadcast, but that was it. And he was probably doing the broadcast routine only because he was disappointed and angry.

Josie wished she could turn back time, go straight back to lunch recess. She could find the orange folder on Scott's desk, have the discussion with him right there and drive straight home to Paul after school.

But she couldn't, and anyway, how many times had *he* run late? So when he asked her, "What are you thinking right now?" she went to default: indignation.

"What am I thinking right now? I'm thinking it's pretty messed up that you, of all people, feel you have the right to get angry that I'm late. This one time I show up late, when you've been late hundreds of times."

"Oh, hundreds? Really? Believe it or not, you're not Miss Punctuality yourself. You were late to our first counseling appointment. Marriage! Counseling! Not only did you disrespect me and our relationship by being late, but you disrespected Dr. Strasser. And our bank account. We're paying for that time. You show up late to your weekly Happy Hour with Delaney and Summer every single week. And you've never bothered asking them to move it back ten minutes so you can be on time. You just don't give a shit. You don't give a shit about anyone but yourself."

A thousand tiny thoughts, in fragments, exploded front and center, tiny firecrackers in her mind:

Is he right?

Do people really think that?

Do Summer and Delaney think that?

Why was I late tonight of all nights?

Why was I late to counseling?

What does this say about my motivations?

What are my motivations?

I'm a loser.

I hate Scott Smith.

Manipulative ass.

I hate Dr. Strasser.

Condescending ass.

I hate myself.

Idiot.

But before she could speak, before she could formulate an acceptable apology, Paul threw up his hands. "I'm going back to work. I can't believe I blew the guys off for this. I skipped out on a big search warrant and endured the guys' comments about me being wrapped around your pinky finger, for you to show up late because you were having drinks with your weasel of a boss. Discussing extracurriculars. This is bullshit."

He was gone before she could stop him.

What is going on with me? Josie thought. *Usually I'm much more … argumentative.*

It's just that you know he's right, her inner voice, all practicality, said.

"I need wine," she said to Paul's fake audience. "I've got to shut that bitch up."

The aftershocks of her discussion with Paul continued to hit her throughout the evening. She felt guilty. Selfish. Inadequate as a wife and friend.

Also, she felt beyond positive Scott manipulated her in an attempt to cause damage to her marriage. Not that she could tell Paul that. And even if she could, it would just make the situation worse because she'd fallen for it. She couldn't escape the clutches of her ex-lover to make it home to her husband.

Three glasses into a nice, special-occasion bottle of pinot noir, Josie heard her phone ding, signaling a text message. She went to retrieve it off the couch, hoping the message was from Paul. Nope. She slid back onto her stool.

Delaney: *What's up?*

Josie sighed again, and responded: *What's up with you?*

Delaney: *Where are you?*

Josie: *Home. Why?*

Delaney: *Wondering.*

Josie: *Why?*

Delaney: *Didn't you and Paul have a special date tonight?*

Josie: *Yes. Why?*

Delaney: *Two reasons. First, I saw you at The Pennant. Second, I saw Paul riding around with his team in that irritated pimple of an undercover car. What happened?*

Josie: *Ugh. Are you stalking me, or what?*

Josie rammed her forehead against her fist several times. Softly, but still.

Delaney: *Spill it, sister. Or I'm coming over. You know you can't resist me in person.*

Josie: *Aren't you heating the sheets with Jake Rhoades the Steamy?*

Delaney: *Over and done with. We get started early these days.*

Josie: *OMG.*

Delaney: *So?*

Josie: *So. Scott talked me into drinks. He wanted to talk to me about extracurriculars. I ran a little late. Paul freaked and went back to work.*

Delaney: *Extracurriculars?*

Josie scowled at her phone. Did Delaney have to have the same reaction as Paul?

Josie: *Haha. Funny.*

Delaney: *Why did you let yourself be late?*

"You have to be kidding me," Josie said to Paul's audience. "She's asking why I let myself. As if I had control. And I am talking to a fake audience. God help me."

Josie: *I didn't let myself. It just happened.*

Delaney: *So you couldn't leave The Pennant at 4:45?*

Josie: *Scott ordered another round. I drank it.*

Delaney: *Couldn't let the vodka cran go to waste?*

Josie: *Exactly.*

Delaney: *So he was mad, huh?*

Josie: *Yep.*

Why did Delaney have to force her to experience the evening all over again?

Delaney: *And he just left? No romance?*

Josie: *No romance.*

Delaney: *So when I texted you just now, did you think it was Paul?*

Josie: *Yep.*

Delaney: *Disappointed?*

Josie: *Well…*

Delaney: *Yep.*

Josie: *Yep.*

Josie poured herself a fourth glass of the pinot noir.

Delaney: *Sorry. But you've got to own this one.*

Josie: *I know. I felt so bad about it, and of course I lashed out. Reminded him about all his shortcomings. Shit.*

Delaney: *Shit. Well, one step forward, one step back.*

Josie: *Something like that.*

Delaney: *Okay, I'm going to say something, and I am pretty sure you're not going to like it. Don't throw your phone against the wall.*

"How did she know?" Josie said. "The woman is practically clairvoyant."

Josie: *I won't. What is it?*

Delaney: *You've got to show Paul you're serious about making this work. You have to be on time. I know you have a habit of being late. But Paul is a cop. He's always early-on-time. So being late is a huge insult. I learned that from you. You should know better. Let's make it two steps forward. Okay?*

"Ugh!" Josie said again. She felt her fingers curling tightly around the edges of her phone. Automatic response. "The woman is dead on."

Josie: *Fine.*

Delaney: *LOL. Fine. Don't make me come over there.*

Josie: *Fine.*

After finishing the pinot noir, Josie felt a sudden need to be honest with Summer and Delaney. Really honest. She started a group text, noting with a smile that their last group text conversation had revolved around how Delaney should let Jake know what kind of ring she liked.

Josie had said: *Just give him a picture you cut out of a magazine.* Summer had advised: *Take him to the jewelry store. Shit. If you don't start telling him what you want now, you may as well kiss it all good-bye.*

The next day, Delaney made a little photo collage for Jake, and then took him to The Lucky Emerald for an engagement ring tour.

That evening, she texted the girls: *Well, he didn't pull out the credit card, but I could see his wheels turning. A proposal is imminent, I can feel it.*

Summer and Josie had each texted back a smiley face.

For a moment, Josie felt guilty about tainting those happy moments with her confession. But it had to be done. She took a deep breath and began typing.

There is something I need to tell you guys. It may come as somewhat of a shock.

Neither Summer nor Delaney responded for what seemed like forever. But when she checked the time stamp on her phone, she realized only three minutes had passed when Summer answered first.

Summer: *You're actually an alien? Which explains your unnatural beauty and sexy curves?*

Delaney: *Good one, Summer. That would explain it.*

Josie smiled. Her fingers hesitated above her phone's keyboard. She didn't want to tell them. A tiny voice inside her head was shouting, "Abort! Abort!" But she had to tell someone. She couldn't keep this secret anymore.

Finally, she typed: *I had a fling with Scott Smith. Before I married Paul. It was very intense. I didn't know he was going to be my boss. Well, not at first. By the time he told me, it was too late. Head over ass and all that. We ended it that first school year he started at Juniper Elementary, but there has always been … chemistry.*

This time, neither of her friends answered for more than five minutes. It felt like an eternity.

Anything? she typed.

Finally, Delaney mustered up the courage to respond.

Delaney: *Whoa.*

Summer: *I mean, whooooa, Nelly.*

Delaney: *Why haven't you ever told us?*

Summer: *Yeah. I mean, why haven't you?*

Josie: *It was right after my mom died. I thought you guys would think it was inappropriate and I knew you'd say my emotions were messed up, especially because I thought he might be my soul mate. It was such a short relationship. When we discovered he was going to be my boss, we agreed it had to end. Plus, he asked me to keep it a secret.*

That wasn't exactly how the true story went. Scott had known all along he'd be her boss when the school year started. He just hadn't revealed it to Josie right away. And since she was reliving the true story, she felt a little pang of hurt when she remembered how it had been Scott who said they couldn't be together. They never really agreed on that.

Summer: *When was this? I mean, RIGHT after your mom died?*

Josie: *It was right before I met Paul.*

Summer: *OMG! Is this when you got that mysterious flu thing that kept coming and going like some kind of freak monsoon storm?*

Josie: *One and the same. I thought that was a pretty good excuse. Too obvious?*

Delaney: *I can't believe you lied to us for what? Like 4 weeks? 5? Plus, like, three quarters of a decade! It wasn't obvious at the time...*

Summer: *I also can't believe you lied to us.*

Josie waited. She couldn't believe it, either. It was the first secret she had ever kept from them.

Delaney: *This is the first secret you've ever kept from us. Right? Or are there others?*

Josie: *It's the one and only. Oh! Besides the time I stuffed my bra with my brother's gloves the first day of freshman year. You guys were both so nervous you didn't even notice.*

Summer: *You did that?*

Josie: *Yep.*

Delaney: *Stay on topic, ladies. So you've been forced to face Scott Smith every day since this magical love affair that gave you mysterious flu-like symptoms?*

Josie: *Pretty much.*

Summer: *Oh, honey.*

Josie: *I. Know.*

Delaney: *So. Why didn't you tell us?*

Josie: *Shit! I don't know!*

Actually, she did know. Scott swore her to secrecy. On a pinky promise or something. But she wouldn't tell them that, either. When she looked at that fact from their point of view, she realized he really did seem manipulative.

As Josie prepared for bed that night, alone, her inner voice repeated a single word over and over again: manipulative. The thought made her squeeze the toothpaste tube so hard she squirted toothpaste on the counter. It made her pop a button off her pajama shirt. The realization had begun to dawn on her a long time ago, disguised as a strange feeling in the pit of her stomach whenever she thought about Scott. At first, she attributed it to nerves. Nerves about being around Scott, nerves about her role as the principal of Juniper Elementary next year, nerves about her marriage failing.

But now that she looked back on it she realized it wasn't nerves at all. It was the feeling of losing control of her own life, one small event at a time.

It was the feeling of being manipulated.

Turning off the lights in the house one by one, she ticked off a list of instances in which she felt out of control.

She experienced it when Scott talked her into going for drinks earlier that afternoon, when she should have come home to Paul. The time Scott told her their being together would ruin both their careers. The moment she saw that orange folder on his passenger seat, and years ago when he dipped a hand below her waistband at the back of the auditorium during the fifth-grade play.

Darkness now blanketed the house, and Josie felt sick to her stomach again.

Had Scott ever really cared about her? Or had every single move, every touch, every conversation been some sort of power play?

Josie pulled the comforter up to her chin, and whispered to Paul's imaginary audience, "I know what I have to do."

CHAPTER THIRTEEN

"You're actually on time for Happy Hour," Summer said. "I guess Paul's going back to work the other night really sent a message."

"Cotton-Eye Joe" played over the speakers, making Rowdy's feel particularly festive. Josie remembered dancing to that song years ago, interlacing her arms with Summer's and Delaney's and scooting across the dance floor.

"Hey," Josie said. "I'm going to make sure it's not a happy hour for you if you don't watch it."

Gratitude washed over Josie. Everything seemed normal. Summer didn't seem too affected by her admission the other night.

"So," Delaney said, and Josie felt the air rush out of her lungs.

Benjamin arrived at the table, tray on his shoulder. Josie pointed at the spot in front of her, and he obliged, putting her vodka cranberry down first. She winked at him, and he set a second drink in front of her, shaking his head as he set down Delaney's Guinness and Summer's water.

"I can tell when you're in a mood, woman," he said. "And I don't want to be the recipient of your bad temper."

Summer and Delaney laughed as Benjamin walked away.

"Where were we?" Delaney said. "Oh, yeah. So. Josie. You've got to dish on this Scott Smith thing. A confession by text isn't going to cut it."

Josie nodded. She had expected this. Hoping the girls weren't distressed by the confession was probably hoping for too much.

"I can't believe we didn't even know," Summer said to Delaney. "I mean, how could we not have known? Does this mean I'm going to be a terrible lie-detector when Sarah's a teenager?"

"Of course not," Josie said. "You probably thought I was grieving my mom, which I was. You probably wanted to give me space. Plus, I have adult-level deception skills. Sarah's will be teenage-level. You'll be fine."

"Let's hope you're right," Summer said. "I hope you haven't rubbed off on her. Remember that time junior year when you called into school three separate times, pretending to be each of our moms, reporting us sick? So we could go to the mall for shopping and pedicures?"

"I still regret that tangerine color I picked for my toenails," Josie said. "Anyway. That was teenage stuff. If that's the worst Miss Sarah does, you're doing great. We all got good grades and got into college."

"Good point," Summer said.

Delaney said, "Anyway. Speaking of adult-level deception skills, back to your big secret. Spill the details."

Josie obliged. She knew there was no point in avoiding this conversation. The girls would get it out of her eventually. They had twenty years of practice.

She told them about how she met Scott at the square, and how charming he was, and how her response to the way he spoke and acted went against everything her mother had taught her about men. How it drew her in, and how she wanted to prove to her mom that poetry and flowers from a man could mean real love.

At first, Summer and Delaney made little "awww," and "ooooh" sounds, appreciative of the romance, the sex and the tragedy of the impending end.

But when Josie backtracked a bit, and got around to the part she was putting off, the part where Scott didn't initially reveal he was going to be her boss and that fact precluded them from having a long term relationship, things changed. Her best friends, each of them so beautiful in her own way, wore matching expressions of anger. Their eyebrows drew together, their mouths frowned and they took matching swigs of their beverages.

"That jerk," Delaney said. "Why didn't he tell you immediately?"

"He says it's because he was so infatuated he didn't want to end it before it even began."

Delaney responded with a "Psh" sound, and Summer echoed her.

Josie added, "He says it's because he'd rather spend a few weeks together than no time at all."

"Oh, yessss," Summer said, and hearing the sarcastic tone of her voice, Josie braced herself for what came next. "The whole, 'It's better to have loved and lost than to never have loved at all' thing, right? That's bull."

Whew. I'm so glad they're taking my side.

"I know you think we're taking your side on this one," Summer said.

Shit.

"But we've talked," Delaney said. "And we agree that—because the feelings were so strong and you still see Scott Smith every single day—you need to bring this up at your next marriage counseling appointment."

No. Nooooo. Josie imagined her inner voice falling off a cliff. The cliff of surprise.

After taking a moment to gather her wits, she spluttered, "Absolutely not. That would be the last straw. I got stuck having drinks with Scott just this week, and then I reveal I had a fling with him? A hot-and-heavy fling? I don't think so."

"Wait," Delaney said. "Did you tell Paul you were discussing extracurriculars?"

She put finger quotes on "extracurriculars," and when Josie nodded, Delaney practically spit out the drink of beer she'd taken.

"Shit. I guess you can't tell him," Delaney said.

"Delaney!" Summer said. "Of course she can. If this little meeting, or discussion, or drinks date, or whatever the hell it was, was above board, then there is no reason she shouldn't tell him. And if it was not above board, and was more along the lines of a secret tryst … well, then I'll say it again: there is no reason she shouldn't tell him. *Capisce?*"

Properly chastised, Delaney hung her head. She was smiling a bit when she looked up at Josie under her eyelashes.

"I guess you'd better tell him," she said.

"And Dr. Strasser," Summer added.

Delaney nodded. "And Dr. Strasser."

Once the girls finally took their claws out of her relationship with Scott, Josie thought she was in the clear. She thought they might talk more about Summer's band or Delaney's impending proposal.

No such luck.

"I hate to hammer you about The Marriage Intervention, Josie," Summer said, "but—"

"I can see the light shining in your eyes, Summer," Josie said. "You love this."

"She does love it," Delaney said. "Her greatest calling in life is to be a mother, and now she can mother you, too."

They all laughed, but the hilarity came to a screeching halt when Summer said, "We're going to the gym this weekend. Yoga. Nine a.m. Saturday. No buts about it."

Josie put her head down on the table.

"I hate yoga."

"We know," Summer said. "Just be glad we're not making you go to hot yoga. You sweat a lot in hot yoga."

Delaney rolled her eyes. "Which is why Summer loves it. I'm going to hate yoga as much as you do, Josie, but it's going to be good for both of us. I have to look good in a wedding dress. And you have to look good naked in bed with your husband."

"And you also have to look so good Scott Smith can't keep his jaw off the floor," Summer said. "Rat bastard."

THE QUESTION REALLY ISN'T, "Should I or shouldn't I?" It's, "will I or won't I?"

Josie stood in the staff bathroom at work, brushing her hair. She knew Summer and Delaney were right. She should tell Paul and Dr. Strasser she had a fling with Scott. Yes, it was old news. But it was also affecting her now. Maybe talking it out would help.

Or maybe it will just make things worse.

"I don't know what to do," she said to her reflection.

She took her loose powder out of her bag and began brushing it onto her face. One of the toilets flushed, and Josie jumped. Susie Lockhart, the teacher who introduced Josie to Paul, emerged.

"Heard you talking to yourself," she said, grinning at Josie in the mirror. "What's the dilemma?"

The two of them weren't best friends or even confidants. But Josie genuinely liked Susie. They often sat together at potluck lunches, sipping water to choke down dry scones and making jokes about sneaking in vodka in a flask. According to Susie, she'd prefer white wine, but if Josie brought the hard stuff, she wouldn't turn it down.

Susie had broken eye contact. She was washing her hands. Josie knew she could brush off Susie's question with a quick joke. But for some reason, she wanted to confide in her.

Probably because you want a third opinion and you're hoping it's different from Summer's and Delaney's.

"The thing is," Josie began. "I had a relationship a while back. Before you introduced me to Paul. It's in the past. Way in the past. Ancient history. But for some reason I've been thinking of it more lately. Paul and I have started going to marriage counseling, you know, just to work on things. My two best friends think that since I keep thinking about Mr. History, I should bring it up in counseling. They think Paul deserves to know, especially since I sometimes run into Mr. History in town."

Susie didn't have to know Mr. History was just downstairs in this very building at this very moment.

Scrubbing her hands vigorously, Susie pursed her full lips. When she nodded, her shiny blond curls bobbed.

"You know, I have to say, I agree with your friends."

Darn it.

As Josie applied her lip gloss, she watched Susie turn off the water and pull way too many paper towels out of the dispenser.

"I can tell that's not what you wanted to hear," Susie said. "But I've actually been through this before. Maybe you're thinking about Mr. History because you're missing a certain aspect of your relationship with him. If you can figure out what it is, you can work on finding closure or bringing more of that aspect into your relationship with Paul."

She tossed her used paper towels into the garbage can. Josie zipped her makeup back into its little bag.

"You know, you surprise me, Susie," she said. "I expected you to say something about bringing vodka to our next counseling appointment. But you've gone and gotten all deep on me this afternoon."

Susie shrugged at Josie in the mirror. "For once I'm thinking like a responsible adult instead of a second grader. Please forgive me. We'll talk wine on Monday."

They both giggled.

As they passed through the bathroom door and into the hallway of the third floor, Susie paused and put a hand on Josie's arm. "Seriously, though. If it really is ancient history, talking about it can only help."

Is it really ancient history?

Josie sighed. "I guess so. Thanks, Susie."

CHAPTER FOURTEEN

Will I, or won't I?

Josie had asked herself the question countless times since Happy Hour on Thursday. She asked it when she walked past Scott Smith's office Friday. She asked it during yoga class Saturday morning as she groaned her way into downward dog. She asked it Sunday afternoon when Paul watched the Suns game and she graded papers on the couch.

Somehow the two of them managed to avoid any real conversations during the days that passed between her late arrival for their romantic evening and Monday morning when she left for work.

Which meant the next time they'd talk would be at their appointment with Dr. Strasser that afternoon.

When the bell rang to signal the end of the school day, Josie packed up her bag and left immediately, jogging down the stairs and breezing out, breathing a sigh of relief when she saw Scott on the phone in his office.

She arrived in Dr. Strasser's parking lot thirty minutes before their appointment, and worked on the rest of the week's lesson plans until five minutes 'til four. Of course, Paul was already in the reception area when she walked in.

"Hey," she said.

He didn't look up. "Hey."

Josie sat down in the chair next to his. Still, he didn't look up.

Which was good and bad, she thought, because it gave her more time to consider whether she should talk about Scott during today's session.

If she did talk about Scott, the big elephant in the corner would finally stroll out of the room, leaving her marriage in peace. But Paul would be upset. She wouldn't live it down for the rest of the school year and Paul would undoubtedly point out, daily, that she saw Scott, daily, and it made him uncomfortable.

She couldn't blame him. It made *her* uncomfortable.

If she didn't talk about Scott, she'd probably continue to think about him, to daydream about him and put him on some kind of sick pedestal where her romantic, er, impractical side believed his manipulation was a sign of his undying love for her. Forever. But Paul would never know, would never even have an inkling that she'd felt so strongly about Scott.

Josie had enough emotional intelligence to see that the reason she didn't want to talk about Scott was because she still had some feelings for him. And she realized, too, that she could probably use some professional help in coping with those feelings, resolving them.

Dr. Strasser opened the door to his office. He stood there for a moment, and Josie pretended not to notice him. She assumed he was assessing the way she and Paul sat there, without touching, speaking or acknowledging each other's presence. She wondered what he'd make of that.

She didn't have to wonder long. Dr. Strasser cleared his throat, and Paul jumped. Dr. Strasser motioned for them to come into his office, and they both stood up. Paul stepped back to let her walk in front of him, and she took that as a positive sign.

When they were settled, Dr. Strasser spoke.

"I noticed the two of you weren't speaking out there. Your body language suggests some tension."

Josie sighed, loudly, before she realized she was doing it. She glanced at Paul, and found him staring at her. Yep, he'd noticed.

"It's my fault," she said.

Might as well plunge in.

"The other night, we were supposed to have a romantic evening in, and I was late getting home. Hypocritical, I know. Paul was pissed, went back to work and we haven't spoken since. I mean, we've exchanged pleasantries, but that's about it."

In the moment that followed her plunge, Josie could hear Dr. Strasser's air conditioner running. She could hear the clock ticking. She could hear Paul breathing next to her.

Dr. Strasser put his elbows on his desk and steepled his fingers, resting his chin on them. He looked at Josie for a span of time that felt longer than the final five minutes of the last school day of the year. His gaze flicked to her husband.

"Paul? Give me your version of events."

"Same as she said. She was late. And hypocrisy really gets to me. I came home early, left my team out on a search warrant one man short. And she's off having drinks with her boss. Talking about extracurriculars."

A spoon would have stood up in the word "extracurriculars." Possibly even a shovel. Why did everyone make such a big deal of that?

Again, Dr. Strasser let the silence breathe between them, the tension like oxygen to a flame. A dangerous one.

You're about to burn this shit up, Dr. Strasser.

This would be a good time to mention her relationship with Scott. Talk about how she obliged him for drinks that evening because he said she broke his heart when she married Paul.

Wait. That's way too much information. Don't say all that.

She obliged him for drinks as a last hurrah. She obliged him for drinks because she didn't know how to say no to his charms? Because he'd always been able to manipulate her?

Hmmm… None of those options will come out quite right.

"Why did you go for drinks with this … uh …"

"Scott Smith," Paul supplied.

"Right. Scott Smith. Josie, why did you go for drinks with Scott Smith when you knew Paul was waiting for you?"

Josie sighed again, then realized she sounded like a petulant teenager.

"He asked me to join him so we could discuss some of my duties for next year, when I take over as principal. I didn't expect it to take as long as it did."

"Why couldn't you meet at the office? At school?" Paul wanted to know.

They waited for her answer.

"I— I don't know," she said, shrugging.

Because Scott has always had a hold over me and I couldn't say no.

"Was this truly a mistake, Josie, or did you want to be late for your evening with Paul? Can you think of a reason you would have wanted to be late? Perhaps to get back at him for being late so many times in the past? Give him a taste of his own medicine?"

He's needling me! Is this what marriage counselors do? How the hell can Summer love this guy so much?

"No, not at all," she said. "Geez, I feel like one of my students when I've caught him with his hand in the treat jar behind my back."

"Did you have your hand in the treat jar, Josie?" Paul asked.

Shit.

"No!" *Too insistent. Tone it down.* "No. Bad analogy. I just meant that I feel kind of, you know, on the spot. It was just drinks with a colleague, that's all. More time passed than I realized. Truly an oversight."

Then Paul said something that surprised her.

"That Scott Smith has always held a flame for you, Josie. You know it as well as I do. A smart woman like you? If you didn't notice, you're playing dumb."

Josie didn't answer.

"Paul, you believing this Scott Smith fellow has feelings for Josie explains your anger over her being late after having drinks with him. Have you seen evidence of his feelings for her?"

"I'm a cop. Observer of human behavior."

"Give us some concrete examples," Dr. Strasser said.

"You should see the way that man looks at her during staff parties. Like he wants to lick her like an ice cream cone."

Dr. Strasser raised his eyebrows.

"I didn't mean it to sound sexual," Paul hurried to say. "I just meant he wants to eat her up."

He does. This would be a good time to 'fess up.

"Josie? What's your take on this?"

She could practically feel Summer and Delaney, twin angels sitting on one shoulder, whispering, "Tell him, tell him!"

"I—uh, I'm not sure."

"See?" Paul pointed at her and raised his eyebrows at Dr. Strasser. "She knows. She probably likes it."

"If I do, it's only because he actually pays attention to me. He actually asks me for drinks. He actually talks to me, Paul. He—"

"He *what*, Josie?"

"Nothing."

"Josie, I'm sensing you feel like you're not getting the attention you want to from Paul."

Wow. Did you use your Mega Doctor Senses to make that observation?

"That's true," she said.

She glanced up at the clock. Only five minutes until the session ended. She could still slip in a confession. What was she confessing, exactly? That she'd had a relationship before she met Paul? Big deal.

Only … it was a big deal. Because she saw Scott every single day and she'd never revealed it to her husband. And of course, the secret had just grown.

"What could Paul do to show you the attention you want?" Dr. Strasser said.

"Something," Josie said. "Anything."

"Be specific."

"He could ask how my day was," she said.

"I do ask how her day was!" Paul said, pointing at her. "Every time I walk in the door."

"While looking at your phone. He doesn't even make eye contact with me! He doesn't even care how my day was. He just asks by rote."

"Now we're getting somewhere," Dr. Strasser said. "Do you see the breakdown here, you guys? Josie, Paul believes he is meeting your needs by asking how your day was. However, Paul, Josie doesn't feel like you're genuinely interested because you aren't looking at her. Sound about right?"

Josie nodded. Out the corner of her eye, she could see Paul nodding, too.

Four more minutes.

Dr. Strasser forced them to go through an exercise. They had to turn their chairs toward each other, look into each other's eyes, and tell each other what they needed more of.

Paul went first. Apparently, he needed Josie to be more understanding and supportive. He needed her to hug him more (Josie almost laughed out loud at this, since it was on Summer and Delaney's list of The Rules for The Marriage Intervention). He needed to hear her say she appreciated him working so hard for them.

Three more minutes. She could blurt it out now, before telling Paul what she needed more of.

"I need attention. I need to feel like I take priority over your work. That's it."

Dr. Strasser nodded.

"Now I'd like each of you to explain precisely what the other could do to give you what you need."

"Look, before we finish this exercise, there's something I have to say."

SHE DIDN'T TELL THEM. She finally worked up the courage to spill her guts and Dr. Strasser stopped her. He made them finish the exercise first.

By the time they were done, the session was over.

But she wasn't off the hook. Paul's detective skills never rested unless he was looking for the ketchup in the fridge. His ears perked up when she tried to interrupt that final exercise. She could see it in his expression, in the way his lips pressed together and his eyes narrowed.

He wouldn't forget about it, and he wouldn't just let it go.

So when they walked out to the parking lot together, after she explained how she wished he could stay home when he got a call-out and he explained how he wished she wouldn't ask him to stay home when he got a call-out (and how do you rectify that? she wondered), he stopped her before she could get into her car.

"What were you going to say, before?" he asked.

"Before what?"

"You know. Before we finished our session with two completely contradictory requests."

He smiled at her and for a moment, she felt an uptick in her heart rate, just as she had when they first met, every time they made eye contact.

Maybe that's why I miss the eye contact so much. I miss feeling like this. Shit. Maybe Dr. Strasser's onto something.

She grinned back.

"It's nothing," she said. "We can talk about it at our session next week."

"No," he said. "We can't. What was it? I could tell you were nervous. It must be important."

It's now or never.

"It's about something that happened before we got together." She cleared her throat.

She always could read him, too, and she saw the knowledge roll into his eyes exactly the way a monsoon storm rolled into town on a summer day. Ominous, threatening, and eventually exploding.

"You had a thing with Scott Smith."

Paul was a good cop. So good, in fact, that his supervisors had already begun grooming him for a sergeant detective position. Just a few weeks ago, he completed a training on interview and interrogation. He loved it. Came home raving about it. He may be a good cop, but Josie saw him mentally slip into the bad cop interrogator role the instant he announced his revelation.

When Josie didn't answer, Paul leaned against the driver's door of her car and crossed his arms. She wasn't going anywhere. Neither was he.

"So. Tell me about it."

Josie felt the blood whirring through her body, whooshing in her ears.

Why am I so nervous? It's over.

She licked her lips, shifted her weight from her right foot to her left.

"There's not too much to tell, really," she said. "We met several weeks before school started that year, and ended things on the first day of school."

Never mind the fact that I broke down and cried at recess and after school every day for a week.

"Why did you end things?"

"He was my supervisor."

"So?" He didn't give her time to answer. "Why are you so nervous?"

"What? I'm not."

"You keep licking your lips."

Josie pressed her lips together.

"See? It's a nervous habit," he said. "So why are you nervous? You still have a thing for this guy, or what?"

"Fine," she said. "I *am* nervous! I'm nervous, Paul, because you're *interrogating* me. I've known all along that if you knew Scott and I had a fling, you'd hate that I was seeing him every day. You'd ask me about it all the time, you'd want to know why I wore a certain skirt or certain shoes."

He seemed to consider that for a moment, and then he nodded.

"Probably. You're right. I would do those things. But what am I supposed to think now, after you were late getting home because you spent an afternoon having drinks with this guy, discussing *extracurriculars*? It all seems very suspicious. Especially when it was your idea to work on our marriage. Or whatever. You know what? I'm calling bullshit. You're probably using this marriage counseling thing as a decoy so you can keep rubbing elbows, or whichever body parts, with Scott."

"Absolutely not!" Josie said. "I just went to have drinks with Scott because he asked me to. Excuse me if I'm susceptible to actual attention from a man, since I get absolutely none from you."

"Oh, don't you dare turn this around on me. This is so completely your fault."

"My fault? My fault? Now we're placing blame? What is my fault, exactly, Paul?"

"It's your fault this marriage is where it is right now. You've obviously got one foot in the grave, here, and one foot in Scott Smith's office. And you have since we got together. We were doomed from the start."

"That's not true!"

Josie heard her voice approaching the tenor of the shrill wail of a siren, and took a deep breath to calm herself.

"That's not true," she said again. "It was over with me and Scott before I even met you."

"If it was, you wouldn't have been so nervous to talk to me about it. You wouldn't have hidden it all this time."

She had nothing to say to that.

"You have nothing to say to that, do you?" Paul said.

"Ugh." She rubbed a hand over her forehead.

Paul stepped aside so she could get into her car.

"I guess we're done here," he said. "And you're on your own with Dr. Strasser from now on. I don't want to waste my time."

He got into his car and drove away.

Josie felt as if the wind had been taken out of her sails. She blamed life, her husband and Scott.

The original plan was for the two of them to meet at home for dinner in a couple of hours, after she went to the gym and he went to the shooting range for some target practice. But now she had no idea whether he'd show up.

With country music blasting, Josie pulled out of Dr. Strasser's parking lot and drove toward the gym, even though it was the absolute last place she wanted to go.

Everything Paul said was true. Since that first time she met Scott, he had a hold over her. There was just something about him. There was always that question in the back of her mind: "Is he my soul mate?"

It was foolish of her to deny it.

She hit a red light and pounded her fist on the steering wheel, then turned up the music.

Despite the fact that she'd always had Scott in the back of her mind, she chose Paul. Didn't that mean something?

Or did it mean nothing, since Scott had been the one to end their relationship? Would she have continued dating him if he hadn't ended it?

At the intersection of Highway Twenty-Three and Pinecone Road, where Delaney had met Jake, Josie turned left when she should have turned right to meet the girls. She knew she'd pay for it later, when Summer and Delaney held her accountable, or whatever they were calling it these days, but for now she relished the thinking time. She needed it.

Old Copper Mine Highway wound up into the mountains that

stood guard around Juniper, twisting and curving, forcing Josie to drive like she imagined a race car driver would.

She pulled off at a lookout point, from which she could see the velvety green of the pine trees unrolling below her.

Nothing but quiet out here.

Yes, Josie would love a little more attention from Paul. She would love a little more eye contact. She would love to feel like a priority. She wanted him to choose her over his work for once, to act like it was a possibility rather than just slipping into that default position.

"Ugh," Josie said when she realized she was actually crying.

But he *was* a great husband in so many ways. He did dishes, laundry, even ironing. He did everything she asked. He was sensitive. To her moods, to her needs in bed, to what she wanted for dinner and whether she wanted to cook.

What was wrong with her? Really, he had just the one tiny flaw. And really, didn't it show his dedication and commitment to work? At least he wasn't a deadbeat.

Her phone buzzed. A text. She sighed and ignored it. She knew it was Summer or Delaney. Probably both of them, calling her out for not showing up at the gym. It buzzed again and she took it out of her pocket. Sure enough, she had one text from each of her friends, asking where she was. Feeling lonely and in need of their company even though she knew she risked a good chastising, she told them. They pulled up fifteen minutes later. Delaney's short pigtails had little curls springing out of them, and sweat spread over the back of Summer's t-shirt.

"Have a good workout?" Josie asked.

"Oh my gosh, have you been crying?" Delaney wanted to know.

Josie rubbed a knuckle under her nose. "Yeah."

"What's going on?" Summer said.

Summer and Delaney sat down, one on either side of her, and within a moment, she was wrapped in their arms, her body relaxing like warm caramel. Josie explained the fallout from her confession during their session with Dr. Strasser, and her friends remained silent for a few moments when she finished. Summer went back to her car to get a tissue and came back with a wadded up piece of toilet paper, shrugging.

"Not sure if this has been used or not, but it doesn't feel crunchy."

Josie laughed and wiped her eyes and nose.

"So, we were talking on the way over here," Delaney said.

"And?" Josie said.

"And we agree that you're not following The Rules of The Marriage Intervention."

Wait," Josie said. "So you're telling me this, right here, is an intervention for The Marriage Intervention?"

Delaney and Summer looked at each other, shrugged, then looked back at Josie and nodded.

"You've got to follow The Rules," Summer said. "We put them in place for your own good. I cannot believe you were late for your romantic evening with Paul. Especially when you were having drinks with your ex-lover! You have to put as much into your marriage as you say you want to."

Not for the first time, Josie felt like a teenager whose mother caught her drinking cheap white zin in her bedroom after lights out.

"I know you're right," Josie said. "It's just that I'm afraid it's not going to work. All this *trying* with Paul. It seems like he's checked out. And when it fails, I'll feel so *stupid*."

"I know," Delaney said. "Summer's been through that with Derek, right, Summer?"

"I have," Summer said. "I understand. But even when he seems like he's at a standstill, *especially* when he seems like he's at a standstill, you have to keep trying. That's the only way a marriage can work."

If the conversation had ended with Summer giving her some solid marriage advice, Josie would have driven home feeling somewhat bolstered.

But after the girls sat in silence for a few moments, the brilliant watercolor sunset fading to a dusky rose, Summer cleared her throat.

"Not to change the subject," she said, "but we have something to tell you."

"Great," Josie said. "Now that you set it up like that, I can hardly wait."

Delaney laughed. "It's no big deal. It's just that, per The Marriage Intervention Rules, we signed you up for a race."

Josie groaned. "A running race? Or, like, a wine-drinking race?"

"Running," Summer said into her shoulder. "But there's wine involved."

"Great," Josie said. "As if this whole marriage thing wasn't taking enough of a toll on my mental state? Now I have to stress over a race, too?"

Summer began rubbing Josie's back.

"It's going to be a super fun race," Delaney said. "It has a wine and chocolate theme. They hand you a glass of wine and a bar of dark chocolate when you cross the finish line. You have two months to train for it."

Well, that doesn't sound too bad.

"Fine," Josie said.

"Fine," Summer and Delaney said.

"It's a good thing too," Delaney added, "Because we already paid for it. We'll send you the link to the website. Your login name is your email address and of course, your password is bigpenis, all one word."

CHAPTER FIFTEEN

A week had passed since Josie revealed her secret to her husband and Dr. Strasser. Paul had not spoken to her. Not surprisingly, he spent all his time at work, coming home only to shower, eat and sleep, and then only during school hours when he knew Josie would be gone.

He probably racked up about thirty hours of overtime. Normally, they daydreamed together about what they'd buy with the big paycheck, but not this week. This week they passed like ships in the night. Only, Josie thought, they weren't even on the same sea.

Now she sat in Dr. Strasser's spotless waiting room.

The past week had held one bright spot: the owners of the cute cottage near Juniper Elementary School had accepted her application. She was the new lessee of the space for the Carla Garcia Community Center. The real work would start now, with permits and construction and marketing. She'd imagined being beyond ecstatic if the property owners accepted her application, but because of everything that was going on with Paul, the excitement just wasn't there.

Dr. Strasser, standing in the doorway to his office, interrupted her thoughts when cleared his throat.

Josie followed him in and sat down in her normal seat, staring at a palm frond just to the left of Dr. Strasser's bald head. She could never get plants to grow, and she hoped that curse didn't carry over to children. That is, if she and Paul ever spoke again, much less procreated.

"Paul's not coming," she said when the clock showed five after four. "He warned me last week, but I didn't believe him."

"So why did you come alone?" Dr. Strasser asked, steepling his fingers and resting his chin on them.

Must be his go-to position. Do I have a go-to position?

"What? Oh, I came because ..." *Because Summer and Delaney insisted.*

The clock ticked. The air conditioner clicked on. The palm frond shifted. Dr. Strasser waited.

"I came because I thought it would be a good idea to talk to you about a past relationship. One I had before I met Paul."

"Go on," Dr. Strasser said.

"Coincidentally" (or not coincidentally) "it was with that same guy I had drinks with last week. The drinks that made me late for my romantic evening with Paul."

Once she started, she had difficulty stopping. She went on and on, the words rising in the air like steam from the espresso machine at Umbrella Coffee. She explained how she met Scott, how they had a very intense relationship for a short time, and how she continued to feel a bit of sexual tension even to this day.

"And the reason Paul isn't here today is because I never told him about this relationship until last week after our session. In the parking lot."

Now she burst into tears, and kept talking. "I know I should have told him years ago, but I kept putting it off. And since I kept putting it off, it felt like a bigger and bigger secret."

"Why do you think you didn't want to tell him?" Dr. Strasser asked.

Why, indeed.

"That's what I'm not sure of," Josie said. "When Scott and I dated, he insisted we keep it a secret. He was the new principal at the school and didn't want anyone to know we'd been together. He thought they might think he was giving me preferential treatment. Or that he was distracted by our relationship. So at first, it seemed like a special secret we shared. It bonded us. I think I always thought of it as confidential."

"Did you ever feel like you should share that information with Paul?"

"I felt like I should, yes. Not because my fling with Scott was a huge deal, but because I knew he'd want to know since I see Scott every day at work."

"What stopped you from telling him?"

"I don't know. I'm not sure," Josie said again.

Dr. Strasser leaned forward now, his elbows on his desk. He looked straight at Josie. "Give me some guesses," he said.

"I thought he'd be angry."

"Why would he be angry? Lots of people have relationships before they get married. Surely Paul did, too."

Josie nodded. "He'd be angry because I still see Scott every day."

"Why would that make him angry?"

"I don't really know." She felt her shoulders lift into a shrug and hoped the movement didn't come off as disrespectful.

"Give me some guesses."

"Because he'd think I couldn't get over Scott if I still saw him every day? Because he wouldn't like me interacting with Scott, remembering the, um, things we shared?"

"Do you remember those things fondly?"

A beat of silence ensued. Then Josie nodded. "Yeah, I do."

"And I take it Scott is different from Paul? The relationship you shared with him was different as well?"

Josie nodded.

Dr. Strasser continued. "So when things are tough with Paul, do you find yourself comparing?"

"Isn't it inevitable?"

"Is it?"

An entirely new kind of feeling was spreading throughout Josie Garcia's body, and she didn't know what do make of the unfamiliar sensation.

Guilt. Guilt over her enduring feelings for Scott. Dr. Strasser hadn't said as much, but his questions definitely got her wheels turning. Why hadn't she told Paul about her relationship with Scott? Would he really be jealous? Would he really think she couldn't get over it?

Probably not. He was a reasonable guy, and yes, he had past relationships, too. Josie hadn't told him because *she* thought she couldn't get over it. The secret started out as a tiny seed, planted just after she met Paul. Every day, she watered it when she saw Scott at school. It grew and grew, its tendrils, in the form of comparison, curling into every aspect of her marriage.

If Paul came home late, Josie told herself Scott would always be on time. If Paul got called out, Josie told herself Scott would stay home. If Paul was too tired for sex because he'd worked an extra-long shift, Josie told herself Scott would never turn her down. She became angry and resentful, picking apart Paul's every move.

In this way, she constantly tore down their marriage, one event, one criticism at a time.

How had this happened? Why hadn't she seen the situation this way before?

IF SUMMER and Delaney were going to insist that she run that stupid race, Josie needed the proper attire. Tuesday afternoon, she hit the mall. Although she had vivid memories of her reaction to Delaney shopping for office supplies and a new suit when she was supposed to be writing her resume and applying for jobs, she walked from the parking lot to the shoe store with growing excitement.

Shopping always warmed her up from the inside out like a bowl of her mother's tortilla soup on a winter day. When she told the salesman (who was actually a sales-teenager with a wispy goatee) she needed running shoes, he pointed to the treadmill.

"Let's get an analysis of your stride," he said.

Josie froze. "I didn't realize this was actually going to involve running. I thought I was just shopping."

The kid laughed.

"We like to analyze your stride so we can select the right shoe for you. It prevents injury. Obviously, you can't run in those heels." He laughed and she glared at him. "Let's start with a neutral shoe. What size do you wear?"

When he disappeared into the back room, anxiety took root in Josie's stomach. She sat down on the metal bench and took off her three-inch heels. There was no getting out of this. The kid reemerged, introduced himself as Mark, and handed her a pair of running socks and some cushy-looking, gaudy shoes slathered in fluorescent pinks and oranges. She cringed, but dutifully put them on and stepped onto the treadmill. Mark pressed the start button and the machine gave a tiny jolt. Josie jumped.

"Just relax, now," Mark said. "I'm going to put it on four miles per hour, which should be a comfortable jogging pace for you."

Josie nodded, gripping the handrails as the belt sped up. She was already out of breath. When she saw the speed indicator reach four miles per hour, she took her hands off the handrails.

Mark walked back to a computer in the corner. "I'm just going to get a quick video."

"A video?" Josie shrieked. "You are *not* getting this on video!"

He laughed. "Just your feet. To see how you strike. Keep jogging."

Josie nodded, and noticed she hadn't even run a tenth of a mile yet. Why did she feel so tired? She plodded along, waiting for Mark to tell her she could stop. After what seemed like several minutes (but was, according to the machine's timer, less than two), Mark reappeared at her side and pushed the stop button.

More than anything, Josie wanted to put her hands on her knees to catch her breath. Instead, she played it cool, inhaling through her nose and exhaling through her mouth like that twig of a yoga instructor always told them to do. A few minutes later, she walked out of the shoe store with a new pair of neutral shoes and a package of fancy running socks designed to prevent blisters (*as if I'll be doing that much running! Ha!*).

She spent the next hour shopping for leggings, tank tops and sports bras, and was pleasantly surprised to discover some genius had designed underwear specifically for running. Everything came in a variety of colorful patterns, fancy fabrics and complete outfits, and Josie felt a rush of pleasure putting together a full running wardrobe. Maybe this whole running thing wouldn't be so bad, after all.

As she walked to her car, arms loaded with shopping bags, she said, to herself or maybe to Paul's invisible audience, "Well, I've got my workout in for today. I'm on my way to a ten K."

• • •

SHE SHOULD HAVE KNOWN it would be a disaster. Josie never had enjoyed running, and even a great outfit couldn't take away from the fact that it made her feel like she was drowning. Or like she was a fish in honey. A snail in peanut butter. Whatever.

The Internet research she did on running suggested morning was the best time to exercise. And so what if researching running rather than actually doing it looked a bit like procrastination?

Thursday morning, Josie set her alarm to go off an hour earlier than normal. Paul wasn't in bed.

She turned on the lights and pulled on some leopard print leggings and a black tank top. The temperature outside felt balmy, and she walked for a few minutes to warm up.

"I can do this," she whispered to the rising sun, which was just peeking up over the horizon.

With that, she started jogging. Slowly, yes, but jogging nonetheless.

"Summer and Delaney would be so proud," she said.

One foot in front of the other.

Her lungs began to burn.

Breathe in through the nose, out through the mouth.

Her legs began to burn.

Right, left, right, left.

This sucks.

I hate this.

I can't do this.

Keep going. Right, left, right, left. One foot in front of the other.

It felt as though a half-hour had passed, but Josie's lying watch told her it was three minutes. She groaned, but forced herself to lift her feet, keep moving forward.

A car passed. She wondered how stupid she looked, a curvy girl barely able to get her feet off the ground to run a measly two miles per hour.

Why had she let Summer and Delaney force her to agree to running a race? She should have taken on some kind of exercise contest, like hula hooping or something.

Another car passed. The driver was probably wondering what the hell she was doing out here at this time of day. The sun had ascended past the mountains now, and it burned her eyes. Why hadn't she worn sunglasses?

Her eyes watered. Her lungs protested. Her legs weighed a million pounds each.

Half a block ahead, an old lady walked her tiny white poodle. The woman's back was slightly hunched, and her white hair stood out brightly against the gray of the early morning.

Josie wasn't even gaining on the woman. Her jogging speed was the same as the old lady's walking speed. The moment that realization dawned on her, she stopped. She stood there on the sidewalk, her hands interlaced on top of her head and her breath whooshing in and out like a dragon breathing fire.

When she walked home a few minutes later, she noted that she'd jogged only a couple of blocks. How could the girls expect her to run six-point-two miles? She could barely run six-point-two blocks. She felt like vomiting and crying at the same time. She growled instead.

OKAY, so maybe Summer and Delaney were onto something. The two-and-a-half-block run this morning felt truly awful, and she felt truly grumpy as she trudged home. But after showering, drinking a few cups of hot coffee and eating a veggie scramble, Josie felt refreshed and even a little accomplished.

So what if she was a terrible runner?

She'd get better. Little by little. Step by step.

She hated to admit it, but after the run, or half-run, or whatever she decided to call it, her mood felt lighter. Summer said something about exercise creating endorphins. Was is possible the phenomenon was real?

All morning, she thought about Paul, and the memories played in her mind like a movie reel, viewed through a filter of endorphins.

One fall night they went to the county fair, determined to recreate their teenage years. They took shots of tequila in the parking lot, licking salt off each other's necks and wrists, matching each other shot for shot, until they were buzzed and warm and giggling.

Then they bought wristbands and corn dogs and lemonades and went on every ride, some twice. They went on the Ferris wheel three times, making out like hormone-crazed kids whenever they rounded the top.

They shared funnel cake in the grandstands while they watched the demolition derby. When it was over, they sat in the silence, ears ringing, discussing their plans for the future: a house with a pool, a Goldendoodle puppy, and a couple of kids. Annual camping trips to the beach, family movie nights and long weekends in the mountains.

By the time they sobered up and drove home, it was almost light out. They tumbled into bed, had lazy, slow-motion sex and slept until after noon. Josie remembered thinking several times that night how lucky she was, how much she loved him and how she couldn't wait to experience their future together.

One winter, they borrowed a friend's four-wheel drive truck and went north for a day. They planned on sledding, but when they arrived in the tiny mountain town a couple of hours from Juniper, they realized Paul had forgotten to pack the sleds. Since this was the first big snow of the season, the stores in town were all sold out. So they grabbed some supplies, got a cozy hotel room and spent the evening watching the snowfall, roasting marshmallows over the fire pit and making love in the gorgeous Jacuzzi tub.

Sure, they'd bickered over the forgotten sleds at first. He blamed her for distracting him by insisting on a coffee run before they left Juniper and she blamed him for not packing them in the first place. But they made up and turned it into one of the best one-night getaways ever.

A couple of months later in the spring, they had gone to a kite-flying event at the Juniper library. The mayor of Juniper wanted to beat some record for the number of kites flying all at once, and Josie convinced Paul they should go. She went out and bought a fancy kite—a dragon with a long plastic tail that supposedly shimmered in the breeze when the sunlight caught it. Only, the kite wouldn't fly.

While Paul held the dragon by its belly, Josie took the string and ran as fast as she could so he could release the kite. It would soar up, looking so promising, its short tongue fluttering … and then it would plummet. Over and over again.

The wind carried Paul's various curse words to Josie's ears as she reeled the string back in at least a dozen times. When they finally called it quits, they were laughing so hard they couldn't stop. They pulled an old blanket out of the car and laid on the grass, watching the 847 other kite-flyers beat the standing record for the number of people flying their kites at the same time. Afterward, they went for pizza and beer, breaking into giggles several times as they relived the disastrous incident. When they realized other patrons were glaring at them, they got their food to go and giggled all the way home.

"I guess kite-flying won't be on the list of skills we teach our kids," Paul said that night as they laid in bed in the dark.

They laughed again, and Josie drifted off to sleep in his arms thinking about their future children, girls with her black hair and his blue eyes, boys with his strong chin and her slow smile.

What had happened to that couple?

It was as if, several years ago, they came to a fork in the road of their marriage and took two different paths. Maybe the paths were parallel, heading in the same direction but never intersecting. Or worse, maybe they headed in completely opposite directions.

JOSIE OWED PAUL AN APOLOGY.

She'd kept a big secret, for a long time. And during that time, which spanned their entire marriage, she probably acted and reacted in ways that weren't normal for her because of that secret. How could she not have realized that?

In addition to apologizing, she needed to reassure Paul that at the end of this school year, Scott would be gone and out of her life for good. Would he accept her apology? Would he forgive her?

It was lunch recess, and Josie sat in the teachers' lounge tapping her fork against the edge of the Tupperware that held her salad.

"You gonna eat that salad, or just make music?"

Susie Lighthouse, sweet as a summer day in her pink dress, breezed into the lounge and slid into the seat across from Josie. "What's going on in that pretty head of yours, woman? You look so serious."

Josie sighed.

"Have you ever done something you regretted, Susie?"

Susie unwrapped her sandwich and took a bite before nodding. "Yeah," she said when she finally swallowed. "Toilet papering Stephanie Hall's house sophomore year of high school."

"Really?" Josie wrinkled her nose. "That's all you've got?"

"Oh! This one time, I played doorbell ditch with my friends, and we rang Mrs. MacMillan's doorbell. She was my next-door neighbor. She was really old. I mean, like almost a hundred. Poor lady. It took her seven minutes to answer the door, and then we were gone. My friends convinced me to hide in Mrs. MacMillan's shrubs, and they were laughing like loons as she stood there calling, 'Who's there?' over and over again. She looked so sad when she finally shut the door. I still feel really bad about that."

"Really, Susie? That's it? You're married, aren't you?"

"Well, yeah, but I don't regret that!"

Josie laughed. "That's not what I meant. Haven't you ever done anything you regret, in your marriage?"

Susie looked thoughtful for a minute.

"Well, you know," she said. "I've been short with Rick, or turned him down for sex." She giggled. "I've criticized him for wearing mismatched socks with shorts. Of course I experience guilt or remorse, but just little twinges. I wouldn't say I regret those things. You know? Like, real regret?"

When Josie didn't respond, and instead took a few bites of salad, Susie's brow furrowed.

"What's going on, Josie? What's wrong?"

Josie shook her head. "It's nothing."

"I know it's not nothing," Susie said. Then, like a trained ninja interrogator, or a teacher, she waited.

"Fine," Josie finally said. "Fine. It's just that lately, I've experienced a lot of regret when it comes to my marriage. I know I've done so many things wrong. I want to fix it, but I don't know how. I don't know what to do. I mean, I want to apologize. But is that it? What then? An apology is one thing, but how do I change?"

"You just change." Susie said, as if changing were the simplest thing in the world. "You make the choice, in every situation, to be the new Josie. To make the change. One choice at a time."

"I can do that," Josie said. "Thanks, Susie. Really. That's good advice."

The new Josie was prepared to conquer this change. But she wasn't prepared for what she saw when she left school that afternoon.

. . .

BECAUSE SHE HADN'T FINISHED her work until an hour after the final bell rang, Josie thought she was the last teacher to leave. But when she walked downstairs, she discovered a scene that made her hackles rise.

Blair Upton perched on the edge of Scott Smith's desk, her tiny hip draped in a bright orange skirt. Josie could see her from the back, and her perfectly coiffed French twist moved snappily from left to right.

Blair was threatening Scott just as she had done to Josie.

The adrenaline started pumping through Josie's veins. Her hands shook. She gripped the banister hard, already planning what she would say. After she finished throttling Blair and her skinny little neck. Expletives aside, Josie would ask Blair how she slept at night, why she couldn't just leave them alone, and why she'd always had it out for Josie.

But as she descended the final stairs to the bottom floor, she got a wider view of what was happening in that office, and she suddenly felt more intrigued than angry. Blair Upton's arm reached out to Scott Smith's waist, and her talon-like hand wrapped around his belt. Her fingertips were inside his pants, and she was leaning forward, pulling him towards her seductively.

For his part, Scott Smith didn't look like he minded at all.

Hmm. Interesting.

Josie wondered how long this had been going on. Instead of confronting Blair, she started to form a plan, and she made a mental note to take the first step as soon as possible.

CHAPTER SIXTEEN

THE CHILI SIMMERED ON THE STOVE, FILLING THE HOUSE WITH THE SCENT of onion and garlic. Acoustic music played on the stereo, and Josie took sips from a glass of wine as she added the beans, tomato sauce and seasonings to the pot. Cornbread muffins baked in the oven, and Negro Modelo chilled in the fridge.

Josie had her apology all planned out.

Paul should be home any time now, and she'd welcome him with a nice, hot dinner, a good, cold beer and the speech she'd worked on throughout the day. She heard his car pull into the driveway, and she took a deep gulp of wine and an even deeper breath.

You can do this, Garcia.

Apologies didn't come easy to Josie. They never had. Once, when she'd pinched her brother's arm until she drew blood (because he got mud on her brand new jean jacket), her mother had said she had to stay in her room until she apologized.

Three days. Three entire days Josie sat on her bed, intermittently staring at the wall and reading a book, leaving her room only to go to the bathroom. Finally, boredom forced her into Juan's room.

A simple, "I'm sorry for pinching you," would have sufficed, but she added on, "But it was your fault."

"Back to your room, Josefina Maria Esperanza Garcia!" their mother said. She'd sneaked into the hallway the moment she heard

Josie's door open. "You don't put a qualifier on an apology. You should not have pinched your brother and that's that."

The second stint had been shorter. Two days.

But she was all grown up now, she reminded herself as she stirred the chili and put the lid on it. Josie jumped when she heard a knock at the door.

Why would Paul knock? Maybe it was a delivery. Or a neighbor coming over for a cup of sugar. Sometimes Lynnie from across the street needed to borrow wine.

"For cooking," she always said, her wrinkled face twisting into an expression Josie couldn't quite read. Was it mischievous or just grateful? Josie wiped her hands on a dish towel and went to answer the door. She simultaneously noticed the patrol car in the driveway, pulled the door open and realized what the car—not Paul's undercover jalopy—and the knock meant.

That split-second realization dawned just in time for her to brace herself against the door as her vision began to gray around the edges.

Two uniformed police officers stood on the stoop, looking nervous. One of them played with a button on his shirt, and the other clenched and unclenched his hands.

"Is Paul—" she began, but found that her voice wouldn't come out.

"He's alive, ma'am," the hand-clencher said.

Josie exhaled.

The other cop took a deep breath. "Comstock, er, your husband, Paul, was in a car accident, Ms. Garcia," he said. "He's at Juniper Medical center now. He sustained significant injuries, including abrasions to the side of his face and a laceration on his forehead."

"What does that mean?"

The hand-clencher cleared his throat. "He's cut up pretty good, Ms. Garcia. We're going to take you to the hospital right away."

The back of the hand-clencher's patrol car smelled like vomit and urine. Josie almost gagged when she got in. Within seconds, the car was speeding through town, lights and sirens blaring, and Josie was sliding across the back seat every time they took a corner.

At the house, an eerie sense of calm came over her when the officers told her Paul had been in an accident. The world went silent, and her movements became slow and deliberate, like she was walking along the bottom of a swimming pool.

Turn off the stove.

Put the cork in the wine bottle.

Get your phone.

Turn off the stereo.

Turn on the porch light.

Put on some shoes.

Grab a jacket.

Lock the front door.

As the wife of a police officer, she always half-expected someone to knock on her door, just as the hand-clencher and his button-fondling sidekick had done this evening. She had played the moment out so many times in her head that she felt almost prepared for it.

Still, the ride to the hospital felt interminable.

Josie texted Summer and Delaney: *Paul's been in an accident. The guys who came to tell me said he's alive, but they're taking me to the hospital to see him. I'll keep you posted.*

Of course, both of them responded immediately.

Summer: *Oh, honey, are you okay?*

Delaney: *Have you talked to him?*

Josie answered that yes, she was fine and no, she hadn't talked to Paul.

Summer: *Keep us posted, okay?*

Delaney: *Hang in there.*

Josie wanted nothing more than to be with Paul in person, to see for herself that he was all right, to make things right between them. What if the crash had been fatal, and he'd died not knowing she was sorry for her juvenile secret-keeping, petty behaviors and childish pet peeves? He had to know, immediately. Josie had to tell him he was the most important person in her life, and that she'd do anything to sustain their marriage.

Finally, the hand-clencher parked at the Emergency Room entrance. Josie wanted to fling the door open, but had to wait for the button-fondler to open it for her.

When he did, she jumped out, already in a half-jog. The button-fondler grabbed her wrist.

"Ma'am? He doesn't look good. Okay? I know you're anxious to see him, and you've got to believe us that his injuries are mostly minor. But I want you to have fair warning that he looks pretty beat up."

Josie nodded and he released her wrist. She gathered herself and walked calmly to the front desk. A tall, skinny nurse who looked not much older than a high schooler led her to Paul's room. She saw his name scrawled on a whiteboard outside the door. The nurse, whose name tag identified her as Joan, gestured for her to go in.

Paul looked horrible. Awful. His left eye was swollen completely shut, enveloping the long eyelashes she so loved, and he had a neat row of stitches above his left eyebrow, in the same spot where he'd gotten hooked with a fish hook as a kid. A dark purple bruise covered the entire left side of his face.

Even though he was wearing a hospital gown, Josie could see another bruise on his left shoulder and a scrape running along the back of his arm.

Her first reaction was anger. She would find the person who did this, and she would wring his neck. At least. She wanted to yell, "Who did this to you?" but instead, she tiptoed over to the bed and sat on its edge. An IV entered Paul's arm at the inside of his elbow, and she wasn't sure if she could hold his hand.

"Hey, baby," he said.

Josie jumped.

"I didn't know you were awake," she said.

He took her hand. "I am. Just resting my eyes."

"What happened?"

Paul took a deep breath. "We were making a left turn from Coal Mine Road onto Boulder Drive and someone hit us. Ran a red light."

"Was he drunk?"

"No." He swallowed. "It was a lady. She wasn't drunk. Just distracted. Probably texting or something, didn't look up in time. This is why I tell you not to text and drive."

Josie, a bit irritated, nodded. "I only text—"

"Summer and Delaney, I know," he said.

"And it's always voice to text," they said at the same time.

"But you look pretty banged up for such a small collision," she said.

He laughed. The sound came out strangled, and he winced. "She was going pretty fast."

A beat of silence passed.

"Listen, Paul, there's something I need to say to you."

"Geez, Josie, give a guy a break. Can this wait until tomorrow? They want to keep me overnight in case I have a concussion or something."

Or something? she wanted to say. *What else could it be?*

She was terrified. But instead of asking more questions, she nodded. "Of course. I'm so sorry. You're probably exhausted."

He nodded, the movement stiff and barely visible.

Even from inside the cubicle, Josie could hear a commotion coming down the hallway toward them. When she distinguished the frantic footsteps from the frantic whispers, she smiled.

"Summer and Delaney are here," she said to Paul.

He smiled, too. "Better go out and greet my fan club."

IT WAS TIME FOR A DO-OVER.

The day after Paul's accident, doctors cleared him for discharge. Josie took the day off from work and drove him home around noon. Naturally, a shower was the first thing he wanted, so she put her famous chili back on the stove and waited for him to come out.

She braced herself when she heard him turn off the water. He never took long to dress, which meant her big moment was imminent.

"Keep it simple," she whispered to herself.

Breathe in through your nose, out through your mouth.

She set bowls of shredded cheddar, chopped green onions and sour cream on the counter. Not the most romantic dish, but it did fit in the comfort food category. Paul's steps sounded in the hallway, and Josie smoothed her shirt and rearranged the bowls of condiments.

He walked in, wearing sweat pants and a tight black t-shirt. He looked like he'd been in some kind of bar brawl. For the first time in their marriage, Josie felt awkward, self-conscious. She wanted to go to him, hug him, repeat, "I'm sorry," until her voice went hoarse. But she didn't know how he'd react. He didn't even know what she was sorry for.

So instead, she said, rather stupidly, "I made chili."

"Smells good," he said.

He leaned against the counter. She lined the bowls up compulsively. Spoons. She needed spoons. And a butter knife, and butter, too.

"You look good," she said.

He snorted. "Shut up."

"No, really. It's just so good to see you up and moving."

"This looks great."

"Look, Paul, there's something I need to say."

"Is this the thing from last night?" he said.

Why do I feel like crying all the time lately?

"Yes." Josie heard her own voice break and hated herself for it. "I just feel like I need to apologize."

"For what?" he said, although she could practically hear him creating a mental list of all her recent infractions.

She nodded, as if to answer his unspoken thought.

"For everything," she said. "For constantly bitching at you, for complaining about your work schedule, for working just as much as you do but not admitting it." She let out a laugh. "For ruining our marriage, basically."

He didn't respond immediately. Instead, he walked gingerly over to the stove and picked up the ladle to taste the chili, like he always did. Since he wasn't speaking, she felt compelled to go on: "Last night, when those guys showed up at my door, I had a moment of clarity. Actually, I had this big speech planned already, but you being in the accident made it even more important that I tell you. I want to fix things. I want to start fresh, push the reset button. Can we do that?"

Paul froze, holding the ladle just above the chili pot. Josie could hear the bubbling soup. She could smell the chipotle chili powder she'd put in, and she could see the setting sun shining in through the kitchen window, slanting onto Paul's still form.

"It brought me some clarity, too," he finally said, ladling chili into his empty bowl.

She waited while he sprinkled cheese and green onions, spooned on sour cream. Finally, he turned to face her, his bowl in one hand.

"Did you get any beer?" he asked.

She inclined her head toward the fridge, where the Negro Modelo waited. The moments ticked by, painstakingly slow.

Why isn't he answering?

While Josie dished up her own chili, she listened to Paul open the drawer, take out the bottle opener, open his beer and take the first sip. A few moments later, they sat at the kitchen counter, side by side.

"So, what was your big moment of clarity all about?" Josie asked.

"Can we eat first?"

Josie nodded. Paul nodded, too, and crumbled his cornbread muffin into his chili. They ate. It took forever.

"Good chili," Paul said, more than once.

"Thanks," Josie said each time.

He pushed his empty bowl away from him.

"I've been thinking," he said. "I'm going to move out."

CHAPTER SEVENTEEN

If she were watching the scene from the outside, or if she were a cockroach on the floor, Josie would have marveled at how it all unfolded exactly like a soap opera.

Her spoon clattered to the countertop next to her bowl, leaving droplets of chili that would harden there for days. *Close-up on the spoon.* She seemed momentarily paralyzed. *Cut to Josie, frozen in place due to shock.*

Paul put his elbows on the counter and his head in his hands. Then he flinched, apparently having forgotten about all the bruising and the stitches. Neither of them spoke as the shadows in the house grew longer and then faded into the deep gray that precedes total darkness. *Cue sad, romantic music that conveys regret.*

"Have you been thinking about this?" Josie said into the silence stretching between them like taffy. *Wide view of counter.*

Paul nodded. "I've been thinking about it for a few days. But the accident brought everything into focus."

"Why didn't you say something sooner?" Josie said.

She felt Paul sigh beside her.

"I didn't know sooner," he said. *Zoom in on Paul's face.* "Lately, working so much, being away from home" (she noticed he didn't say, "away from you," but she knew that's what he meant) "I've felt more, I don't know, comfortable. You're not breathing down my neck every second, waiting for me to mess up so you can call me on it. It's been so peaceful."

Ouch. It took a moment to absorb the sting. *Zoom in on Josie's face.*

"You haven't been lonely?" she asked, for lack of anything better to say.

"Babe," he said, "I started feeling lonely a long time ago. I'm past that. I feel almost relieved. And then last night, I was so glad to see you. So glad. But I also felt like we need to fix this or move on. You know? And the best way, for us to do that, I think, is to spend some time apart." *Close up on Josie's reaction.*

When she put her forehead on the counter, he rubbed her back, long strokes up and down her spine. He must have felt her crying, because he scooted his stool closer to her and wrapped an arm around her. *Wide angle.*

"I'm not saying it's over," he said. "I just think some time apart would be good for both of us. It would give you time to get over that skinny, big-toothed Scott Smith asshole," here he chuckled, a little too heartily, in Josie's opinion, "and it would give me time to think about my priorities."

"But I was apologizing," she said (*close up on Josie*), hating the whine in her voice. "I want to make things better."

"I think the first step toward making things better is to give each other the space we need. So we can get back to appreciating each other."

All the time, Paul kept rubbing Josie's back, which only made her more upset.

"I'll stay here tonight," he said. He kissed her on the temple. *Close up.* "And pack my things tomorrow. Go on to bed, and I'll clean up. Great chili, by the way."

Josie went straight to bed without undressing, brushing her teeth or washing her face. *Pan out while she exits.*

People always said things look better in the morning, but Josie sincerely doubted that would be the case. Unless, of course, she woke up and discovered this was a nightmare and in her real life, her husband wanted to spend every spare moment side by side with her.

But as she drifted off feeling miserably sorry for herself, that practical little voice whispered: *This is your real life, honey. You'd better suck it up.*

And … cut.

Morning still came. For the first time in Josie's life, laying awake all night did not slow the clock.

Resentment crept in as she listened to Paul's even breathing. Why was he sleeping so well? Why hadn't he been up all night, fretting over the impending failure of their marriage? It seemed so unfair. Her alarm went off, but she stayed in bed. What would Paul do for an alarm when he moved out? Where would he go? Who would he wake up next to? She heard his breathing change and looked over to see him touching his face, exploring the row of stitches and pressing lightly on the swelling on his left eye.

"Good morning," he said.

Why was he so friendly now, on their last morning together?

"Good morning," she answered. She could hear the pout in her own voice.

"Babe, don't do this," he said, sitting up and turning toward her.

"Don't do what? Say good morning to you?"

"You're talking so grumpy."

"Of course I am. You're moving out. With practically no warning. After you almost died. I had this big moment of clarity, and you did, too, and they're opposing. I'm upset. I just realized how much I've messed up, but obviously, your heart isn't really in it."

On a loud sigh, Paul stood up. Even in this moment, Josie could appreciate his washboard abs and well-defined quads. She felt herself flush at the thought of an early morning romp. *When was the last time we did* that? She bit down on her lip and looked away.

She said, "Remember that time we got drunk and went to the fair?"

To her surprise, he laughed. "How could I forget? I ate so much that night between the corn dogs and the funnel cake I thought I was going to toss my cookies on one of our rides on the Ferris wheel."

"What about the time we went for a sledding trip without any sleds?" she said. She didn't know if this was self-torture or just a conversation.

"But we loved the Jacuzzi tub, right? That was a great night."

Suddenly, he was beside her on the bed again, holding one of her hands in both of his, staring into her eyes.

"Josie, this isn't the end of our marriage, okay? This is just some breathing space. That's all this is."

A loud sob escaped her, and she turned away and got out of bed.

"I don't want breathing space. Breathing space always ends in divorce, don't you know that?"

Paul sighed again, and to Josie's disappointment, stood up and began pulling clothes out of the dresser and stacking them on the bed.

"Where are you going to stay, anyway?" she asked. She leaned against the wall that opened into the bathroom and crossed her arms.

"Uh, well, I'm going to stay with Schmidt," he said, looking down and scratching the back of his neck.

"Terry Schmidt?"

"Yeah." He didn't look up. "Terry Schmidt."

"The lifelong bachelor Terry Schmidt?"

"The one and only."

"Paul!" Josie threw her hands up and turned to walk into the bathroom and start the shower.

Paul followed her, and answered as she stripped down. "He's the only one I can stay with. McAdams' wife just had a baby, Willis has about eight kids, crazy bastard, and Drew and his wife are trying to get pregnant. I guess they're having sex, like, every other night or whatever, all over the damned house. He says it gets pretty monotonous so they have to spice things up by doing it, you know, on the kitchen counter or whatever. I ain't eating off their counters. And those are the only guys I'd stay with."

Josie poked her head around the shower curtain and shook it.

"Terry Schmidt's going to have you converted to bachelorhood in less than twenty-four hours."

"He's a nice guy. Did you know Terry Schmidt is the one who helped me pick out your engagement ring?"

That stopped Josie's ire in its tracks.

"No, I didn't know that."

"Did you know he's the one who helped me pull off the way I gave it to you?"

"Nope. Didn't know that, either," Josie said.

"He's a good guy, okay? He's not against marriage or anything. He just hasn't found the right woman. He's actually got a really romantic heart."

Because she didn't know what else to do, Josie tugged the shower curtain closed.

PAUL'S actual proposal had been absolutely no-frills. About as far from romantic as a person could get. He didn't even have a ring.

Josie always thought it represented the way he loved her, though: straightforward and no nonsense. He didn't need flowers and candlelight to set the scene to ask her to spend the rest of her life with him. He didn't need accessories to prove his affection or his devotion.

But he swept her off her feet when he gave her the ring.

Because she was so in love with him—stupid in love with him—she never even thought about that little detail when he proposed, until someone asked. Then, she'd only shrugged and said, "I'll be happy with a plain wedding band once we're married." And it was true. She was practical. She didn't need him to spend hundreds or thousands of dollars on a piece of jewelry. "Put that money towards a down payment for a new house," she told him when he asked what kind of a sparkler she wanted.

Then one Friday afternoon shortly after the proposal, he picked her up from work in a rented Mustang convertible. He had her leave her car key in the office, and a friend of his—Terry Schmidt—delivered her car back to the house.

They arrived in San Diego six hours later, and checked into the Bayside Manor, a bed and breakfast that overlooked the ocean and had a private beach.

Summer and Delaney helped him pack several outfits, including her favorite sundress. She wore it to dinner at Ray's, a swanky steakhouse where they sat on the patio and soaked up the warm, brilliant sunset. They sipped cold white wine until long after dark, and then went back to the hotel and passed out side by side on the huge four-poster bed, still in their clothes.

The next day, they ordered room service for breakfast, and then

Paul took Josie to Clam Shell Cove, an amusement park on the beach. He seemed a little jumpy throughout the morning, but she assumed it was the typical hyperawareness most cops experience in crowded public places.

Just before lunch, though, Paul pointed to the Sky Ride, which took people from one end of the park to the other in colorful cars suspended on cables fifty feet above the ground.

They sat across from each other in the hanging car, and Paul smiled at Josie as the ride attendant latched the door. She smiled back, looking so forward to the spectacular sky-high ocean view that she didn't notice the gleam in his eyes. With the salty breeze blowing Josie's hair back from her face and the sun shining high in the sky, Paul pulled a red velvet pouch from his shirt pocket.

Josie didn't even have time to wonder what was in it before Paul dropped the ring into his hand and held it out on his palm. The round cut diamond and the sapphires surrounding it sparkled in the sunlight, winking on his palm like planets in the nighttime sky.

Josie's breath caught.

I'm so not a romantic, but I so love this man.

When she didn't speak, Paul laughed. "For once, I've made Josie Garcia speechless. Put it on."

"You put it on me," she said, holding out her hand.

He laughed again and slipped it onto her finger. She held up her hand, admiring the ring from different angles, watching it shine and sparkle in the sunlight.

"Like it?"

She nodded, then put her hands on either side of his face and pulled him in for a long kiss.

"I know you said you didn't need an engagement ring, but I wanted you to have one. It's a symbol of how I feel about you, like you're my sun, the center of my universe. You're the diamond to my sapphires. I want to be near you, surrounding you, all the time."

As the beach sailed by underneath them and the cool ocean air swirled around them, they kissed again.

This is what it's all about. This moment right here.

CHAPTER EIGHTEEN

"Wow, Josie, you're here first," Benjamin tipped his hat at her as she slid onto her stool at the usual table at Rowdy's. "It's a modern-day miracle. One of each?"

When he sauntered off to fetch the drinks, she realized she was holding onto another secret. She tried to think of how to avoid talking to the girls about her marriage all together. Not that she didn't want to tell them Paul moved out. She simply wasn't ready to tell them just yet. They'd be so disappointed that their Marriage Intervention hadn't worked. By not telling them, she was actually protecting their feelings. This wasn't about her. Benjamin returned with a water and a bowl of green olives for Summer and a Guinness for Delaney. He set Josie's vodka cranberry on the table in front of her, and when she downed it in one gulp he held up two fingers and raised his eyebrows. She nodded, and he returned a few seconds later with number two.

Summer came in next, but she was on the phone and didn't even make eye contact with Josie when she sat down. She was speaking quietly and Josie sensed this wasn't a conversation on which to eavesdrop. To give Summer some privacy, she took a bathroom break. As she walked through the bar on her way back to the table, she noticed that Summer's pregnancy was starting to show. Not just the tiny bump where you weren't sure whether she was pregnant or just slightly overweight, but the mini-watermelon shaped bulge that left no question a baby was growing in there.

Josie smiled to herself, but felt the smile slide off her face when she saw the expression on Summer's. She was pale, and she was biting her bottom lip, which was always a sign of worry. Josie quickened her pace, and was reaching for Summer's arm when Delaney came through Rowdy's front door, practically dancing.

Summer and Josie had enough time to exchange a quick glance, during which Summer gave Josie a tiny "don't worry about me" head shake. The moment passed quickly, swallowed up by Delaney's excitement. She giggled maniacally, holding her left hand up, wiggling her fingers.

"He did it! It happened! He proposed! I said yes! We're getting married!"

Josie noticed Summer take a deep breath and visibly shake off whatever was bothering her, and she followed suit. They stood up to hug Delaney, shouting congratulations and signaling for champagne.

"So he says, 'I know you saw the brochure in the junk drawer,' and I just start laughing," Delaney said, her eyes glowing with excitement. "And I say, 'I don't know what you're talking about.'"

"Then we're both just laughing, and he takes my face in his hands and he says, 'I love you, Delaney Collins.'"

Delaney started to giggle-cry and Summer handed her a bar napkin.

"Of course I said, 'I love you, too, Jake Rhoades the Dreamy,' and then we're both laughing again."

"And then?" Josie prompted. "Did he get down on one knee or anything?"

"No!" Delaney said. "Then he walked away! It was the strangest thing. He just left me standing there in the kitchen!"

"So ... did he actually propose, or not?" Summer wanted to know.

Delaney laughed.

"No! That was yesterday. I was flummoxed. Seriously. But he did it today. Right before I came here. He showed up at Dr. Rick's office, they're friends, you know? And I think she's known it was coming all day. She's been grinning like the Cheshire Cat or the cat who ate the canary or whomever. Anyway, he's waiting by the car when I come out, and he's holding a bouquet of tiger lilies, just like he gave me after our first date. It was so cute, you guys. He looked almost sheepish. And he held out the ring, no box, no nothing, just the ring, and he said, 'Delaney Collins, I'd be honored if you'd be my wife. Will you marry me?'"

Summer and Josie responded with appropriate "Awwww" and "Ohhhh" sounds, and Delaney stretched her arm across the table so they could admire the ring. Again.

The solitaire diamond shone, and the image began to waver when Josie's eyes filled. A fat tear dropped onto her arm, and Summer handed her a bar napkin, too.

"Our Delaney's growing up," she said, blowing her nose.

Josie nodded, "We're so happy for you, Dee."

"Are you actually crying?" Delaney said. "Josie Garcia is crying over an engagement? This deserves a toast of its own."

Delaney raised her glass, and before she could speak, Josie said, "To Delaney and Jake, and a long, happy marriage."

How was it possible to feel so sad—no, make that devastated—and so happy at the same time?

Josie's chest was practically exploding with happiness for Delaney, who, just a few months ago, was dating every loser with a stained necktie who walked into Rowdy's with a soggy sob story. But Jake matched her perfectly.

At the same time, Josie felt like she was being ripped apart at the seams in her own marriage. She supposed it wasn't a simple ninety-degree right or left turn that had sent it down the course toward … wherever they were now. It was probably one very slight turn after another, until they ended up traveling in a completely different direction than the one in which they started.

She remembered showing her ring to Summer and Delaney after Paul took her on that surprise trip to San Diego. She danced her way into an impromptu emergency Happy Hour meeting the next Monday evening, and used every opportunity available to show off her ring.

She pointed at a new rodeo photograph on the wall, acted out one of her co-workers' rants about not being selected for the choir teacher position, and lifted her glass way more often than usual, all with the diamond and sapphires sparkling from her left hand.

By the end of that evening, the girls had been hysterical, asking Josie every question they could think of to get her to use her hand again. For some reason, they spoke in Southern accents, fanning themselves with coasters.

"Excuse me, madam, could you please point me to the ladies room?"

"Where did you say the sun sets? The east? No? Well, by golly, ma'am, could you point the way to the west, then?"

"Could you please hand me a napkin, sweetheart? Bless your little heart."

"Oh, darlin', you have something on your face, there, on the left side. No, up a little, down a little. Yes, you've got it."

Now it was Delaney's turn, and Josie could practically feel that same happiness again.

For the next couple of hours, Josie basked in it, listening to wedding plans, color choices, flower options and honeymoon destinations, giving her advice and engaging in thoughtful discussions about whether to serve lunch or dinner, whether to get live music or a DJ, and whether each layer of the cake should be a different flavor or they should all be the same.

Delaney, anxious to get back home to Jake and get his opinions on roses versus calla lilies, floated out of Rowdy's at six p.m. sharp, leaving Summer and Josie alone in silence.

"Who called right before Delaney got here?" Josie asked. The question came out as more of a demand than a conversation starter, and Summer jumped off her stool.

"It's—uh, it's nothing. No one. Look, I've gotta go."

Summer was gone in a cloud of vanilla scented lotion. Josie scrambled to follow her to the door. Summer never acted like this. Josie's usual tactic would be to interrogate her until she opened up. But tonight, she found herself taking a new approach. After all, wasn't she keeping secrets, too? When they stepped out into the cool evening air, Josie put a hand on Summer's shoulder. Summer stopped, but Josie could feel her entire being aching to walk down the sidewalk to her van.

"I know it's not nothing," Josie said.

When Summer opened her mouth to deny it, Josie held up a hand to stop her.

"I know it's not nothing," she repeated. "But I understand if you're not ready to talk about it right now. Just remember I'll be here when you are. Okay?"

Summer bit her bottom lip and her chin quivered, sure signs she was about to cry. She nodded, pulled Josie in for a quick hug and walked away.

Standing alone on the sidewalk, Josie congratulated herself for keeping her secret and for letting Summer keep hers. Neither of them wanted to taint Delaney's happiness.

CHAPTER NINETEEN

"EVEN THOUGH I KNEW HE WAS PLANNING TO PACK HIS STUFF, I WAS surprised when I got home and discovered he took the single serve coffeemaker."

Josie sat in Dr. Strasser's office, watching the palm fronds sway in the air conditioner's breeze.

"How did that make you feel?" Dr. Strasser asked.

Josie took a deep breath. "Lonely. Sad. Like a failure. But then I kept reminding myself that he said this is just a break. It's not forever. He wants to keep trying. So that bolstered me a little, even when I saw so many of his clothes were gone."

Dr. Strasser nodded, his chin, as always, resting on his fingertips.

"I just don't know what he wants from me," Josie said.

"Don't you?"

Do I?

"Kind of, I guess."

"What I heard Paul saying was that you seemed unhappy, impossible to please. Can you think of examples of how that manifested in your communications with him?"

Plenty.

She ticked through a mental list of her constant complaints: about what time he came home and where he put his boots, about how he forgot to use the splatter guard when he cooked bacon and how he made so much noise when she was sleeping. Each of these points seemed valid, in the moment. But now, looking back on them, she could see how they had a cumulative effect.

"A few, yes," she said.

"Can you think of ways to change the nature of those communications?"

Stop being so horrible?

"Yeah, I guess so."

"Look, Josie. It doesn't really matter why you act the way you do. It's become a habit, hasn't it?" He didn't wait for her to answer. "What matters is that you realize you do it, and you make the choice, each time you interact with Paul, to change that habit."

FOR MONTHS JOSIE hounded Paul about never being around, but he was almost always in bed when she woke up. When her alarm went off he'd raise a heavy arm, drape it over her and pull her in close to his body. And if he wasn't there, she knew he would be within twenty-four hours.

Not today, though. Josie wished she could stay under the covers until he decided to move back in.

In his texts throughout the day yesterday, he said he was recovering well and wasn't in much pain. His sergeant had him riding a desk and he was bored out of his mind. He didn't say anything about missing her.

Josie chose an orange blouse, hoping the cheerful color would buoy her mood.

Scott Smith spotted Josie the moment she walked into the school building. He was on his computer, but his gaze snapped from his screen to her torso faster than a third grader could stash a piece of gum under his desk.

Where Paul would say something like, "Oh, you're wearing orange today. Need some cheering up?" Scott nodded at her and said, "That shirt really shows off your waistline."

"Inappropriate, Scott," Josie said.

Suddenly, he was up and walking around the side of his desk with a sense of urgency that had her backing up as he approached her. She almost yelped when he grabbed her upper arms arms.

Her memory flashed on that damn extracurriculars folder sitting on the passenger seat of his car and then on Blair Upton's hand inside his waistband.

"Could we have another meeting?" he asked. "To discuss the extracurriculars?"

Suddenly, she felt revolted. He *was* manipulative. Complimenting her on her waistline now, rubbing Blair's waistline later. Anger flared up, and she felt heat rise to her face.

Although she was desperate to call him out on the Blair Affair (she'd have to trademark that, it was pretty good), she decided to keep it close for now. She would save that card until she really needed it. She had to enact her plan, gather evidence, first.

"Can't you just put it in an email? You know how it is this time of year. I'm really busy."

Scott's shoulders drooped in a cartoonish way Josie found mildly comical.

He rubbed a hand across his forehead as if it pained him to even consider putting the information in an email. Finally, he said, "Yeah, I guess so. I just thought it'd be easier to explain in person."

"I'm a visual person, so seeing it in print would be better for me anyway," she said.

"Yeah. Okay."

Josie turned to leave.

"Listen, Josie?"

She bit back an exasperated sigh and stopped in the doorway. She didn't turn around. "Yes, Scott?"

"Would you want to go out for drinks one more time? Just once?"

This time she let the sigh come rushing out of her mouth and she hoped he could read her frustration. "No. Thank you, Scott."

TOO BAD SHOPPING was not an acceptable long-term stress relief solution. Josie pulled on a pair of bright pink leggings and a black tank top with pink piping. Summer swore she'd read that running would make Josie nicer (well, she hadn't used those exact words). Josie felt doubtful.

Still. As she admired the outfit in the mirror, she thought she could get into running just for the clothes, if it wasn't for the panting and the side aches. She clipped on her Mp3 player and filled her water bottle. All geared up.

"All the gear in the world isn't going to burn calories or produce endorphins, Garcia," she said aloud.

She wondered if Paul's fake audience was still here, or if they'd hitched a ride in his suitcase and were, at this very moment, watching him gesture wildly in Terry Schmidt's leather-and-steel bachelor pad as Paul described the reasons he had moved out.

After a lengthy internal debate, Josie had ended up choosing black and white running shoes. The same style had come in a fluorescent orange, but she opted for something that would match all her new leggings.

"Maybe I should get a pet," she said. "A dog. To run with."

Although it was tempting to go to the shelter and adopt one immediately instead of going for a run, Josie grabbed her water bottle and headed out the door. At first, it felt like she was trudging rather than walking. She took a deep breath and thought about how Summer would tell her to bring in the positive energy.

"Visualize the light entering your body," she would say.

It seemed to work, at least a little.

After walking for a few minutes, Josie found the running playlist she'd created on her Mp3 player and began to jog to the dance remix of, "I've Had the Time of My Life."

Absolutely nothing about this felt like the time of her life. Her skin tingled and all those body parts Summer and Delaney referred to as curves jiggled or bounced with every step she took. Infuriating. How the hell did people run marathons?

"You've got to make it through at least one song, Garcia."

One of their neighbors, an ultra-fit blond Barbie, walked out her front door to her mailbox as Josie approached. She waved and smiled, but her smile contained that level of concern she'd have if she were looking at someone who appeared to be on the verge of fainting or throwing up.

Well, I guess I fit into both categories.

Josie smiled. Then she took it a step further and waved aggressively.

Just after she passed Barbie's house, it happened: her foot caught on an uneven sidewalk panel. One minute she was jogging and the next thing she knew she was on all fours, her palms and knees burning.

Quickly, she glanced behind her to see if Barbie had seen the spectacle. Fortunately, she was already inside.

Probably watching through the window. Probably saw everything.

Josie hadn't fallen since childhood, and was surprised at how jarring it felt. She climbed to her feet, one at a time, and noted with some surprise that her body already felt stiff. She'd ripped holes in both knees of her leggings. Those holes revealed huge, bloody scrapes. Although she wanted to open her mouth and wail at this misfortune, she picked her way back towards her house, trying to act like she felt normal, but failing miserably.

How did people think running reduced stress? It was stupid. It hurt. You fell. You ripped your brand new, expensive leggings.

Forget the stupid race. She'd pay Summer and Delaney back for the entry fee. She could do something else. Something where you didn't move at high speeds. Yoga, maybe.

I hate yoga.

Okay, maybe the elliptical.

Speaking of quitting, The Marriage Intervention was as stupid as running. She would quit that, too. It wasn't working, anyway. Summer and Delaney had high hopes, but they didn't know their plan had created results opposite from what they intended. They still didn't know Paul had moved out. They didn't know she had failed.

The moment she walked in the door of her house, Josie gave in. She burst into tears.

CHAPTER TWENTY

Froth, Juniper's only bridal boutique, sat one block off the downtown square in a remodeled Victorian house with an English flower garden out front. The owner, Debra Mills, served brides and their friends chilled champagne and fancy crackers while they pored over design books.

Saturday morning, Josie and Summer flanked Delaney as they approached Froth, the three of them walking completely in sync, arms linked, just like they'd done in junior high and high school.

"It never gets old. I love shopping for wedding dresses," Summer said.

"I love shopping for wedding dresses and drinking the bubbly," Josie said.

She stepped forward to open the door, and gestured for Delaney to go in ahead of her. Debra greeted them with champagne flutes on a tray.

"Isn't your mother coming?" she asked Delaney.

Delaney nodded. "She'll be here soon. She and Dad just got back from Scotland. Jet lag. She wanted to sleep just a little longer, but she said she wouldn't miss it for the world."

Josie felt her eyes sting at that. Her own mother hadn't been there for any of Josie's wedding festivities. She blinked away the tears and took a sip from her flute.

This morning, when the girls met in the small parking lot Froth shared with The Barkery, Summer had casually asked Josie, "What's Paul doing today?"

Josie knew it was the perfect opportunity to mention that he was staying at Terry Schmidt's and was probably watching sports and drinking cheap beer. But she didn't. Delaney's wedding dress shopping day was hardly the backdrop for that particular piece of news.

Josie said, "Just hanging around the house."

Now, she downed her champagne during the short between Froth's entrance and library, and although Debra raised her eyebrows, she refilled it without comment before pulling a stack of oversized books off a shelf and setting them on the table at the center of the room.

"So we have traditional here, and contemporary here," she said. "Where would you like to begin, Delaney?"

They spent the next several hours looking through dresses, discussing what Debra called "important considerations," like how difficult it would be to go to the bathroom in a full skirt, how much wedding cake Delaney would be able to eat in a tight dress and how challenging it would be at the end of the night for Jake to get Delaney out of a gown with a thousand buttons.

At some point, Camille came in, looking cozy in a wool sweater and boots, and giving each girl a kiss on the cheek before dabbing her eyes with one of Debra's soft handkerchiefs.

Josie noticed with no little satisfaction that Camille downed the alcohol as quickly as she did, if not even faster, and she wondered whether she'd ever have a daughter to send off into wedded bliss.

Although Summer involved herself fully in each question of whether a waistline was too high or too dramatic or too plunge-y, her eyes remained shuttered and Josie knew the topic of that phone call during Happy Hour was still eating away at her.

They finally narrowed the choices down to a contemporary dress with slim straps, a scooped neckline, and a semi-full skirt.

"It's the best of all worlds," Delaney said. "It's slimming and it should also show off the few curves I have."

"I think I have a few similar styles in stock," Debra said. "You're welcome to try them on."

Josie, Summer and Camille grinned at each other, and Delaney blushed.

"That's exactly the reaction you had freshman year when Matty Donovan sent you a note at lunchtime asking to kiss you after school," Josie said.

They laughed, Camille looked scandalized. They made their way to the fitting salon. Camille went into the changing suite with Delaney, and Summer and Josie sat on the plush leather couch at the back of the salon.

For once, they didn't speak, and neither of them made a big deal of it.

The girls had come to Froth to find Josie a wedding dress six and a half years ago. Her memories of that day were slightly fuzzy, thanks to Debra's champagne. To the girls' mutual surprise, Josie had been a relatively easy-to-please bride. Considering her taste for fashion, it was astonishing that she chose her dress in a matter of minutes.

"I want to look like a princess," she said when she sat down at Debra's library table.

Debra answered, "I have just the thing."

It was just the thing, too. With a silky satin bodice and lace from here to Texas, the dress suited her as if the designer had climbed right into the eight-year-old-Josie's imagination and created the perfect princess bridal gown.

Everyone in the fitting salon gasped when she emerged from the changing area. Summer burst into tears.

Before her mother died, Josie always wondered whether her practical nature would take the fun out of finding an expensive and completely impractical wedding gown that she planned to wear for only half of a single day. But even Carla Garcia would have cried her eyes out when she saw Josie in that dress. She would have taken back everything she'd ever said about the benefits of a courthouse wedding.

When Josie and Summer heard the door to the changing suite begin to open, they both sat up a little straighter.

Delaney's skirt came through the door first, and Josie noticed Summer inhale, holding her breath and ready to make some sort of exclamation. When the rest of Delaney followed, though, it was met with silence. On the couch, Summer gripped Josie's hand.

The hopeful expression on Delaney's face died away instantly, and when she turned around and stepped onto the pedestal to look into the three-way mirror, she let out a loud, barking laugh.

"Well, if that isn't the worst fit for me I've ever seen, I don't know what is," she said.

Camille nodded. "Back to the drawing board," she said.

Was it as simple as that? Back to the drawing board? Trying on wedding dresses was a bit different from repairing a marriage, but Camille's remark struck a chord with Josie. Back to the drawing board. No, it couldn't be that simple. Josie refused to believe it.

DELANEY CRIED mercy after trying on three dresses, each of which had a strength and a weakness. She claimed the third one lifted her cleavage to the moon but made her stomach look like a sausage.

"I didn't realize how exhausting this process would be," she said. "Besides, it gives us an excuse to come back and drink champagne." At a dark look from Summer, she added, "Well, Josie and mom and me, anyway."

They went to the Red Lantern for lunch and had a good laugh telling Camille about the time Josie and Summer had stalked Delaney and the awful guy she was dating, Mitchell, when they went there for dinner one evening. The whole escapade had started a fight between them.

"What can I say? I really was in need of that intervention," Delaney said.

They ate their cashew chicken and Mongolian beef in silence for a few moments, Summer laughing every time Josie used her free hand to pick up pieces of broccoli and sneak them into her mouth instead of using her chopsticks.

"Speaking of interventions," Delaney said, and Josie felt the weight of three pairs of eyes land on her face. "How's the running going, Josie?"

Josie cringed.

"Well, to tell you the truth, it's not going very well."

She told them about her most recent fail, tripping on the sidewalk and scraping both knees and ripping her leggings. She ended the story with a somewhat feeble, "I'm thinking about taking a break from running." Which was silly, since she hadn't really gotten started yet.

"You were pissed about the leggings, weren't you?" Summer said.

Josie nodded. "Yeah, I was! They were expensive, and they made my ass look really good."

"That *is* disappointing," Camille said.

"Anyway," Delaney said. "We wanted you to have the support you need to continue working out and to train for the chocolate and wine race."

Summer nodded, quite vigorously. Josie's sixth sense started to wake up, and within a split second, it was shouting, *ding ding ding*!

"So we hired you a personal trainer! Isn't that great?"

"Oh, that's so nice of you girls," Camille said. Josie was grateful for her interjection because it distracted Summer and Delaney from seeing the steam that was probably coming out of her ears.

"A personal trainer?" Josie said.

Crickets.

Summer's nodding became less vigorous.

"We just got you a package," Delaney said. "Like, a package of eight sessions. Eight weekly sessions? Two months? Don't kill us, Josie! It's for your own good. We know you don't like working out. You only have to go eight times. We thought it would be good for you."

The tiny, satisfying flame of anger began to burn, and she smiled.

"Uh oh," Summer said to Delaney. "That is not a friendly, I-love-you-guys, you-guys-are-the-best smile."

Delaney shook her head.

"I appreciate the sentiment," Josie said. "But I'm not going to see a personal trainer. Why don't you just tell Dr. Strasser to give me some exercises? Don't you think one stranger working on my life is enough?"

She set her napkin down, placed a twenty-dollar bill on the table and stood up. This was her moment of truth.

"And, I've been meaning to tell you guys something else, too."

Summer froze, her chopsticks halfway to her mouth. Delaney froze, too, but didn't have as much poise as Summer did. She squeezed her chopsticks too hard and a cashew popped out of their grasp, zinging across the restaurant and hitting the wall. A few people turned to find the source of the sound. Camille wiped her mouth and put her napkin back on her lap.

They all blinked up at Josie, waiting.

Oh, shit. Shit, shit, shit. Why did I even say that?

She could practically hear a clock ticking.

Well, they'd always considered her the irrational one.

"Never mind. I'm leaving."

She stalked out of the restaurant and heard Delaney stage-whisper to Summer, "I think this place has bad juju for us."

It's not bad juju. It's just that the three of us need to butt out of each other's lives.

Josie should have known her friends would come after her. It was just the way they worked. As she drove home from the Red Lantern, she thought about why she didn't want to tell them Paul moved out. She could imagine the surprised looks on their faces: Summer's eyes would go wide and her eyebrows would shoot up towards her hairline before she had the chance to get her expression under control. And Delaney, who was slightly worse at hiding her feelings, would open her mouth and then close it quickly, her nostrils flaring. Then—and this was the worst part—the pity would set in. Summer's forehead would crinkle and her eyebrows would arch into little seagull shapes. Delaney's eyes would get all squinty.

They would exclaim, "I'm so sorry, Josie," and, "What happened?" and, worst of all, "Why didn't you tell us?"

Just as she imagined herself screaming in exasperation, she spotted Summer's van in her rearview mirror. She picked up her phone and pressed the voice-to-text button.

"You should have driven Delaney's car. It's much less conspicuous."

Summer: *Delaney's still tipsy from the champagne. You knew we'd come after you, anyway.*

Delaney: *Yeah.*

Josie shook her head, then answered, "I have things to do, guys."
Like going home and wallowing in my misery.
Summer: *We're sure you do.*
Delaney: *Like wallowing in your misery.*

Summer pulled up next to Josie in the driveway. To her surprise, neither Summer nor Delaney spoke as they followed her into the house.

"Paul get called out?" Summer said after Josie shut the door behind them.

"I don't know, why?"

"Because his car's not here," Summer said, her tone indicating Josie was an idiot.

"Oh, I didn't even notice," Josie said.

"You're lying," Delaney said, pointing at her. "You're looking down and to the left, and you're pulling on the ends of your hair."

"Gives you away every time, Josie," Summer said.

"Ugh! Why can't I learn to control that stupid habit?" Josie said.

An idea flitted through her mind and she seized on it. "Listen," she said. "I need to ask you guys a favor."

Summer looked suspicious. Delaney said, "Of course. Anything."

"So, Delaney, remember when Summer and I spied on you?"

"How could I forget?"

"That was so funny," Summer said. "The look on your face when we coincidentally ended up at the Red Lantern with you and that sleazy Mitchell guy was priceless. Seriously."

"Well, I need you to use those spy skills again," Josie said.

Summer narrowed her eyes. "I will not spy on Paul."

Josie laughed. "No, it's not him. It's that Blair Upton creature who's trying to sabotage my job for next year."

"Yes!" Delaney said, quickly adding, "Sorry," when Josie and Summer looked surprised at her fist pump. "It's just that I've wanted revenge on her for months."

"Now is your chance," Josie said. "She's been threatening to tell the school board Scott and I had a fling. Even though it was years ago."

"How does she know?" Summer said.

"She saw him groping me outside the auditorium one time."

Summer rolled her eyes. "Juvenile."

"I know. She's awful," Josie said.

"I meant you and Scott."

Josie felt herself blush. "Right. Anyway. So I was hoping you could get some photos of her."

"Why?" Delaney asked. "She's awful. I don't want her on paper. Or disk. Or anywhere."

"She's having an affair with Scott."

Summer and Delaney looked at each other.

"What?" Josie said.

"Josie," Summer said, in her mom voice. "Is this about Blair, or about Scott?"

Josie looked at the floor. "It's about Blair," she mumbled.

"Hmm. So you want photos of her and Scott in the act," Summer said.

"Stop using your mommy voice on me," Josie said to Summer. "You sound so disapproving. She thinks that if I lose the principal position, she'll get it. She came out second on the list. But if I have proof that she is having an affair with Scott, she'll have the same disqualifying factor. It will be pointless for her to rat me out because I can turn around and do the same to her."

Delaney laughed. "We'll do it. I can't wait to get back at that awful woman."

Summer shook her head. "We'll do it, but I don't believe this is really about Blair. Just for the record."

"Thanks, guys," Josie said. "It means a lot."

They stood there in silence for a moment.

"So, where's Paul?" Summer and Delaney said in unison.

There was no point in putting off the inevitable for any longer than she already had.

"Paul moved out."

"I knew it!" Delaney said, almost triumphantly.

"I thought so," Summer said.

Wow. This is going so much differently than I imagined it would. Where's the surprise? Where's the pity?

"You guys don't sound surprised."

"You've got to hit rock bottom," Summer said. She shrugged one shoulder, and Delaney nodded.

"Oh," Josie said. "Well. So. Obviously this stupid Marriage Intervention thing isn't working out. I quit."

Summer and Delaney responded to Josie's declaration of withdrawal from The Marriage Intervention with uncharacteristic nonchalance, nodding as if she were crazy and they had to indulge her, while helping themselves to the brownies on the counter.

They made small talk for an hour, and Josie noticed Summer avoided talking about phone calls or news of any sort. Josie knew she could play dirty and bring up the mysterious phone call while Delaney was here, just to get information out of Summer. But something about the expression on Summer's face when she'd turned away from Josie at Rowdy's stopped her. She'd looked stricken and pale. Her lips drew tight, just like they did that lunchtime sophomore year when she sought out Josie and Delaney to tell them her grandmother had died.

Summer would tell them in time. So Josie went along with the idle chitchat about the windy weather, Sarah's science fair project and Delaney's disgust at having to drain an abscess on a horse's rib cage the week before.

"It was so juicy. I mean, sooo juicy! I had to wear goggles. And I should have worn one of those plastic parka thingies."

Josie wasn't fooled into thinking they planned to let her off the hook with The Marriage Intervention. They were just biding their time.

But you take what you can get.

After they left, Josie spent the rest of Saturday grading papers, planning lessons and researching her ideas for the Carla Garcia Community Center. And thinking about a personal trainer.

A personal trainer was simply someone else—some muscle-bound teeny bopper, more than likely—telling her what she was doing wrong.

"I don't know if I can hang with that," she said to herself several times throughout the day. "Nope, probably not," her self answered, each time providing reasons that kind of relationship wouldn't work. First of all, she was predisposed to dislike anyone who tried to encourage her to work out (i.e. break a sweat). Second, she didn't really have time to add another weekly meeting to her schedule. Third, she hated people who liked working out. And didn't all trainers like working out? They were gluttons for punishment. They liked that feeling of their muscles burning. They liked sweating, breathing hard and feeling terrible.

It made absolutely no sense.

Therefore, hooking Josie up with one of these crazy people was a waste of Summer and Delaney's money. Just before she fell asleep, she resolved to call and cancel first thing Monday morning.

CHAPTER TWENTY-ONE

Josie woke up Sunday morning to a text from Paul: *Lunch tomorrow?*

"Tomorrow" really meant today, she realized when the sleep fog cleared from her brain. He'd texted last night after she fell asleep. She felt her stomach lurch and butterfly wings flapped wildly inside it.

Why did he want to have lunch with her? Did he plan to give her even more bad news? To ask for a divorce? To tell her he'd found someone else? Maybe he'd decided he loved the bachelor life. Maybe he'd decided he wanted to move in with Terry, to escape the piles of mail and papers Josie stacked at various places all over the house.

She texted him back: *Sure. Where do you want to go?*

Paul: *Sand Witch?*

Josie: *No, Delaney says the owner wipes the sweat off his forehead with the same towel he uses to dry the glasses.*

Paul: *Ha. Okay. How about that pizza place?*

Josie: *Pizza Palace?*

Paul: *Yeah.*

Josie: *Okay. Noon?*

Paul: *Sure.*

She wanted to add so many other messages: *I miss you, I love you, Please come home, pretty please with sugar on top.* But she didn't.

Josie spent an entire hour and a half preparing for their lunch date. She exfoliated her legs and put on Paul's favorite vanilla-and-lemon-scented lotion. It was still too early to leave for lunch, and she felt lonely, so she indulged herself with a batch of chocolate chip cookies and felt only slightly ashamed when she set them on the counter next to the plate of brownies.

No one ever had to know. She'd eat it all before she had any more guests. Including her husband.

Is he a guest now?

She wondered what Paul had done last night. Probably played poker with Terry Schmidt. Or watched a UFC fight. Or ordered his favorite takeout—pork carnitas from Tito's—since she never let him order it when they were together.

Finally, Josie pulled on a pair of dark skinny jeans and a peach sweater, and spent way longer than necessary searching for her black and white infinity scarf, which she eventually found under the bed.

Once she'd positioned it carefully around her neck and applied another layer of mascara, she felt pretty good.

Lunch would go well. She could feel it.

Josie and Paul always joked about how fun it would be to show up at a bar, separately, and pretend they weren't married. They'd leave their wedding rings in their cars and pretend one of them was picking up the other, asking if that seat was taken and sitting down to make flirtatious small talk.

When their marriage was going well, the scenario sounded fun and romantic. But now, when they met for lunch at The Pizza Palace, Josie felt like they actually *were* strangers. Not in a good way. Paul waited for her in a corner booth. He sat there, sipping his Dr. Pepper (he never ordered anything else) and perusing the menu as if he didn't know he'd order sausage and pineapple like he always did.

She was relieved to see his expression soften when he saw her. Maybe there was still hope. She sat down across from him as she had a million times. This time, it felt different. Maybe because they arrived separately. Or maybe because she had no idea whether he was really drinking Dr. Pepper. He always ordered it, but what if he'd changed his mind about soda, just like he'd changed his mind about living with her?

She forced a smile. "Hey."

"Hey," he said. "I already ordered. I hope that's okay."

"Pineapple and sausage?"

"Yeah. And breadsticks."

Okay, some things did remain the same.

"Perfect," she said. She felt a goofy but authentic smile spreading across her face and for once, didn't try to stop it, to play it cool.

"I miss you," Paul said.

Josie surveyed him carefully. The stitches stood out against his skin, and the bruising all over his face had dulled to a gray-blue color. She wanted, more than anything, to hold his head against her chest, to offer him comfort, to run her fingertips along his injuries. But of course, she couldn't. Not now.

Instead, she stretched her arm out so their fingertips touched and said, "I miss you, too."

The waiter came then, to ask if Josie wanted anything, and Josie pulled her hand away, as if she'd been caught doing something illicit.

When he left, Josie said, "Why don't you come home?"

Paul smiled. It wasn't a condescending smile like she expected. Rather, it was a kind, apologetic smile that broke her heart one single beat at a time.

"Josie," he said. "It hasn't even been three full days since I moved out. I really think we need a bit of time away from each other. Time to think, time to breathe. You know?"

"I get it. I understand," she said. "I just don't like it."

Paul sighed. The waiter brought their pizza.

"I'm sorry," Paul said, separating a slice off the pie for each of them, the cheese stretching from the tray to each plate. "I don't like either, but I think it'll do us some good. Okay?"

"Okay. I'm just afraid you won't want to come back."

CHAPTER TWENTY-TWO

She wasn't going to go. If Josie had been smarter, one step ahead of the game, she would have ignored Summer's text on Tuesday afternoon, pretended she never got it. But lately it seemed like life was always one step ahead of her, dancing to a slightly faster song than she was.

And so, she responded to Summer's *Your personal training appointment is at 5 p.m. Call me after* with something stupid like *What? Huh? I don't know what you're talking about.*

If she had been smarter, she would have gotten caught up in something at work, like grading papers or erasing that day's lesson on bees and honey off the whiteboard. Or scraping gum off the bottoms of her students' desks with the edge of a ruler.

But out of some need to please Summer and Delaney, especially after seeing the closed-off look on Summer's face the past few times they'd been together, she put on some of the new leggings she hadn't ripped and a matching tank top and went to the gym. On time.

She could just cancel after this initial appointment. Blame it on the trainer.

The girl at the front desk didn't look exactly like a gym rat. She looked almost manly with her short, gel-spiked hair and her broad shoulders. Big muscles, though, accentuated by a tight light blue t-shirt tucked into a pair of shiny black gym shorts.

Josie felt only slightly intimidated, less than she would if the receptionist had been a skinny tan girl in a leather catsuit.

"You must be Josie," she said when the embarrassingly loud electronic doorbell signaled Josie's entrance. "I'm Ronnie. I'm going to get you started. Your personal trainer's—uh, running a little late. New guy."

Oh, great. She was getting the new guy. Just what she needed.

Ronnie laughed then, a "heh, heh, heh" sound Josie always associated with video game designers in a dark room. "And then have the giant dragon come out from behind that building and attack the protagonist. Heh heh heh," or, "Ooh, what if we fill that river with invisible boiling lava that burns the guy's feet, only he can't actually SEE it? Heh heh heh."

"First we're going to do a body fat analysis," Ronnie said. She chuckled when Josie grimaced.

"Don't worry," Ronnie said. "It's painless. I promise. It's just to give you a baseline, a starting point. So you can see your improvement."

Josie snorted.

Ronnie laughed again. "We're going to get along just fine. When I first started coming to the gym two years ago, I had an attitude similar to yours. I was definitely put off by the body fat analysis." She shook her head as she remembered it. "I snorted exactly like you just did. But I've seen myself make big strides, and it feels really good. Let's go."

Josie followed Ronnie to a little room just off the weights area. Fortunately, it had a door, which gave Josie privacy as Ronnie used a caliper to measure the fat on her stomach, her triceps and her thighs.

"You're right at thirty-one percent," Ronnie said. "Just a little bit above normal for your age range. Not bad."

She gave Josie's upper arm a friendly pat, then checked her watch.

"Okay, we still have a few more minutes. Let's hop on the treadmill and get a baseline for your fitness level."

Josie groaned.

"I'll go easy on you," Ronnie said.

She took Josie's heart rate before she got on and set the treadmill at four miles per hour just like the sales-teenager had done at the shoe store. Josie's mind wandered to her personal trainer. She wasn't sure how she felt about it being a guy. The gym's personal trainers ran the gamut from young and muscly to old and sprightly. Did "new guy" mean fresh out of college? That would be embarrassing. She stepped onto the treadmill, Ronnie pressed the Start button, and Josie began to jog.

No uneven sidewalk here.

Why did they put mirrors right in front of the treadmills? She hated that she could see her face, her bouncing curves, and her swinging ponytail with every step she took.

Think about something else.

An old man personal trainer would be okay, she thought. A fatherly or grandfatherly type. She could handle that. Her heart rate sped up, but she didn't feel too bad. Yet. Ronnie increased the speed to five miles per hour.

"Just a few more minutes," she said loudly. "Then we'll take your heart rate again."

Josie nodded, and wondered if Ronnie could tell with all the bouncing. "Okay," she huffed out, just to be sure.

Ronnie had noticed her bad attitude, and no doubt that would be a turn-off to her new personal trainer. She had to get that under control.

I don't know why I care. This isn't going to last.

But again, a vision of Summer's face, pale and sad, flashed into her mind, and she decided she'd go through with this personal training crap even if she didn't do the stupid chocolate and wine race or the even stupider Marriage Intervention. For Summer. It was only eight weeks. Just then she saw a reflection in the mirror. Someone walking across the back of the room behind her.

Scott Smith.

It couldn't be Scott. This had happened to her for years. In the movie theater, she'd see a tall, thin man walking up the stairs to find a seat. At the park, she'd see a dark-haired man throwing a frisbee to a buddy across the lawn. At the grocery store, she'd see a pair of Converse in produce. She'd think, "Scott," and then feel a quick hit of disappointment when she realized it wasn't him. Swiftly followed by equal parts embarrassment and self-hatred when she realized how stupid it was that she saw his ghost everywhere. Ronnie pushed the Stop button, and Josie slowed to a walk and then stepped down. This was mortifying. After only a few minutes of light jogging, Josie was completely out of breath. She was panting like a dog on a hot summer day.

"Heart rate," Ronnie said. Josie lifted her wrist and Ronnie held it between a thumb and two fingers, looking at her watch the whole time.

Josie was so focused on what Ronnie was doing that she hadn't even noticed someone walk up behind her.

Ronnie turned around, squinted at his name tag and turned back to Josie.

"Ah, here he is now. The man of the hour. The new guy. Heh, heh, heh."

Ronnie turned back to Josie, oblivious to the horrified look on Josie's face.

"Josie, this is your new personal trainer."

"Scott," Josie said.

"Josie," Scott said. He couldn't quite stop himself from smiling.

"So … you guys know each other, then?" Ronnie looked perplexed.

Josie and Scott nodded. "Work together," Josie said, at the same time as Scott said, "We used to date."

Silence descended like a heavy fog. Ronnie handed Scott the clipboard and she and her sculpted calf muscles ducked out, probably in search of clear skies.

"What the hell are you doing here?" Josie said to Scott, at the same time as he said, "Pretty cool that you're my first client, right?"

They answered at the same time: "I'm working here," Scott said, and Josie said, "Um, no, actually. Not very cool at all."

Scott laughed, an awkward, horsey laugh Josie had never heard before. Josie kicked at something invisible on the floor.

"I thought you were moving," Josie said.

"I was. I mean, I am. Eventually. But I put it on hold. I wanted to do something carefree for a while."

Josie just shook her head. "I didn't even know you were getting certified."

"You don't know everything about me, Josie," Scott said.

Her mind flashed to the image of Scott and Blair in his office. She didn't answer. Scott's bright blue workout shorts and black workout top were obviously brand new, exactly like her own outfit. She could tell he'd selected them carefully with the goal of looking athletic. It was too much to take in.

"I can't do this," she said. "I can't have you as a personal trainer. This stupid working out stuff is hard enough as it is."

Scott nodded as if he knew just what she was thinking.

"The sexual tension is pretty strong, isn't it?" he said.

When she only stared at him, he barked out a loud laugh. "Kidding, Josie. Kidding. I mean, I've always been attracted to you—you know that—but I'm sure we can keep this strictly professional. Hands above the desk."

Josie left Scott standing next to the treadmill, the clipboard dangling stupidly from his hand.

Ronnie looked up from some paperwork that had her deep in thought. "Everything okay?" she asked.

"No, actually," Josie said. "I need a different trainer."

"Why? What's wrong? Did the new guy do something?"

Josie didn't want to work out with Scott, but she didn't want to ruin his new career, either.

"No, not at all," she said. "It's just that I'd prefer a female trainer. In fact, I believe I checked that box on my intake forms."

She couldn't be sure, since Summer and Delaney had filled out the forms. But she figured Ronnie didn't know and even if she did, she wouldn't call her on it.

"Okay," she said slowly. "Let me check the schedule and see when our next available appointment is."

Josie wondered if Scott was still standing by the treadmills. She hoped she hadn't hurt his feelings. She hated herself for hoping that. Ronnie tapped a finger on the desk next to the computer mouse.

"Actually, it looks like our next available appointment with a female trainer is four weeks out. Do you want to wait that long?"

Josie grimaced.

"I know," Ronnie said. "We've been really busy. That's why we hired another personal trainer. Um, Scott."

Josie nodded. Summer and Delaney would absolutely not be satisfied with Josie waiting four weeks to begin working out. That would give her only a few weeks to prepare for the stupid race. Even if she didn't plan on actually running it, Summer and Delaney thought she did, and she'd make sure they thought so until the day before it actually happened.

Could she train with Scott? She would see him eight times. Eight hours of her entire life.

In addition to seeing him at work every single day.

Couldn't she handle that?

The romantic part of her said that she absolutely could not.

The practical part argued that of course she could. She had quashed her feelings for him and the two of them could easily engage in this simple working relationship.

"Josie?" Ronnie said.

"Sorry!" Josie said. "No. I don't want to wait four weeks. I can work with Scott. It's fine."

When Ronnie nodded, Josie quickly added, "It's not ideal. But it's fine."

Scott was standing next to the treadmill in the exact spot where Josie left him. He smiled when she approached him, and the way he looked so unsure of himself brought on a pang of some unidentifiable emotion.

"Well, I guess it's you and me for today," she said to him.

His smile became more confident, and he nodded. "Let's get to work. What are your fitness goals?"

He looked so earnest and so out of his element that Josie laughed. "Summer and Delaney have signed me up for a race in about two months. It's about six miles. So I need to be able to run, or, jog, or limp, six miles or so."

Scott nodded.

"I can't believe you're here," she said as he wrote some notes on her chart.

"I know," he said without looking up. "You're as surprised as I am, but I just couldn't leave Juniper again."

"What about your career?" Josie asked.

Scott shrugged. "It's still there," he said. "And I can come back to it. But for now, I want to be right here, doing this."

Once Scott finished quizzing her on her fitness aspirations, he showed Josie how to use the weight machines, and he had her run on the treadmill again. Although she experienced inevitable feelings of intimacy when he leaned over to adjust the weight on a machine or touch the muscles she was supposed to be working, she thought she did a pretty decent job of pretending he was just a personal trainer and the history between them wasn't suffocating her.

"Why personal training?" she asked as she did bicep curls, even though she already knew the answer.

"Remember how we used to always say we should work out? Get in shape?"

Josie nodded. She remembered. Together, they had been dreamers. Not doers. They talked about a lot of things they should do, but they never actually did them.

"I should drink less," she said on more than one occasion, while emptying yet another vodka bottle into a glass of cranberry juice. Or Scott would say, "I know you said you should cut back on sugar," while handing her a carton of ice cream he picked up at the grocery store. Extreme Moose Tracks.

In that sense, Josie was the worst version of herself when they were together.

"I was the best version of myself when I was with you," Scott said.

Josie had just completed a set of hamstring curls and wondered if Scott was checking out her ass. She disentangled herself from the machine and stood up to face him.

He went on, "You always encouraged me to do what I really love."

"Did I?"

He nodded.

"That's one of the things I miss about you," he said.

He talked about missing her so casually. Like he was talking about what he had for breakfast or what color socks he was wearing.

Did Paul miss her? What was he doing at this very moment, while she stood across from her ex-boyfriend, wearing leggings that made her ass look incredible?

"Don't talk about missing me," Josie said.

Scott nodded. "Okay."

They spent the rest of her session in near-silence.

CHAPTER TWENTY-THREE

"So, how was your first training session?" Summer asked as she walked up to their table at Rowdy's. Josie noticed she didn't breeze up, radiant, like she usually did, but again, made the conscious decision not to ask about it.

Instead, she said, "Wait. Before I tell you, I want serious props for being the first one here, again."

Summer laughed. "Okay. Props, my sister. I can tell you're making an effort to be on time."

She popped a green olive into her mouth. "So?" she said.

"How'd you know I went?" Josie said.

College kids streamed into Rowdy's, thirsty soldiers on the march at the beginning of their three-day weekend. The bar always felt festive on Thursdays, so much so that Josie often showed up at school on Fridays feeling a bit cheated, like it should be the weekend already.

"First of all," Summer said, "I knew you'd go out of guilt, after I texted to remind you. Second of all, I called Ronnie to make sure you showed up. I was fully prepared to come find you and drag your stubborn ass over there, myself, if I had to."

Josie nodded. "It was fine," she said.

Summer waited for a beat, and when Josie didn't elaborate she said, "And?"

"Well, I did some running and lifted some weights. You know. So, you know Ronnie?"

Summer nodded. "Don't you remember? She was my lab partner in college biology. We dissected a fetal pig together. Some bonds just can't be broken."

Delaney rushed in then, wearing surgical scrubs. Josie was so distracted by the ensemble that she forgot to finish the conversation about Summer knowing Ronnie. Later she would wonder why no alarm bells went off when Summer had said, so casually, like it was no biggie, "Some bonds just can't be broken." She would tell herself she was distracted by Delaney's choice of Happy Hour outfit. She would kick herself for being so clothing-conscious.

"Sorry, guys," she said. "I'm not myself today. I almost forgot about Happy Hour. Can you believe it? We've been doing this for what, like thirteen years, and I almost forgot!"

She laughed. Summer spoke the very thought Josie was thinking: "You sound a bit insane, Dee. Is everything all right?"

"What? Oh, yeah. Of course."

"Why are you wearing those … things?" Josie asked. "I mean, I love the dog and bone print, it really brings out your eyes. But what the hell?"

Delaney rolled her eyes. "Can I have one of those?" she said to Summer, pointing at the dish of olives that sat next to Summer's water glass.

Summer shrugged and nodded. "Sure."

Delaney's eyes rolled back as she chewed. "This is so good," she said, drawing out the word "so." "I can't believe I've never shared these with you before."

In that moment, everything dropped away: the chatter of the college kids who were swigging beers and munching on chips and salsa, the giggles of the girls next to them, who kept waving at a group of guys sitting the corner, and the sound of the blaring TVs, which were showing a few different basketball games. One of them cut to a puppy food commercial and Josie thought again about getting a puppy.

Josie and Summer looked at each other. Summer grabbed Delaney's hand.

"Delaney, you're pregnant."

At first, Delaney didn't respond. She chewed on another olive as if Summer hadn't spoken.

Summer looked at Josie as if to ask so many questions at once. Did she hear me? Should I repeat myself? What should we do? Should we take her beer away? Will she be happy?

Just as Josie slid Delaney's beer across the table to the empty spot, Delaney heaved a big, dramatic sigh.

"It explains everything," she said. Her eyes filled with tears.

"SERIOUSLY," Delaney said. "I can't believe this is the first time we've ever done this. We're thirty-four, we've known each other since we were fourteen and we've never come to the drug store for a pregnancy test."

The three of them were crowded into the Good Health Pharmacy's single bathroom stall, which smelled overwhelmingly of cinnamon spice air freshener and toilet cleaner.

"Remember when Summer first got pregnant with Sarah?" Josie said. "You showed up at Happy Hour with a bottle of sparkling cider and had the whole place cheering. I loved that moment."

Summer sighed, and Josie noticed she had placed a hand on her lower abdomen.

"Me too," Delaney and Summer said.

"How much longer?" Josie asked. "Should we have set a timer for this bad boy?"

"Probably," Summer said. "It can't have been more than a minute and we're supposed to wait what, like five?"

"Four," Delaney said. "You should know."

The last three words came out a mumble.

"Oh, my gosh, Delaney's nervous!" Josie said. "I've never seen you this nervous."

"Yeah, you have," Summer said. "The first time she went to prom. Remember? She was practically throwing up until we got to the restaurant."

Josie laughed. Delaney groaned.

"I just can't believe I might be pregnant when I'm supposed to be shopping for wedding dresses. I mean, the timing is pretty crazy, right?"

Summer nodded. "What will Jake think?"

Delaney groaned again. "I'm not sure. I mean, we want to have kids and everything. We just hadn't really talked about the timing. You know? Since we're not even married yet. I just imagined a very romantic honeymoon with lots of Guinness."

"He can have lots of Guinness," Josie said. "And you can watch."

"Maybe it's just nerves making me crazy forgetful," Delaney said.

When Summer and Josie looked at each other over the top of her head, Delaney laughed.

"I think it's time to check it," Summer said.

Delaney put her hands over her face. "You guys check it. I can't."

Josie lifted the pregnancy test off the top of the toilet paper dispenser, being careful to hold it parallel to the floor, and to avert her eyes so she and Summer could look at the same time.

Summer counted to three, and because the bathroom's fluorescent lighting was so dim, they both squinted to see the little plastic window.

Josie felt a smile spread across her face, and looked up at Summer to see a matching grin on hers.

They both looked at Delaney at the same time, and each of them reached for one of her hands.

"Congratulations, Dee," they said. Summer started to cry. "You're a mommy."

CHAPTER TWENTY-FOUR

AFTER HER FIRST PERSONAL TRAINING SESSION WITH SCOTT, JOSIE
debated (again) whether she should find a different trainer. Even
now, a week later as she drove to the gym to meet with him, she
went over both sides of the argument in her mind. Scott was obviously new to personal training, and she could use that as an excuse
for quitting when she explained it to Summer and Delaney. She
didn't even have to mention his name. She could just explain that
Ronnie had called her trainer, "The new guy."

On the other hand, if she did quit Scott, it would take a while to
get another trainer. And by the time she did, that stupid race would
be coming up really fast, and she wouldn't have time to train
properly.

More importantly, Josie felt traitorous hogging the limelight with
her insignificant marriage and exercise issues when Delaney was
now planning for a wedding *and* a baby.

She pulled into the gym parking lot and chose a spot at the far
side to force herself to walk farther and burn more calories. Before
she got out, she carefully applied lip gloss. Nothing too flashy, just
enough to give her some shine.

Squaring her shoulders, she walked through the parking lot. *It's
only seven more weeks.* She pulled open the front door, and smiled at
Ronnie, who gave her a friendly wave before pointing to the free

weights area where Scott waited. He was flipping through the papers on his clipboard.

What will Paul think?

Well, she didn't want to think about that. Did it matter? Who knew if he'd ever move back home? She certainly didn't. And wouldn't it be good for her to have someone … um, special… to hold her accountable to working out?

Summer and Delaney would never know. Paul would never know. She walked toward him, raising her chin just a little to convey some kind of confidence. Then Scott smiled at her. The thought of keeping yet another secret, and worse, another secret with Scott, did send Josie's stomach churning like the disgusting smoothies Summer made in her high tech blender. But what if she didn't think of it as a secret? She could instead consider this personal training thing small potatoes. Not a big enough deal to even mention.

She smiled back.

Seven more weeks. She could do this.

"HOW LONG DOES a wife keep coming to marriage counseling alone?" Josie didn't expect Dr. Strasser to give her an answer, which was why she asked her reflection in his office's bathroom mirror. She shrugged. "As long as it takes, I guess."

Dr. Strasser didn't smile at her when she sat down on the opposite side of his desk. Always so distant, so separate. Josie found herself wanting to get a rise out of him. Unfortunately, he could probably read that kind of behavior fairly well, as he had a PhD in figuring out why people act stupid.

"No Paul today?"

"No, he's still giving me time to work on my own issues," Josie said.

"Ah. I see." Dr. Strasser leaned back in his chair, but kept his fingertips together. What are those issues?"

"I'll just be honest, here."

"That's a good start." Now he smiled. Ice cold.

"I still have kind of a crush on my ex-boyfriend. Scott. The guy I dated right before Paul. Well, it's not really a crush. I don't know what to call it."

"The principal?"

"Good memory." Josie had the insane urge to tap the side of her nose. *Right on the nose, Dr. Strasser.*

"What does this crush" (finger quotes) "mean for your marriage?"

"It means Paul's pissed off at me, is what it means," Josie said. "It means he thinks I can't work on our marriage just yet because I still have feelings for someone else."

"Is that true?"

Josie shrugged. "It's not that I have feelings for him. It's just that I remember our time together fondly. And then I see him every day. And then, when he asks me out for drinks I have a hard time turning him down because of that."

"Even though you know it upsets Paul?"

"I almost want to upset Paul."

Now that the words were out there, Josie felt kind of free. Ah, this must be what it felt like to experience that famous *aha!* moment people talked about. Dr. Strasser nodded, as if he'd known this all along.

A bit smug, aren't you?

"Go on," he said. "Why do you want to upset him?"

Josie sighed. She'd walked through the proverbial door and there was no turning back. *No Exit.*

"I can think of a couple of reasons," she said. "First, it means he cares enough about our marriage to be upset about something. Jealous, even. Second, it feels a tiny bit nice knowing he feels threatened. Like, knowing he knows he's not meeting my needs. And if he knows, then won't he make a change?"

Dr. Strasser didn't answer right away, which compelled Josie to keep talking. "I mean, I know it's childish, but there you have it."

It took a conscious effort not to babble, so Josie pressed her lips together and waited.

"Josie. I think it's time you communicated your needs to Paul directly, instead of sending him messages in the form of what you call childish behavior. Aside from your time here, have you ever actually told him he's not meeting your needs?"

The silence stretched between them. Josie's throat constricted. Now that she thought about it, she probably hadn't ever put the idea into plain words. Like a child, she'd thrown little jabs, little barbed comments designed to deflate his sense of well-being as a husband.

"Oh, my God. I hate myself."

"Now, Josie, there's no need for that. You're here because you want to fix things, right?"

Still too shocked at her revelation to speak, Josie nodded.

"So instead of focusing on the mistakes you've made in the past, let's focus on moving forward. How do you think you can do that?"

The next five minutes passed so slowly it was excruciating. Dr. Strasser insisted on a role-playing exercise that made Josie feel like she was six years old, but she participated just for the sake of getting it over with. Meanwhile, she felt herself edging closer and closer to the brink of tears with each tick of the second hand on Dr. Strasser's clock.

Fortunately, Dr. Strasser had another client to see immediately after Josie, and she was able to lock herself in the bathroom for a good ten minutes to sob into a wadded up paper towel. Her eyes actually ached from crying when she finally walked to her car. The more she thought about it, the more she realized the blame for her problems with Paul fell squarely on her shoulders. Because the sun scorched her eyelids, even through the dark lenses of her sunglasses, Josie didn't notice Paul standing next to her car until she was practically bumping into him.

"Way to be aware of your surroundings," he said.

She jumped.

"What are you doing here?" she asked. Then, realizing her tone hadn't been very welcoming, she added, "I mean, I thought you weren't coming. The appointment is over."

Paul lifted her sunglasses, and when he saw she'd been crying he pulled her against him.

"What's wrong, babe?"

"I miss you, and I just want to fix things, that's all," she said. "But I'm not sure how."

"Start with dinner?"

Josie nodded against his chest. "Tonight?"

He sighed. "We can aim for tonight, but the guys have a dealer coming out of Phoenix. I might get called in."

A tiny, resentful voice in the back of Josie's mind piped up to point out that this, right here, was actually the root of their problems. She tamped it down. When Paul had gone undercover, they'd discussed the position at length. They both knew call-outs and late nights were a possibility, but it was something he wanted to do and, more importantly, it was better to get it out of the way before they decided to start a family.

The same resentful voice told Josie that imagining a situation before it happens is different from actually living it. Which was true.

"I've got a couple of errands to run," Paul said, "but let's tentatively plan to meet at the Mexican place at six. I'll call or text you if I end up getting called out. Does that sound good?"

It would have to do.

THE BEST AND the worst thing about best friends is that they hold you accountable. Josie should have expected—no, scratch that—she should have *known* Summer and Delaney would begin keeping tabs on her at some point as she and Summer had done to Delaney during The Dating Intervention.

Even after the stressful, embarrassing, horrifying evening she'd had after her appointment with Dr. Strasser, Josie felt her lips twist into a smile as she lay in bed alone (again), remembering The Dating Intervention and what they'd put Delaney through. For her own good, of course.

One night when Delaney was still tending bar at Rowdy's, Josie and Summer sat in the darkest corner of the saloon and spied on her as she flirted with a depressed, drunk, floppy-haired loser. When the two girls realized the inevitability of Delaney taking him home, Summer had raced to Delaney's house and intercepted them, forcing Delaney to put him in a taxi and send him on his way.

Another evening, they followed her and a different guy, another obvious mismatch, through town, ending up at the Golden Lantern to call Delaney on her inability to follow their Rules and stop dating the wrong guys.

Delaney must have felt terrorized. She did, if Josie remembered right. To the point of insanity. Josie followed Delaney into the bathroom and found her talking to the serene Chinese woman in the painting on the wall.

Now, tonight, it was Josie's turn.

After Paul left Dr. Strasser's parking lot to run his errands, Josie decided to go for a drive. She turned the air conditioner on full blast, and headed for Copper Mine Road. While she drove, she used voice-to-text to send Delaney and Summer a text message.

"Had kind of a breakthrough today with Dr. S. Planning dinner with Paul at six, unless he flakes."

She deleted that last word and said, "gets called in."

Looking back, she wasn't sure why she felt the need to text them. It's not like they needed to know her minute-by-minute plans.

Summer responded first: *Sounds great! Keep us posted.*

And then Delaney: *Good luck, and yes, keep us posted.*

"Will do," Josie said to her phone.

Despite Paul's warning, Josie's hopes were crushed when he texted her just before six to tell her he had to go into work after all. Disappointment hit her like a bucket of ice cold water being thrown over her head, traveling from her shoulders to the pit of her stomach where it sat, freezing.

During her appointment with Dr. Strasser, she felt ready to accept almost full responsibility for their marriage problems. And then this. Couldn't he turn down a call-out? Couldn't he choose their marriage over his work, this one night?

Apparently not. He didn't even spare a moment to call.

She received his message while she was driving back down Copper Mine Road. She dropped her phone onto her lap, and then tumbled onto the floor. She reached for it and almost ran off the road. Despite the loud sound the phone made when it hit the door, the screen wasn't cracked and the case was still intact.

Then she made a decision. She didn't know why she made the choice she did. Maybe it was to get back at Paul for going into work after they'd planned dinner. So what if he'd warned her. Maybe it was because she was lonely and wanted company. Maybe it was because she had her heart set on Mexican food and didn't want to eat alone.

There's a reason they say hindsight is twenty-twenty, she'd think later as she drifted off to sleep on waves of uneasiness.

But when she dialed Scott Smith's number, she wasn't using hindsight. He answered on the first ring. She picked him up ten minutes later, and just seven minutes after that, they sat at The Blue Fish in a two-person booth with a window looking out onto downtown.

"Best guacamole in town," Josie said to Scott, scooping a creamy bite of it onto a tortilla chip.

He nodded, and in a move so intimate it curled her toes, gave her chills and made her want to run home to Paul (if he had been there), he wiped a bit of that guacamole off the corner of her lip and inserted his finger in her mouth.

In what she'd later call reflex, she sucked the guacamole off his finger.

Josie's "usual" hadn't changed since she and Scott dated, and he ordered for both of them so casually the waiter referred to her as "La Señora" for the rest of the meal.

They both giggled every time the phrase rolled off his tongue.

So what if Josie downed three margaritas within an hour? So what if she touched Scott's arm or his hand so frequently it became obvious she was doing it on purpose? She was having a good time. Isn't that what really mattered?

Her two very best friends didn't think so.

After Josie finished that third margarita, she made a trip to the ladies'. She pulled up short when Summer emerged from the center stall. Her mouth dropped open when Delaney, too, emerged from the center stall.

"Oh. Um, hi, guys," Josie said.

"Hey, Josie," Summer said. "How's your date with Paul going?"

Josie's mind scanned her friends' respective calendars. Monday night. Summer should be delivering Sarah to archery lessons and Delaney should be home with Jake doing wedding planning stuff.

"It's fine. But who has Sarah? And aren't you and Jake picking out your centerpieces tonight?"

"'It's fine'? Really?" Delaney said. "Because I didn't see Paul when I came in. What happened? Did he get called to work? Or was your text earlier just an elaborate cover-up to throw us off your devious trail?"

Josie's mind flashed to the view from the front door of the restaurant. Colorful tiles on the walls, huge pots on strategically placed shelves. The back of Josie's head in that window booth ... and undoubtedly, Scott Smith's face staring adoringly at her.

Josie sighed.

"Caught," she said. She smiled in a self-deprecating way she hoped they'd find humorous.

From the identical looks of disgust on their faces, though, she knew they weren't amused. Not even slightly. Then Summer clapped her hands together in front of her chest.

"Ohmygosh I just have to say." She laughed a bit wildly. "I feel like I should be drumming my fingers together and saying, in a witchy voice, 'Well, well, well, what do we have here?'"

"It's the thrill of the hunt, is it?" Josie said. She could feel the heat of humiliation making its way up the back of her neck.

Delaney giggled and Summer answered, still in a witchy voice, "No, no, no, my dear girl! It's the thrill of the *capture!*"

Josie closed her eyes, wishing she could disappear.

"What are you guys doing here?"

"Spying on you, of course," Delaney said. "You didn't think you'd get away with doing The Marriage Intervention without us infringing on your privacy at least once, did you?"

"You don't trust me," Josie said.

"Should we?" Summer and Delaney said.

"This would never stand up in police work."

"Good thing we're not police," Summer said.

Delaney interrupted her: "But we are very good investigators. We got that photo evidence you wanted. You can thank us later."

Josie opened her mouth to ask how they'd gotten the evidence, and what the photos were of, but Summer held up a hand. "We're your best friends, Josie," she said. "Which also means we can tell you to go out there, right now, and tell Scott Smith to go home."

"What will I tell him?"

"Oh, I suppose it doesn't matter," Delaney said. "He saw us come in. He'll know."

Josie felt her whole body droop.

"And if you must tell him something, stick with your old stand-by," Summer said.

"Just tell him you have a yeast infection," both girls said, their voices rising in hilarity.

I can't believe I told Delaney to use that as an emergency escape plan on awful dates. I should have known it would come back to bite me.

Josie knew better than to stall or argue. If the girls had any communication with Scott, she risked exposing the whole personal training issue.

"You guys are having way too much fun with this," Josie said. She pushed open the bathroom door and went to tell Scott the date was over.

Unlike Paul, Scott did not insist on paying for dinner. Josie couldn't tell whether he was hurt or angry or both, but when she walked back into the dining room and told him she had to cut the evening short, he put his napkin on the bench seat next to him and left without saying another word … and without throwing down a couple of bills.

While Summer and Delaney waited in the car, Josie paid for the meal. They'd come out of the bathroom as soon as Scott left, and Josie figured they probably followed him to the parking lot to make sure he was actually leaving. They had the audacity to follow her home and right into the house, she assumed because they wanted to run interference if she'd made a secret plan to meet Scott there. Her dinner date with Scott had shown poor judgment, but she wasn't *that* foolish.

"We think you need to get a puppy," Delaney said the moment Josie shut the door behind them. Josie had planned to bring up the photographic evidence of Blair and Scott, but Delaney's announcement brought her up short.

"What?"

"We think you need to get a puppy," Summer said.

"I heard. I just don't know what that has to do with anything," Josie said. She put her keys in the bowl on the entry table, and walked into the kitchen with the girls trailing behind her.

She poured herself a glass of wine, not that she needed another beverage after the Margarita binge during dinner. Automatically, she gestured to the bottle to ask if Summer or Delaney wanted a glass, then laughed, not kindly, when she remembered they were both pregnant.

"You guys are going to have new babies soon. What do I need a puppy for? I can just increase my auntie responsibilities. I'll have to babysit while you and Jake honeymoon, Delaney."

Summer shook her head. "You need supervision. And a puppy is the best answer. Thursday, instead of going to Rowdy's for Happy Hour, we're going to the shelter. It's final. Now, shall we watch a movie?"

Josie shook her head. "Fine," she said. "But first tell me about the photo evidence you collected."

Delaney practically squealed. "You would be so impressed with our spying skills," she said.

"You would," Summer said. "Definitely."

"Well, don't hold out on me!"

"So," Summer said. "We went into the school just before the kids' lunch time. You know how the office ladies are never in there just before lunch?"

Josie nodded and made a "hurry up" motion with her hand.

Delaney picked up where Summer left off. "So we went in, really quietly, and we saw them! Blair Upton was in Scott's office, and they were totally making out."

"This happened on your first try?" Josie said. This was the kind of luck that made her suspicious.

"Oh, no," Delaney said. "That was, like, our third or fourth trip in there."

"Anyway," Summer said, "I pretended to be waiting for the office ladies while Delaney stood behind me and pretended to text people. But really, she was taking photos through the window."

"Well, text them to me!" Josie said, although she didn't really want to see them.

"Not to worry," Delaney said. "It's already been taken care of. I don't think Blair Upton will bother you again. Now, as Summer said, shall we watch a movie?"

"Wait. What did you do?" Josie asked.

"So, it was kind of infantile," Summer said. "But it was Delaney's idea."

Delaney shrugged. "It was. So remember in junior high, people would write those chain letters and they'd cut words out of magazines and paste them on the paper so no one would recognize their handwriting?"

When Josie nodded, Delaney said, "Well I did that!"

She looked so proud of herself Josie chuckled.

"What?" Delaney said. "It was genius. I cut out a bunch of words and letters and glued them onto a piece of paper. '*You've been spotted, and you've been warned. Hypocrisy doesn't look good on you. Neither does jealousy. Neither does the shade of pink you're wearing in these photos. Bring up Scott's relationship with Josie and these pictures go viral.*'"

"That should do it," Josie said.

Delaney nodded. All three of them dissolved into laughter. They doubled over, giggling like teenagers.

When they finally gained control of themselves, Josie said, "You guys are better than a strawberry shake."

The analogy had been born after Delaney suffered through massive humiliation in junior high when her crush told their entire class she'd asked him out—and then pronounced that there was no way he'd ever go out with her. Summer had insisted on going out for shakes, and Delaney wondered aloud what was wrong with her. "You're better than a strawberry shake," Summer told her.

Now, Delaney opened the fridge and said, "Summer, we should have included stocking the fridge in Josie's intervention. There's nothing to eat in here."

Josie, wiping tears from the corners of her eyes, pulled a bag of popcorn out of the pantry and handed it to Delaney. "Make me some popcorn and I'll dig out some green olives, you weirdos."

Just as "Legally Blonde" ended, Paul texted Josie: *Try again for dinner? Tomorrow at The Blue Fish?*

She texted back: *Sure.*

Of course, before they left for the evening, Summer and Delaney had to look at her phone to verify that she was really communicating with Paul, and not Scott.

"I can't show up to babysit you tomorrow," Summer said to Josie as they stood in the doorway. "So please behave yourself."

"I will," Josie said. "Promise."

CHAPTER TWENTY-FIVE

"So how do you feel about expanding our family?"

Paul nearly choked on the guacamole-covered chip he'd just put in his mouth and Josie wished for a margarita despite having sworn them off after this morning's hangover. She was far too old for hangovers.

She was slightly offended he choked on a chip over the thought of having children, but she decided not to latch onto that particular angle. She let him off the hook for now.

"Geez, Paul." She hoped her tone sounded light and humorous. "I was talking about a puppy. How do you feel about getting a puppy?"

"A puppy?"

"You know, four legs, puppy breath, soft fur. A puppy," she said.

"Dog hair, accidents, fleas," he said. "Sounds like pure heaven."

"Paul! Puppies are so cute!"

"Where did you get this idea all of a sudden?" Paul wanted to know. "Wait. Don't answer. I'll bet Summer and Delaney concocted this spectacular scheme."

Josie grinned. As always, he had an unerring knack for reading her.

"They did," she said slowly. "But it's a good one, right?"

"Remember when you and Summer took over Delaney's love

life? And remember how you guys came up with all these good ideas for making her life better? Is that what this is? It reeks of some kind of … intervention."

This time, she laughed. And so what if her laughter bordered on maniacal?

"It is, isn't it?" he said. "They think this will be, like, I don't know, a toddler step toward having a real, actual baby. Or something."

Josie was relieved he didn't know the intervention wasn't baby-related. That was almost normal. If he knew how personal it was, he'd probably be angry. Instead of answering, Josie shrugged.

"Fine. Get a freakin' puppy."

She smiled at him.

"Stop grinning like that," he said. "You're freaking me out."

"Let's talk about names!" Josie said. "How about Harry?"

Paul shook his head. "I don't care what you name it. Name it Penelope for all I care."

"I'm glad you're so invested in our first fur child," Josie said, still forcing a cheerful tone.

"I'll have to meet him or her before I become invested."

The conversation lulled. Josie looked at the tabletop.

"Hey!" Paul said. "What's going on with your community center? You haven't said anything about it."

Immediately, Josie felt her mood lighten. She told him about the lease, and about how she'd hired an interior designer to help her maximize the use of the space. She talked paint colors and furniture styles and snacks and tutors.

As she spoke, she pictured the two of them working together: painting the walls, laying flooring, moving desks and chairs, hanging art. This thought brought tears to her eyes.

"I've asked Summer to start working on designs for the signs and letterhead and a logo. It's going to be so great. I'm so excited. This is, like, my dream come true."

"Wow," Paul said. "It sounds awesome. It's nice to see you this happy."

Again, the conversation lulled.

"Paul, when are you coming home?"

Josie hated the desperation in her voice.

He looked down, ran a finger around the edge of his water glass. The server came and took their plates.

"I don't know, Josie. I mean, I want to come home, spend every evening with you. I miss you. I miss the hell out of you. But has anything really changed? Yes, things are fine here, at The Blue Fish. But what would it be like if we went home right now? I'd feel like I couldn't please you or make you happy, you'd still be working with Scott Smith…"

"Things have changed," Josie said. "I promise. Now I realize the way I was behaving. And as for Scott—I just have to get through the school year, and then he's leaving. I can't very well quit now."

"You've never even admitted you've done anything wrong."

Josie nodded. That was true. She started to speak, to apologize, but Paul cut her off.

"Do you know what last night was about? Last night, we waited on the highway for a drug dealer who has brought hundreds of pounds of meth into our county over the past couple of years. Hundreds of pounds, Josie. You know how much it takes to get high? Like two tenths of a gram. You know what hundreds of pounds can do? You know those kids in your class who never have their homework done or their papers signed? The ones who come to school filthy every day, their fingernails longer than yours because their parents haven't even looked at them in the past week? The ones who fall asleep at their desks and always look just this side of awake?"

She nodded again, thought of Joshua Morton. His parents seemed like good people, but they worked so hard they didn't have the time or energy to care for him beyond his basic needs. The waiter dropped the bill on the table.

When he walked away, Paul continued. "Those are the kids affected by this stuff. The guy we hooked last night had four kids. Cute as fucking buttons. They were all in the car. Wide awake at midnight. Sitting on top of packaged meth. These big eyes, just staring at me. It was a school night! The meth this guy was bringing in, it was going to people who live in Juniper. People with kids. The parents of your students. We arrested him. We stopped him. We removed that scumbag from the streets. We prevented thousands of people from getting high, driving around high. You can't sit there and tell me that's not important, Josie. These are people in our own town. Students in your class."

Not for the first time in recent weeks, Josie felt like bursting into tears.

"It's not that I don't think it's important," she said, casting around for the right words. "It's just that I want to be more important."

She saw him inhale, as if he were preparing a serious response. This time, she cut him off. "I know I'm important to you. And I know you expect me to understand that. But I guess, just once in a while, I'd like to come first."

"You mean, like, so we could have a movie night?"

"Let's keep this civil, Paul. You know that's not what I mean. It's not that a movie night is particularly important. All your late nights and call-outs have a cumulative effect. One, on its own, is not that big of a deal. But when it's the fifth time you've bailed on me in a month, a movie night becomes a big deal. It feels huge."

"You knew this was a possibility when you encouraged me to take this position," Paul said.

"I know. But our discussions were academic. Living it is a whole different animal."

Paul nodded, and his countenance shifted, softened. "Have you talked to Dr. Strasser about this?"

Josie shook her head. All at once, she felt exhausted. "I haven't talked to him about getting a puppy, either."

"You want a puppy, get a puppy," Paul said. He reached across the table and took her hand.

"But I want you to get the puppy with me. When are you coming home?"

Now, he used his thumb to rub circles on the back of her hand, and when he spoke, it was with kindness. "I'll come home soon. I just need a little more time. And I need a commitment from you that you're ready to make a change."

"I am committed, Paul. That's why I'm doing this whole Marriage Intervention thing. Because I'm committed to making things work."

"Ha!" he said, pointing at her with the butter knife he hadn't used. "I knew it!"

Josie put her head down on the table.

"So, they're making over our marriage, huh?" he said.

When she didn't answer, he laughed. "Does this makeover include more frequent hot sex?"

"You'll be happy to know that it does," she said.

He laughed out loud, a short sound that punctuated the conversation. Josie felt herself smiling.

"Well, let's get to it," Paul said.

IT FELT SO good to have Paul back in the house, even if he didn't plan on staying.

They moved around the kitchen together, their bodies in sync as she dropped ice cubes into glasses and poured them drinks and he put away the leftovers and cut up limes for garnish.

Of course he loved her. Of course she was important to him. If not, then why did being together feel so natural, so right, so much like clockwork? Josie cringed when they walked into the bedroom, wondering if Paul would notice the dirty laundry she'd left on the floor. Yesterday's blouse lay crumpled next to the bed, and the past few days' underwear was piled next to the hamper.

"When the cat's away," he said.

He then proceeded to peel her clothes off, one article at a time, in slow, deliberate movements that left her shivering with anticipation. He made a big show of dropping each item into the laundry hamper, and by the time she was undressed, she was smiling and simultaneously aching for him to touch her.

She began to undress him, flinging his clothes across the bedroom so they landed like so many decorations. His shirt draped over a chair, his pants over the headboard, and his underwear over the lampshade.

They stood facing each other. Paul framed Josie's face with his hands and kissed her so gently she thought she'd faint. She put her hands on Paul's waist and he trailed his up and down her sides, calming her and revving her up so that by the time he led her to the bed her body was warm honey and her insides were humming.

They made love slowly. Despite the fact that Josie felt like she was starving for this moment, desperate for the nourishment of her husband's body, she took her time, feasting on his mouth, tasting his skin, savoring it.

He did the same, and when they finished, she felt completely undone. They lay facing each other, and Paul gently tucked Josie's hair behind her ear.

Then, without any warning at all, she felt tears pool in her eyes.

"Was it that bad?" Paul asked.

He was joking, but she could see he was concerned.

"No," Josie said. "It was that good."

"You know, I think that's the first time my mad lovemaking skills have ever moved a woman to tears."

Josie laughed. "Congratulations. I'm glad I could be here for it."

"Seriously," he said. "What's the matter?"

She took a shaky breath. "I just keep thinking about how I screwed up and I wish I could take so much of it back."

Paul said, "We can move forward from here. I'll come back home. I promise. When the time is right."

Suddenly, Josie felt a surge of panic. How would she know when the time was right? What if the time was never right? What if the time was right, now, and he was missing it?

"Don't look so panicked," he said. "I've got to help you raise Penelope, don't I?"

THURSDAY AFTERNOON, the sun shone hot in the sky and Josie squinted as she got out of her car to stand with Delaney in the animal shelter's parking lot. Summer was the last to arrive, and when her kids tumbled out of the car in a jumble of swords and untied shoelaces, Josie clucked her tongue just like her mother would have done.

"You know I love you, Summer," she said, "but I'm not sure bringing the kids was a smart move. You know you're going home with a puppy, right? You cannot have brought all four kids with you and seriously expect to drive away without an extra body in the car. A wiggly, hairy one."

"I had to bring them," Summer said. She blew a loose strand of hair out of her eyes. "No choice. Derek had a job interview. Last minute."

"We're getting a puppy?" Summer's youngest son, Luke, looked up at his mother, awestruck.

"No, Luke," said Sarah, who, at ten, sounded more like an adult every day. "We're here to get Auntie Josie a puppy. Because she's lonely. Because Paul moved out. Temporarily. Well, we hope it's temporary."

"Because Josie is too grumpy," said Nate, Summer's second child, and the one who was prone to blurting out everything he'd heard without regard to other people's feelings.

Sarah elbowed him. "Shut up, Nate."

When Josie shot The Look at Summer, Summer put her hands up like she had no idea where the kids had gotten the gossip. Josie shook her head and took the baby, Hannah, from Summer.

"Give Tía Josie some love," she said, kissing Hannah's chubby cheek. "You won't tell me I'm grumpy, will you?"

"Grumpy!" Hannah squealed.

"That's our girl," Delaney said in a singsongy voice. "C'mon, Josie. Let's go find your second soul mate."

They trooped into the shelter's front office, Nate and Luke sword fighting the whole way, while Sarah kept her nose in a book.

"We have an appointment," Summer told the receptionist.

"We do?" Delaney and Josie said at the same time.

"You're so organized," Josie said.

"I thought it'd be better since we have the kids with us. Anyway, this way they could get all the puppies ready for you."

A teenaged girl, probably a volunteer from Juniper High, came through the door that led to the kennels.

"This is Kelsey," the receptionist said. "She'll be taking care of you today."

Kelsey took in the kids, and said, "Hi guys! Can I help you choose your new puppy?"

They were momentarily stunned into silence, and then naturally, Nate piped up. "We're not here to get a puppy." When Kelsey looked a bit perplexed, he added in a whisper, "We're here to help our Aunt Josie get a puppy. She's lonely. Her husband moved out. We hope it's temporary."

Kelsey's face turned bright red, but to her credit, she recovered quickly.

"Well, I've got all the puppies lined up and ready. Follow me."

"That was embarrassing," Josie whispered to Sarah, who had finally closed her book. Josie was rewarded with a rare smile and Sarah answered, "No kidding. That kid has no filter."

"So we just got this litter in last week," Kelsey said. "Their mom is a Lab, but they're obviously mixed breed. There's seven total. Four boys and three girls."

The kids rushed forward, and Josie followed them. The puppies were adorable. Fat and rollicking, and wiggling all over the place.

When Hannah reached her arms out and shouted, "Dog! Dog!" Josie set her down so she could inspect them, too. One of the puppies, a spotted one with a blue eye and a brown eye, knocked her down and licked her face. Hannah giggled and Josie hoisted her back to her feet.

"They're all so cute," Josie said. "How old did you say they are?"

"Eight weeks," Kelsey said. "Ready to go home today."

"Today?" Josie swallowed.

"Yep! Want to get a closer look?"

Delaney had already knelt in the grass with Luke and Nate, and the three of them tickled a puppy's stomach while the dog thrashed wildly, nipping at their hands.

"Kind of overwhelming, right?" Summer said. "I mean, I only have four and there's seven of these guys."

Josie nodded. "I'm not sure I can handle a puppy. They're so … active."

"They are," Summer said. "Luke, put that puppy down before you drop it."

"You should get the kids one," Josie said.

Summer shook her head. "I'm going to have a newborn in a few months. The last thing I need is a puppy."

"Actually, it'd give the kids something to do while you tend the baby," Josie said. "Remember how guilty you felt when you first had Hannah? You said you were always sitting around nursing and felt bad for the other three."

"Yes, I do remember. But add a puppy to the mix? That's just asking for trouble. I'd have to hop up from nursing the baby so I could clean up accidents. No, thank you."

Nate came running up to them, another furry bundle in his arms. He held it up to Summer's face and it licked her like crazy. She laughed.

"See?" Josie said. "You want one."

Nate held the puppy out to Josie, and she took it from him. Instead of licking her like it had done to Summer, it cozied up against her body and nuzzled her. Then it fell asleep, completely limp and snoring.

Josie sighed, her contentment mirroring the puppy's. "I'll take this one," she said.

The puppy was a dark brindle with short fur and a white spot around her left eye. Her ears looked like they wanted to stand up, but the ends flopped over.

Kelsey nodded and smiled brightly. "I'll get the paperwork."

"What'll you name it?" Sarah asked.

"How about Sarah?" Josie said. Sarah rolled her eyes.

"We don't even know if it's a boy or a girl, Aunt Josie," she said.

"True. Check for me."

"It's a girl. How about Delilah?"

"Perfect."

With unerring sweetness and well-directed guilt trips, Summer's kids talked her into bringing home one of Delilah's brothers, an all-black pup with bright blue eyes. They named him Chuck.

Of course, Delaney couldn't (or wouldn't) be left out of the action, and Summer's kids convinced her, too, to adopt a puppy. She named her Sweetie at Luke's suggestion.

After they filled out all the paperwork, the ten of them—Josie, Delaney, Summer, the four kids and the three puppies—walked back to the parking lot, the kids dancing all the way.

"Make sure to put your swords up, guys, so the puppy doesn't eat them," Summer said.

Even as Summer closed the van door, Josie could hear the kids squealing, calling Chuck's name and laughing. She smiled as she got into her own car and settled Delilah on her lap.

"Let's go and get you some toys," she said to her new family member. "And a bed or something."

Delilah yawned, a great big gaping yawn, as if she'd never been more bored. She climbed onto the passenger seat, turned around a couple of times and flopped down.

"I love your calm demeanor," Josie told her. As if Delilah heard her, she opened an eye, looked at Josie, and then closed it again.

Josie laughed. "You're just right."

CHAPTER TWENTY-SIX

JOSIE ARRIVED AT THE GYM FIVE MINUTES BEFORE HER PERSONAL training appointment and took a moment to watch Scott. He didn't know she was there, but she told herself she wasn't spying. He seemed a little more confident today, judging by the way he casually set his clipboard on the bench in the free weights section and did some jumping jacks and arm circles.

She wondered how his other appointments had gone. Then she wondered why she wondered about that. It wasn't really any of her business, was it? He turned around and saw her then, and his face lit up. He didn't smile, not really, but she could see the excitement in the way his whole energy transformed. When he lifted a hand, she responded in kind and walked toward him.

"Ready to pump some iron?" he asked.

"Of course," she said. "I'm always ready."

Oh my God. Why did you say that?

Josie's memory flashed to a scene in the past—a hot and heavy sex scene. She and Scott had just come back to his place after some fun activity. Josie couldn't remember what, exactly. Go-karts, maybe? Or Skee-Ball at the arcade? Whatever, it didn't matter. For some reason, she had felt really turned on all night. She made so many sexual comments they cut their date short and headed home. He stripped her down right there in the living room, in less than a minute.

"Are you ready?" he said then.

"I'm always ready," she answered.

And then came the super-hot (steamy-hot) sex scene, straight from a romance novel. No, Scott wasn't slow and careful, but he knew exactly what to do and did it every time. No one had ever been able to make things *happen* so quickly for her. Back at the gym, Josie could tell Scott had just experienced the same memory. She smiled, and then shook her head quickly as if to clear the steam from her brain.

"Let's get started," Scott said.

Josie nodded and went to the treadmill for a warm-up. Throughout the workout she experienced a vague feeling someone was watching her. She wrote it off as paranoia, but she found herself glancing over her shoulder and scanning the mirror compulsively. She never saw Summer and Delaney standing in the corner near the lockers, wearing sunglasses and and those trendy trucker hats they all made fun of— the same ones Summer and Josie had worn that night they spied on Delaney at Rowdy's. After Josie completed her warm-up, Scott led her through some stretches, managing to keep a courteous distance.

See? I can keep the sexual tension at a manageable level.

"It's time to run," Scott said.

"I thought I just did," Josie said. They both laughed, because the five minutes she spent warming up was barely more than a fast walk.

"Gotta get you ready for the big race," Scott said.

The two of them walked out to the gym's outdoor track.

"Just take it easy, now," Scott said. "Since your goal is just to finish, not to run the race at a certain speed, let's work on building up your endurance."

Why does everything sound sexual?

Josie bit her lip.

"So I want you to jog, just slowly, for a couple of laps. Okay?"

At first, her body protested as if she were asking it to walk through fire. But she found her rhythm after a few minutes. Maybe she could do this, she thought. Maybe she could run six miles at once without dying or vomiting. Maybe.

"Startin' to sweat," Scott said.

No shit.

She couldn't answer. She didn't have the breath.

"Lookin' good," he said.

Still, she didn't answer. After the first lap, he began jogging beside her. "Breathe in through your nose and out through your mouth," he told her. "Keep your pace nice and steady."

She followed his advice, and before she knew it, she'd gone one mile. Her throat felt a little tight, and she laughed out loud when she realized it was because she was emotional after completing her first full mile.

"What's so funny?" Scott asked.

Josie shook her head.

"You're doing great," he said. "More than a mile down. Great job. Let's go for two."

"Two?" she huffed out.

He laughed. "Yeah. Two. It'll be no problem to work up to six from there. Just settle into the rhythm you've got going."

In through your nose, out through your mouth.

It became a mantra, and one step at a time, she made it to two miles. She couldn't believe it. Then Scott gave her a double thumbs-up and announced, "Cool down time." A stab of disappointment punctured the bubble of her euphoria and she couldn't believe that, either.

"How do you feel?" he asked, after giving her a chance to get her breathing back to normal.

"I feel good," she said. "Great, actually. I can't believe I ran two whole miles."

"I can believe it," Scott said. He put his hand up for a high five.

And just like that, Scott Smith was playing a role in the new and improved Josie Garcia. The new and improved Josie Garcia wasn't sure how she felt about that.

As Josie drove away from the gym, still glowing with pride and more than a little sweat, her phone rang. Paul.

"You sound … breathless," he said when she answered.

"Just got done with my workout. I ran two whole miles."

"Wow. Two whole miles, huh?"

"Geez, Paul. Don't sound so impressed."

He laughed. "Sorry. That's a good job, Josie. Really. Think you'll be ready for your race?"

"Yeah. I think so. I didn't before, but now I think I will."

"What changed?" he asked.

"The girls hired me a personal trainer to hold me accountable. I think he knows what he's doing and I've taxed him with getting me ready, so…" Josie felt herself stalling out, not sure what to say.

"A guy, huh?"

She nodded, relieved he couldn't see the guilty look on her face. "Yep."

"Huh."

"Huh," she echoed.

"Well, anyway," he said. "I'm calling to tell you that I'm going to a training next week."

"Another one?"

"Yeah. Don't sound so impressed," he said, mimicking her. "No, really. You should be excited for me. The PD sends me to all these trainings because I have potential."

"Yeah," Josie said.

"Anyway. I thought I'd come home Friday afternoon. After the training."

"For good?"

"For good."

Immediately, her mood soared again. "Great. That's really great. So, next Friday, then?"

"Yeah," he said. "Next Friday."

"SO, I GOT A PUPPY."

Josie made the announcement to Dr. Strasser expecting some kind of congratulations. Instead, he frowned at her over the top of his glasses.

"For decades, misguided couples have had children in the hopes of saving their marriages," he said.

Josie held up her hands in surrender. "It's a puppy, not a child."

"Did you get the puppy in hopes of strengthening your marriage?"

A long silence followed, during which Josie considered. Finally, she spoke. "I got the puppy because I'm lonely. My friends thought it would help me cope. Also she'll grow into a good running partner if I do decide to continue running. I can play with her every time I feel like calling that guy."

On the word, "guy," she flapped a hand dismissively, as if Scott Smith didn't mean anything to her anyway.

"Did you need a distraction from Scott?"

Oh, crap.

"No. I mean, not really. I just need someone to keep me company."

"Ah. I see," said Dr. Strasser.

"What is that supposed to mean?"

"Why aren't you happy with your own company?" Dr. Strasser said.

It was a good question, actually.

"It's not that," Josie said. "It's just that I got married because I wanted a life partner. But when he's not around, which is a lot, I'm lonely. And I got a dog to keep me company. That's actually better than having a human child at this point, right?"

Dr. Strasser went to his go-to position and rested his chin on his steepled fingers. He didn't answer.

"Well, *I* think it is," Josie said.

"Look, Josie." Now he leaned forward. "I'm glad you're happy with your choice to get a puppy. But I also think it's important for you and Paul to repair your marriage without the various elements a dog adds. So I want you to continue the work you've been doing."

Josie nodded. "Of course. Of course we will."

"Have you thought about the question I asked you the last time you were here?"

"Which one?"

Dr. Strasser smiled an ironic smile. "Have you thought about how you can improve the communication between you and Paul? How you can communicate in a more positive manner so he doesn't feel attacked?"

The truth: she hadn't thought about it. She was so busy thinking about all the moving parts in her own life—the puppy, the community center, working out—that she forgot all about it.

I can't say that to Dr. Strasser. Although he could probably tell from the look on my face.

Just then, a thought crossed her mind, sudden like a drop of bacon grease popping out of a hot pan.

"I have, actually," she said. "I could focus on him more, on how his work and the weird schedules and everything are affecting him. I've been pretty self-absorbed. He probably gets as sick of working as I do of him being gone. I always assume he'd rather be at work, but I realize now that he feels like he can't let his team down. And that's an admirable quality."

Dr. Strasser looked satisfied, and Josie felt smug.

"That's a good insight, Josie," he said. "Well done."

Josie beamed. Unfortunately, that feeling of pride didn't last for long. Summer and Delaney were waiting for her in the parking lot, and they didn't look as proud of Josie as she was of herself. In fact, they looked ready to pounce.

They leaned against the driver's door of her car, arms crossed, sentries protecting the world from the terror that was Josie Garcia. Josie felt the nerves buzzing through her body the moment she saw her friends, and the buzzing crescendoed as she approached them.

"Did we imagine it," Delaney said slowly, "or did we see you with Scott Smith at the gym?"

"Not only with Scott Smith," Summer said, "but receiving a personal training session from him? After we specifically told you to stop seeing him outside of school."

The sun hovered low in the sky, and Josie had to squint to see their faces. The air still felt warm, and Josie noticed the trees along the parking lot's outer edge had tiny buds on them. She didn't know how to answer, so she said, "Did you?"

"Did we see you, or did we tell you not to see him?" Summer said.

Delaney spoke before Josie could answer. "Don't play dumb. Even if we didn't say it, I'm pretty sure it was implied when we saw you at The Blue Fish."

"How did you guys see me? You weren't even at the—oh. You must have been at the gym on Friday."

Because the sun was in her eyes, Josie turned around and stood next to Delaney, leaning against the car and crossing her arms in the same way her friends were.

"Now she's catching on," Summer said. "You were acting so strangely about your personal trainer at first, and then all of a sudden you were fine with it. We thought it seemed really suspicious so we—"

"So you spied on me?" Josie said. She fought hard to keep anger out of her voice. That particular emotion seemed to rise to the surface so easily, and she needed to get it under control. To improve communications.

How do you like that, Dr. Strasser?

"Well, not at first," Summer said. "But when I talked to Ronnie and she mentioned your trainer was the new guy, I had my suspicions. I mean, I have to admit, when we saw Scott and Blair making out, his ass was looking, you know, pretty…"

"Tight," Delaney supplied. "So anyway, *then* we spied on you."

Josie groaned at the ground.

"Yeah. Feels pretty crappy, right?" Delaney said. "But I'll say to you the same thing you said to me when you guys were doing the spying. You need it. Obviously."

"Obviously," Josie said.

"Now, don't pout," Summer said. "We're doing this for your own good. This is an intervention, after all. But you can't recover until you first admit you have a problem."

"What problem?"

Delaney and Summer looked at one another and sighed.

"Just kidding, guys," Josie said. "Okay. Step one. My name is Josie, and I'm addicted to Scott Smith."

"Hi, Josie," Summer and Delaney said.

"My marriage has become unmanageable because I'm powerless over this addiction."

The girls nodded, satisfied.

"Good," Delaney said. "Now we need to find you a different personal trainer in time to train for the race. And I think we need to give good old Scott Smith a talking to."

Panic swept over Josie like wind in the spring, howling through her body and clearing everything else out of its path.

"You can't talk to him. And you can't cancel him. He inspired me!

You probably missed this, because you were spying from afar, but I ran two miles! Two whole miles! Because he inspired me. I need him."

"That's the addiction talking," Summer said. "You don't need him. You ran two miles because of you. Because of your own determination."

Josie kicked at the ground. "But finding a new trainer will hurt his feelings."

"Um, no offense," Delaney said, "but I think your marriage is more important than Scott Smith's feelings."

"Agreed," Summer said.

"Then I should be the one to break the news," Josie said. "Let me talk to him."

As if she weren't there, Summer stage-whispered, "Can we trust her?"

"No," Delaney answered in the same loud whisper. "But we can give her a chance."

Summer nodded, and as one, the girls pushed themselves away from Josie's car and walked to their own cars, each of them sending a quick, "See you Thursday," over her shoulder.

Josie sat in her car for a moment before driving away. She could do this, she thought. No problem. She could tell Scott Smith she had to get a different trainer. He would understand. It was probably too late now to cancel their next appointment, and she didn't wait to taint her own exercise euphoria by telling him while they were together. So she'd do it after that. She had to.

With that matter settled, she drove home, where Delilah greeted her with so much enthusiasm she couldn't help but feel truly loved.

THURSDAY EVENING: Happy Hour at Rowdy's.

"Did you do it?"

Delaney didn't bother with greetings or preamble. She launched right into the nitty gritty.

"No. I told you," Josie said, hearing a cringe-worthy whiny quality in her voice. "I'll do it after our next session. That way I won't miss a session."

Rowdy's was already in full swing, the bartender pouring drinks at a frenzied pace.

"Whatever," Delaney said.

Josie's radar beeped. Why was Delaney acting so grumpy? That was usually Josie's role.

"What's up with you?" Josie said, careful not to sound like she was speaking too carefully.

"Huh? Oh, nothing," Delaney said. "I'm just turning into a fat cow who can't find a wedding dress to save her life. No wonder I looked like a sausage in that one dress at Froth."

"That's what has you acting like a coyote with a burr on his backside?"

"Yeah. Got a problem with that?" Delaney said. "I always pictured myself looking beautiful on my wedding day. Not gonna lie, I'm going to look like a seal. A walrus. A whale. And I'm disappointed."

"There are lots of knocked-up brides these days. They make lots of bridal gowns for—"

"For fat girls?"

"Oh, Delaney. No. Not for fat girls," Josie said. "For glowing pregnant women. I've got you. Let's go back to Froth. Trust me. As you know, fashion is my specialty. This may feel like a lost cause to you, but to me, it's a special challenge. One I'm happy, and honored, to take on."

Summer walked in then, her long ponytail swinging behind her.

"Sorry, guys," she said as she boosted herself onto her stool. "I've been on the phone all day."

"You look tired," Josie said.

"I'll take that as a compliment. Shit."

"What's going on with you?" Delaney asked. As if she was one to talk, Josie thought.

Summer nodded, acknowledging there was something. "I don't want to bother you with it right now," she said. "But I promise to tell you when I have more details. Okay?"

Josie and Delaney tried prodding for a couple of minutes, but she remained tight-lipped.

"Have an olive," Josie said finally, pushing the bowl closer to Summer. "It always makes you feel better."

"Thanks," Summer said, laughing just a bit. "It does."

Josie left the bar that night feeling guilty, herself. Delaney and Summer were both facing down some of the biggest moments of their lives, and Josie was afraid to risk hurting the feelings of a man who supposedly meant nothing to her now? What was really important? Not Scott Smith. Not even running six miles, although the race was symbolic of her commitment to herself.

Her marriage and her friends were the most important things in her life. No exceptions.

CHAPTER TWENTY-SEVEN

Scott jogged up alongside Josie and motioned for her to begin the cool-down. When she slowed, he fell into step beside her. Even a couple of weeks ago, Josie wouldn't have believed it was possible, but here she was, cooling down after three whole miles. Tamping down the urge to pump her fist in the air, or jump up and down, or yell, "wooohoooo!" she grinned at the track as if it were her new best friend.

The white gym towel Scott handed her smelled like bleach, and Josie inhaled as she wiped her face. She couldn't stop smiling. For the first time, six miles didn't seem like a trip around the world. Maybe she *could* do it.

She'd almost forgotten Scott was there when he said, "All right. Let's stretch it out."

As she stretched out her quads, she said to Scott, "I need to talk to you."

He nodded, eager to hear what she had to say.

She said quickly, "Not here. Can you come over?"

His face lit up.

Oh, shit.

"No, not like, 'Can you come over,'" (she waggled her eyebrows) "but, like, 'I need to talk to you in private.'"

Scott's shoulders slumped. "Oh. Okay. Let me just grab my stuff and I'll follow you home."

Josie would later look back and realize—again—that hindsight would have come in handy before she actually put herself in such a vulnerable situation. But again, she wasn't operating in hindsight. In the moment, she thought she was doing what was right: she was giving Scott privacy by talking to him somewhere other than his workplace. Later, though, she'd think that what was right, in this case, was also stupid.

Determined to keep the meeting between her and Scott strictly hands-off, Josie placed Scott's ice water on one side of the bar, and positioned herself opposite him so there was no risk of physical contact.

"So," Scott said. "This is pretty serious, huh?"

Josie sipped her water. "Yes. It is."

Scott drummed his fingers on the countertop. "Okay. Spill it."

"Working with you," she began. "I mean—training with you. Training with you has been good."

When he quirked an eyebrow at her, she amended her statement. "Incredible. I couldn't have run three miles today without your support. And I know I'm on the way to finishing my first race, in large part thanks to you."

Now, he smiled, warmly, and she felt a stab of guilt.

"Josie, I—"

"Wait," she said. "Let me finish. Please. Like I said, it's been great training with you. I know you're going to be a great trainer, and you're going to help people get great results. But."

"I knew there was a 'but' in there," Scott said.

Josie smiled. "But I need to get a different trainer."

He opened his mouth to speak, but again, she stopped him. "With our history, with everything that's happened between us, it's not fair to me, to you, or to Paul for us to be working together in this capacity. I have to put my marriage first."

To his credit, Scott managed to cover his shocked expression pretty quickly.

"I understand," he said, nodding. "I understand."

"It's nothing personal," Josie said, but she wished she hadn't. It was such a cliché, such a go-to phrase. And it was a lie.

"Actually, it's pretty personal," Scott said. "It's absolutely personal."

"You're right," Josie said. "I'm sorry. It is personal. Very personal. Which is exactly why I can't do it anymore."

"I understand," Scott repeated. "No hard feelings."

The clock on the microwave read six-fifteen, which meant Paul should be home in about fifteen minutes. Perfect timing. She set her glass down and moved toward the front door. Scott didn't follow.

"Just one thing, Josie," he said. He leaned a hip against the counter.

She bit back a sigh.

"Yes?"

"Tell me the truth. Do you still have feelings for me?"

What could she say? *Yes, Scott. I do. For some reason I can't identify. Which is a completely inappropriate answer. Shit.*

"It doesn't matter," she said instead. It wasn't a lie. It wasn't the truth. But it was a truth. And she could live with that.

He followed her to the front door, and she opened it. Instead of walking through it, he stopped. He put his hands on her shoulders and turned her to face him.

Without warning, he pulled her to him and crushed her mouth to his. For a split second, her body went limp against his. Her mouth responded without her even being aware of it. Her mind took over then, and she startled like he'd slapped her instead of kissing her with all the thirst of a man who hadn't had any water in weeks. She put her hands on his chest and pushed him away gently. She could see so many things in his expression—questions, heat, passion, even anger. But then she saw surprise.

Scott's eyes flicked over to the driveway, and Josie's gaze followed his. Paul had just pulled up. He was early, and there was no question he'd seen the two of them kissing.

CHAPTER TWENTY-EIGHT

Scott retreated. He scuttled to his car like a tiny crab and Paul advanced in an angry march towards the house. Before she knew it, Josie was standing in the kitchen with her husband as if the two men in her life had been swapped out, interchangeable.

Only, Paul wasn't looking at her in the same way Scott had been. Josie felt more than a little scared.

"What the hell is going on here?" Paul said. "I come home early, to surprise you, and I find you kissing that skinny weasel in our entryway?"

For once, Josie didn't have a witty or scathing comeback. "He kissed me. I wasn't expecting it. I pushed him away."

Paul nodded. So he knew. That was a relief. Josie exhaled.

"I saw you push him away," he said, his tone still angry. "But what the hell was he doing at our house, Josie? Where the hell did he get the impression it was *okay* to kiss you?"

Josie opened her mouth and then closed it again. Fortunately, Delilah chose that moment to come tearing into the kitchen, her legs going triple-time on the tile floor, her tongue hanging madly out of her mouth. She ran up to Paul and put her front paws on his legs. Her entire body shook with the thrill of meeting someone new. As Josie expected, Paul couldn't resist her charms. He laughed and bent down to scratch her behind the ears.

"Meet Delilah," Josie said. She wondered if he could hear the relief in her voice.

"Delilah," he cooed, letting the puppy lick his face. "What the hell was your mommy doing letting a strange man kiss her in the entryway of our house? Do you find that as symbolic as I do? 'Welcome home, Paul. But before you step through the front door to move back in, you'll have to get past me kissing another man.'"

The dog, of course, only became more delighted, and began running in tight circles around Paul.

"Get your toy," Josie told her. She was surprised when Delilah stopped running, looked at her with clarity and darted off into the living room. "Who knows if she'll actually come back with it."

"So what was Scott Smith doing, kissing you in the entryway?" Paul said.

Josie hung her head. "Saying good-bye."

Paul snorted. "Do you always say good-bye like that?"

"No. No, we don't."

She told him the story of how their trainer-trainee relationship unfolded, how she hadn't known he was "the new guy," and how she only went through two appointments with him and had brought him to the house to cancel future appointments. How this little meeting had been like a final meeting, and how Scott had just kissed her—unexpectedly—in the doorway as he went to leave.

"Why didn't you just fire him at the gym? Why did you need this intimate setting?"

"I don't know, Paul," Josie said. "I didn't want his boss or anyone else at the gym to know he was training someone he used to date. It almost seems like that would put a black mark on his record, you know? Plus, I knew he'd be disappointed and I wanted to give him privacy."

"How did you think *I'd* feel when I drove up after being gone and found him here with you? Because I'll tell you something. Disappointment doesn't even cover it."

"I—I don't know. I didn't expect you to be home just yet."

Delilah raced back into the kitchen, the whites of her eyes showing and her toy clamped between her teeth. Paul laughed. "You got her a police officer doll to chew on?"

"I thought it would be funny," Josie said.

Paul took the toy from Delilah and threw it for her. After her little legs scrambled on the floor, she finally gained traction and took off after it.

"It is," Paul said. "At least, it would have been ten minutes ago. Now I think it's a sign, a statement about your wishes for my future."

"I'm sorry, Paul. I really am. I thought I was doing the right thing by inviting Scott here to let him know I needed to get a new trainer. The last thing I expected him to do was to kiss me."

"I believe you," Paul said. "But I saw the way you kissed him back. Even if it was just for a second. That wasn't a good-bye kiss. That was an I-wish-we-were-just-getting-started kiss. And then you pushed him away. But it was there, for a minute."

Denying it would be pointless. Paul specialized in translating the code of her own personal body language. So she waited.

"You're not denying it."

Delilah was back, wiggling so hard she couldn't hold onto her police officer chew toy. She dropped it and picked it up several times before finally getting a good grip on it. Paul laughed and shook his head at her. "You're pretty cute. I'll give you that."

He picked up the doll and tossed it back into the living room, sending the puppy into a frenzy. She dashed off and Paul looked at Josie again. She wanted to look away, but didn't.

Her mom had taught her to look problems straight in the eye. Too bad she didn't have a mirror.

"Josie."

She sighed, and instantly thought of her third graders, trying on adult behaviors like sighing and eye-rolling, especially when she chastised them for sloppy handwriting or talking during spelling tests.

"What."

"I really want to stay married. I really do," Paul said.

"To me?"

"Don't lash out at me," he said. "Obviously. I'm not the one kissing someone else in our doorway."

Heat crept into her face.

"I just don't know if you're ready to really work on this

marriage," he said. "I mean, you can't seem to disengage yourself from that skinny, long-necked asshole, and—"

"He's not an asshole," Josie said.

Delilah wandered back in, sniffed Paul's shoes, turned in a few circles and plopped down with her chin resting on one of his feet.

"One of you is," Paul said, and Josie felt her mouth snap shut. "Anyway. I feel like I'm all in and you're, well, not. I don't know what's going on, why you feel the need to keep seeing Scott Smith the giraffe. But I do know that I can't feel good about working on things if you can't tear yourself away from him. I'm going to keep staying at Terry's, I guess. I'm not sure I even want to work this out anymore. I need some time to think."

He walked out the front door, got into his car and drove away. Her vision went blurry and her hearing seemed to go into overdrive: the sounds of his shoes on the tile floor, the front door creaking open, the chugging sound of his car's engine turning over and the tires rolling off the cement of the driveway and onto the asphalt of the road.

The sound of him getting farther and farther away until she couldn't hear him any more.

Delilah either sensed something was wrong, or was completely worn out from playing so hard. Her head resting on her police officer chew toy, she didn't move from the spot where Paul's foot had been just a moment ago, even when Josie went into the silent living room and sat on the couch.

For the next week, Josie avoided the world. She spent most of her non-working time in the house, either under the covers in bed or on the couch staring at the TV as soap operas played, but not taking in a single word of what the actors said. Now, it was Friday again and for no reason at all, she kept expecting Paul to return home.

For the past hour, as the bright blue daytime sky faded to a dusky purple and then a deep blue, she'd stood at the front window watching the driveway. He was late, and the spot where he parked remained empty. Finally, headlights illuminated the window, sweeping over her stakeout spot. She jumped, not wanting Paul to know she had stood on this spot for hours, frozen with fear.

Before she walked away, she noticed it wasn't his car parking alongside hers. Worse, the driver's door and the passenger door were opening. Her heart rate increased, and black swirls converged on her vision.

A pair of officers came to your house for only two reasons. The first: to inform you if your police officer husband had been hurt or killed. She closed her eyes when she thought about the second reason. Maybe if she didn't answer the door, they couldn't tell her. She walked quickly over to the front door, locked it and leaned back against it. She couldn't breathe. Fear wrapped its bony fingers around her throat and squeezed. As the officers approached her door, she heard them talking in voices so low the actual words sounded muffled. Only sad people talked like that. Or people keeping a secret.

One of them knocked, and in her crazed state she analyzed the speed and force of the knocks for meaning. Maybe Paul was just in the hospital, like he'd been a few weeks ago. He couldn't be dead. She had so many things to say to him. She hadn't had the chance. With an ever-growing sense of dread, she turned around and unlocked the door. Her body swayed as she pulled it open.

The men on her doorstep looked apologetic. One of them was an older guy with a close cropped haircut and steely blue eyes. The other was a mushy-looking forty-something whose forehead scrunched with sympathy.

"Josie Garcia?" said the older guy.

"Yes?"

In that split second before he spoke again, she felt the floor tilt beneath her. She grabbed the doorknob for support.

"I'm serving you with court documents."

Everything stopped.

Court documents? With a shaky hand, she took the envelope from the police officer and opened the seal.

She extracted the sheaf of papers.

Official Summons

"Divorce papers," she whispered. "He's filed for divorce."

"I'm sorry, ma'am," the crinkle-browed officer said, nodding in a way that made him look guilty. As they turned to leave, Josie heard herself say, "Thank God," before her vision went completely blank and she crumpled to the ground.

She came to a few minutes later, steeped in relief that Paul wasn't dead. But he wanted a divorce. He was gone. And Josie didn't know if he was coming back. For the first time since her mom died, Josie felt the kind of loneliness that made it nearly impossible to go on. Paul was right. She couldn't seem to stay away from Scott. But why? Why did she keep going back for more?

Her mom would say romance attracts women like car accidents attract passers-by. You know you shouldn't look but you can't turn away. Actually, that's something Paul would say.

Mama would say romance attracts women like kids to an ice cream truck. There's a creepy guy on the inside, but as soon as you hear the music, your ears perk up and you start looking around for it, your feet moving before you even realize it. Then you're forking over the money, keeping the creepy guy in one-dollar tacos from Jack in the Box. The only thing is, you never know when the creepy guy is going to give you an ice cream with a razor blade inside it.

Practicality? That's a one-gallon carton of ice cream from the grocery store. Get ice cream for your entire family for the same price as you'd pay for a single ice pop out of the truck. No razor blades, no creepy guys. Scott was the ice cream truck, the creepy guy, and the one-dollar taco. Exciting. But definitely not steadfast. Paul was the grocery store. He was ever-present, stable, and could keep her nourished.

So what the hell was she thinking? Why had she even considered it an okay idea to invite Scott to the house? Why had she not thrown the personal training sessions in the trash like she would any other advertisement for crap that would get you skinny and make you feel great ... only, you knew it was a total lie?

The answer came to her then, with clarity so startling she felt like she'd stepped outside on a winter night and was having trouble catching her breath in the freezing air. Because keeping both men in her life was like having a conversation with her mother. It was holding up the options, one in each hand, weighing them for suitability, measuring them for adequacy.

It was hearing Mama read off the weights and measurements, compare them like two apples at the farmer's market. If she let Scott go, let him disappear completely, that conversation was over. And her mother was gone.

CHAPTER TWENTY-NINE

"So remind me again why we're here with you, and Jake isn't?" Josie studied her reflection—and the obvious signs of exhaustion on her face—in the exam room mirror.

Puffiness under the eyes, pale skin, lips pursed, almost in a disapproving way. And for a quick moment, it was her mother staring back at her, disappointment reflected in her eyes.

"I haven't even told Jake yet," Delaney said, edging herself up onto the exam table. "I wanted a medical professional to verify it first."

Summer, who was sitting in the room's single chair with her hand on her lower abdomen, laughed. "Twelve pregnancy tests don't lie, my sister."

Josie pinched her cheeks, hoping to bring some color into them. Delaney laid back on the exam table and put her head on the pillow. The paper liner crinkled.

"I know," she said. "It's just that I wanted to be sure. You know? We've both been so stressed out lately, with the wedding planning, Jake's gallery just opening, and me working full-time at Dr. Rick's. Add a baby into the mix and everything gets even more intense. I don't want to bring it up until I know for sure and have a due date and all that good stuff."

Now Josie pulled lip gloss out of her purse and leaned toward the mirror to apply it. "How far along do you think you are?" she asked Delaney.

Delaney stared at a photo on the ceiling. Josie looked up to see what was holding her interest. Someone had obviously cut it off some scenic calendar: a field of yellow flowers against a celadon sky. Peaceful.

"I have no idea," Delaney said.

"Well, when did you last have your period?" Josie said.

"I honestly can't remember," Delaney said. "Everything's been so busy. I didn't even notice."

"No wonder you looked like a sausage in all those wedding dresses," Josie said.

In her mind it had been a thought, but she realized too late the sentence had actually come out of her mouth. Delaney sat straight up again, the field of yellow flowers obviously not putting her into a state of serenity like it was supposed to. Her face was flushed. Josie flinched, and in the mirror she could see Summer's shocked expression staring back at her.

"You're the one who said it!" Josie said, then quickly added, "I didn't mean it. I'm sorry, Dee. We'll find you the right dress. You didn't look like a sausage. I swear. You said it, right? You're the one that said the sausage thing. I was just using your words."

"What's up with you, Josie?" Summer said. She was suddenly on her feet, standing behind Josie, her hands on her shoulders and her face peering into the mirror right next to Josie's.

"What do you mean?" Josie asked.

"I mean, you're standing over here, examining your face like you're looking for a hidden message or something. You're distracted. You're not yourself. You're obviously stressed out and you're blurting out mean shit because of it. So what's up with you?"

A quiet triple knock sounded at the door, and the three girls jumped.

Summer returned to the seat, and Josie went to stand next to her. Delaney remained sitting up, her hands clasped in her lap. The doctor walked into the room, smiling.

"Well, Ms. Collins," she said. "You're well-fortified."

They all laughed, and the tension from the previous moment dissipated.

"Which is wonderful," she went on, "because you're going to have a big cheering squad."

Silence.

"Congratulations," the doctor said. "You're pregnant."

Summer smiled a smug smile, and Josie reached out to grab Delaney's hand.

"Here's where it gets even better," the doctor said. "You're already at sixteen weeks. So you're through the first trimester. Today we'll get you scheduled for your twenty-week ultrasound."

Delaney went paler than pale. Alabaster. Josie stepped forward quickly and forced Delaney's head down between her knees. Summer pulled a bottled water out of her purse and unscrewed the cap.

"I know. It's a bit of a shock," the doctor said. "You weren't even positive you were pregnant and now you're almost halfway through. Fun stuff."

"Fun stuff," Delaney said, her voice muffled.

"Have some water," Summer said.

Delaney sat up, took the water bottle, drank.

"Shortest pregnancy ever," Summer said. "I'm jealous. It's a good thing, Dee. You still have plenty of time to get ready. I have tons of stuff you can borrow."

"You're having another baby. You can't give me all your stuff."

"We'll throw you a kick-ass shower," Josie said. "We'll get you all set up."

"Is there a Mr. Collins?" the doctor asked.

Josie laughed out loud at the doctor's question. "It's Mr. Rhoades," she said. "They're engaged. Their wedding date is August 5."

Now the doctor laughed out loud, too. "That's your due date, honey. Congratulations."

THE SAND WITCH was so busy the girls had to sit outside at one of the umbrella tables. Josie thought it was a bit windy for sitting outside. Her hair kept getting caught in her lip gloss. But Delaney and Summer didn't seem to mind. They had other things to think about. Like a wedding. New babies. A family.

She had nothing.

"So, you gonna move your wedding date?" Summer said as she scrubbed the glass tabletop with an antibacterial wipe she pulled from her purse.

"I guess I have to," Delaney said.

"Move it up," Josie said. "Let's do it this spring."

"This spring?" Delaney said. "This *is* spring!"

"I know," Josie said. "But we can get it done."

"I agree," Summer said as Blake delivered their sandwiches. "I mean, why not? You guys already plan on getting married, why not do it now?"

"Yeah. Why not?" Josie said.

"She's delirious," Summer said to Josie. "Look at her."

Josie laughed. "I'll call the golf club and see if they can move it up to this month or next month. Let's just start with that. If not, we can always have it at a park or something. I'll look into it. Leave it to me."

This renewed sense of purpose made Josie ravenous, and she took a huge bite of her sandwich. She chewed aggressively, until Summer broke in: "So what is up with you, anyway? You never answered at the doctor's office."

Josie froze mid-chew. She picked up a napkin and wiped her mouth.

"Nothing," she said, then, "Nothing. Why?"

"You know why," Delaney said.

"This is your day," Josie said. "We're celebrating. Let's not talk about me."

"Nice try," Summer said. "Nice. But no."

The chewing continued.

"Go ahead and procrastinate," Delaney said. "But we're cracking this, right here, right now."

"Fine," Josie said. "Paul isn't coming home anytime soon. I thought he was. But he's not. He served me divorce papers."

Here, the girls gasped. At any other moment, Josie would have found that funny. But not today.

"And yes, I'm stressed," she went on. "And no, I don't want to talk about it. Okay? Not only do I not want to ruin this celebratory, happy day, but I also don't want to dwell on it. I'm freaking out. I have no idea what to do."

Delaney and Summer looked at each other.

"You guys! I'm so sick of seeing you guys look at each other like that. Like you're both thinking the same thing but you won't say it to me. What are you thinking?"

They looked at each other again. Josie sighed, and made sure it was extra-loud.

"Things were going so well," Summer said. "What happened? What did you do?"

JOSIE REMEMBERED the moment she realized—no, *knew*—her mom was right about choosing practicality over romance. The conversation with her mother could have ended there. But it didn't. Josie made sure it continued, to her own detriment.

Her mom's funeral was planned for a Friday. Although Scott distracted Josie with fun activities, like having her give him local tours in a city where he'd actually grown up, he had been conspicuously absent whenever it came time to think about funeral details.

He just disappeared. Naturally, Summer stepped in, leading Josie through all the decisions just like she'd lead one of her children through a zoo, carefully, thoughtfully, pointing out details, guiding Josie in the right direction.

When it was all over, Scott returned, never once mentioning Mama's name or asking about her habits, her quirks, her tamales. It was as if she hadn't died. It was as if she hadn't existed. Scott's avoidance of the topic at once numbed Josie and hurt her. Then there was Paul. During one of their dates to The Sand Witch, the place where she sat this very moment with her two best friends, Josie mentioned, in an off-handed way, that her mother had died recently. Paul reached across the table and took her hand. He asked all the questions she wanted him to ask, giving her the opportunity to talk about her mom at length.

She told him how she'd inherited her mother's propensity for laughing when she was angry. She told him how her mom had loved making tortillas, how the scent of flour filled the house every weekend. She told him how crushed she'd been when her mother died, and how she had wished innumerable times that she could tell her how much she loved her. To Josie's own surprise, she even told Paul how her mother had urged her to choose practicality over romance, to ditch the flowers and poetry in favor of someone stable and supportive.

That was the proverbial lightbulb moment.

Everything became clear.

Josie felt herself transform.

She went from being a frenzied, uptight woman in search of something so intangible she could never describe it, to feeling serene, in control, and like she had absolutely everything she wanted and needed, right here at the table in the window of The Sand Witch.

"You really love her, don't you?" Paul said.

His use of the present tense turned her insides into warm candle wax, malleable and soft, and she felt in love with him on the spot. When had she gone from warm candle wax to cold, hard… whatever she had turned into?

Back in present time, Summer and Delaney looked at Josie expectantly.

"What was the question?" she said.

"What went wrong?" Summer said. "Why isn't Paul moving back in?"

All of a sudden, Josie began to cry. She felt her mouth open and her eyes squeeze shut, involuntarily.

She heard Delaney say under her breath, "Oh, my God," and Josie sobbed out a laugh before lapsing into full-on crying again.

"Josie!" Summer said. "What's going on?"

In a rush of words, Josie described everything that had happened recently with Scott in the doorway, with Paul in the kitchen, with Blair at work. Finally, she got to the part about the divorce papers. Delaney grabbed Summer's hand on the tabletop, so hard her knuckles went white.

"My life is a mess," Josie said as she finished. She wasn't crying anymore (she had just cried herself dry in thirty seconds) but she stared at her hands on the table. A period of silence passed.

When she finally looked up at her friends, she realized they had frozen. For the first time she could remember in the twenty years since they'd known each other, they didn't know what to say. Or they did, and they were choosing not to say it.

Josie walked into Juniper Junior High School on the first day of eighth grade, her binder clasped tightly to her chest, her eyes wide as she took in millions of students milling around the quad like so many bees swarming the berries on an overripe strawberry plant.

The buzzing was almost unbearable, and Josie found her feet felt completely stuck, her body immobile with fear.

Why had she let her mom braid her hair? Most of the other girls wore their hair loose and flowing and she felt old-fashioned.

Josie's mother had promised Arizona would provide their family with opportunity far beyond what they'd had in California. Right now, at this very moment, all Josie saw was the opportunity for loneliness. Her school in California was tiny in comparison, a shoebox of a building with only four classrooms compared to this compound, which had at least forty.

She continued to stand in place, becoming increasingly overwhelmed by the noise, the sheer volume of it all. Just as she felt her heart rate begin to rise, two girls approached her. Just like all the others, they wore their hair loose. Just like all the others, their jeans and tennis shoes sharply contrasted Josie's black skirt, white blouse and shiny Mary Jane shoes. What made them different, though, was that they noticed her. And they approached her, smiling with a combination of empathy and curiosity.

Despite her nervousness, she smiled back. It was a tentative smile, a wobbly pressing together of the lips, but it was a smile nonetheless.

"First day, huh?"

Josie nodded. She swallowed the lump that had formed in her throat as a reaction to the girls' kindness.

It was the tall one who spoke first. "I'm Summer," she said, casually, and Josie thought the name fit her perfectly. "And this is Delaney. We both came here last year, in seventh grade. But the first day is always kind of nerve-wracking, right, Dee?"

The shorter one smiled, and Josie noticed a dimple on her left cheek. "It is. Who do you have for homeroom?"

The three of them took out their schedules and formed a little huddle, comparing classes and lunch breaks. They were pleased to find that they all had two classes together—algebra and life science —and the rest of their classes overlapped throughout the day. Just like that, Summer and Delaney enveloped Josie in the fun, funny, steadfast friendship they now took for granted. The first day of eighth grade at Juniper Junior High served as the first example of how, between the three of them, someone always knew just what to say.

When one of the skinny athletic girls teased Josie about her big breasts, Summer said to Josie, "Well, at least the guys can tell you're a girl. She looks like one of them."

Looking back on that day now, twenty years later, it didn't seem like that witty of a remark. But it had worked. The girl never teased Josie again, and Summer's comment infused Josie with a new confidence she hadn't felt before.

A few years later, when Josie's first bonafide boyfriend, Michael Riggs, broke up with her the night before the homecoming dance, shattering her perfect visions of dancing with him to romantic songs like "Kiss From a Rose" and "Have You Ever Really Loved a Woman," while he rubbed her back and pressed his body against hers, Delaney said, "You know what? Homecoming dances are no fun, anyway. Let's just go to the game and then go back to my house and watch movies. We'll have popcorn and chocolate. Way better than a stupid school dance."

The support bolstered Josie immediately, and although the girls offered to stay home, she sent them off to the dance with their dates and had a girls' night with her mom. That night, she felt exactly the opposite of lonely, simply because of what Delaney said.

Throughout their adult life, too, the girls had a knack for saying precisely what Josie needed to hear. Whether it was offering congratulations for a killer interview for the Juniper Elementary third grade teacher position or putting her in her place when she didn't make a big enough deal of Paul's first promotion, they were always straight shooters.

So why now, after all this time, were they speechless? Had she messed up that badly, that they didn't have any positive or scathing-but-educational words to offer?

Oh, God. Maybe she had.

"I—I don't know what to say," Summer said, finally breaking the spell. She and Josie looked expectantly at Delaney, who shrugged.

"I'm at a loss, Josie," Delaney said. "I mean, what were you thinking? Then she looked at Summer and said, "We've failed her."

Silence descended again, although the other deli patrons continued to talk and laugh like nothing momentous had happened. Summer was nodding. She pressed her lips together and kept nodding.

"We have," Summer finally said.

Both girls stared at the table, crestfallen.

Josie heaved a deep breath and said, "I think we were solving the wrong problem. And that's because we didn't know what the right problem—the real problem—was. Is."

They didn't answer immediately, and Josie was almost frozen with fear. She took a bite of her sandwich. Summer and Delaney looked at each other as if Josie were crazy and needed escorting to a psych ward.

"No, really. I didn't," Josie said. "But I've done a lot of soul-searching lately, and I think I know now."

"Please, enlighten us," Delaney said.

Before she knew what had happened, Josie felt tears stinging her eyes. Again.

"My mom always said I should choose practicality over romance. She always said you can't depend on romance. Romance doesn't pay the bills or stick around. You know, my dad was a real romantic. It's why he left. He had that bug. He was a dreamer. He felt called to travel, to try new things. He was constantly infatuated with new ideas, and my mom was just one of them, easily replaced by others. So mom clung to practicality."

"But what does this have to do with you?" they said in unison.

It all seemed so clear now. It was so obvious. But because she'd always kept Scott a secret from her friends, they didn't realize he was a romantic, a dreamer. They didn't realize he was the epitome of what her mom had warned her about. So she told them. She told them how he lured her in with flowery language and big promises. How he thrived on romance, on fancy restaurants and flashy bouquets. She told them how even now, he said things that made him irresistible to her, like, "Love you in that dress."

He never said he loved her when they were dating, so throwing the phrase into a compliment was *this close* to admitting he had.

She explained how Paul was Scott's opposite. He was beyond practical, packing a First Aid kit but forgetting the sled on their first sledding trip. He thrived on quiet moments in private corners, and every event had meaning for him.

He'd say things like, "You look nice," but he didn't mean he wanted to get into her pants. He said it when she walked out of the bedroom in the morning wearing a scowl and his t-shirt. He meant she looked nice. He meant he was proud to be her husband. He meant she was beautiful, all the time.

But he meant it.

"I get that," Summer said. "I get that they're different. But you started out this conversation talking about your mom."

"Right," Josie said. "I'm getting to that."

"Carry on, then," Delaney said.

Now the tears spilled out of Josie's eyes as she told them about how every encounter with Scott, every situation with Paul, was like a conversation between her and her mom.

"It's like she's there with me. She's telling me, 'This is what I warned you about, *mija*,'" Josie said. "'This Scott is a real romantic. S-C-O-T-T spells trouble.' And then with Paul, sometimes she is nodding her head in approval, even when he walks out on a delicious dinner we've been planning all week. 'He's a good provider, *mija*. You should be grateful for that.'"

Josie shook her head, then wiped her eyes and nose with the thin brown deli napkin Summer held out.

Then she continued, "I sometimes want to say to her, 'But practicality is leaving me lonely, Mama.' I know Paul is the one for me. I know it. There are certain things I miss about Scott, but overall, I know Paul is it. But it's like, if I write Scott out of my life, the conversation with my mom is over. And she's gone."

Josie was now crying openly, her chest heaving and hiccups escaping her throat. Delaney handed her another napkin and massaged her shoulder with one hand. Summer was almost in tears, herself.

"You know," Summer said, "you kind of cut us off after your mom passed away. Was it because you were spending so much time with Scott?"

Josie could only nod. Summer went on, "That explains a lot. Did you ever really get the closure you needed around your mom's death? Did you ever really get to say good-bye to her?"

The sobbing and hiccuping threatened to turn into an all-out wail, and Josie took a deep breath. "I don't know." She sniffled. "I don't think I did. I mean, Scott encouraged me to move on. Whenever I brought her up, he changed the subject. At the time, it seemed reasonable. Thinking about her, talking about her, it all made me so sad. I never even spread her ashes." At this, Delaney and Summer exchanged horrified looks. "When I met Paul, I thought I should be over it, you know? I rarely talked about her. Sometimes he would practically beg me to tell him stories, or give him details about what she was like. But you make a good point. I mean, maybe I never did get the closure I needed. And maybe that's why I'm kind of scared to close out this conversation."

"Well, Dee," Summer said. "I guess we've found our new starting point."

Delaney nodded sagely, still rubbing Josie's shoulder. "Yes, we have," she said. "Not to worry, Josie. We can fix this."

Ah. There it was. At her friends' perfect words, Josie burst into a fresh round of tears.

CHAPTER THIRTY

Josie woke before dawn Saturday morning, anticipation giving her the rare gift of watching the sunrise, a peach and lavender quilt, gilded by the sun's rays, intersected by a dark gray jet stream. Wide awake before even having her coffee, she stepped over a still-sleeping Delilah who couldn't be bothered to uncurl her body and instead nuzzled more deeply into her bed.

"Spoiled puppy," Josie whispered.

Spring mornings in the mountains could feel frigid, but the afternoon sun would cause heat waves to rise off the landscape. Josie dressed in layers, wearing the necklace her mom had given her closest to her skin.

She coaxed Delilah outside for a potty break and then fed her breakfast. While the coffee brewed, Josie set out three travel mugs.

Ten minutes later, beams of light swept the inside of Josie's house. The whirling mixture of emotions brought Josie to the brink of tears yet again. She opened the front door before Summer and Delaney even knocked, and they folded her into a long, tight hug.

Delilah apparently decided having company was a good enough reason to be out of bed at this ungodly hour, and she ran around their feet, gyrating and yipping, every once in a while nipping at one of their pant legs.

"Are you ready to do this?" Summer asked.

"I'm ready," Josie said. "Thanks again, you guys. Really. This means more to me than you know."

Josie handed out coffee mugs, loaded Delilah and her food into the car and retrieved the tiny cardboard box the crematorium had given her.

Even now, Josie hated the idea that everything that was her mother could be condensed down into this one little box. Not just her body, but her love for the Spanish soap operas, her tradition of decorating gingerbread houses for Easter and her spending the days ahead of Christmas baking so the house smelled like warm bread and spices and Josie and Juan got sick on cookies. It was all here in this plain brown box.

Once she stowed the box away at Scott's urging, shoved it to the very back of her closet with the carefully-packed photos from her childhood, Josie managed not to think about the actual cremation process or the resulting package.

Now, she felt a profound sense of sadness as she ran her fingertips over the label: *CARLA M. GARCIA*.

"It's time to say good-bye, *Mamacita*," she said.

REDWOOD TREES REACHED toward the azure sky, the reddish-brown of their fuzzy bark contrasting the soft green of their leaves. The afternoon sunlight slanted through the branches, and Josie watched the dust motes dance and sparkle.

"No wonder your mom loved this place so much," Summer said. "It's magical."

"It is," Josie said. "She'd bring us here on her days off, and it was always a respite from the hot fields. We all loved it here."

The girls had dropped Delilah off with Summer's family and then driven twelve hours to the redwood forest of central California. Years ago, this spot provided a calm, shady escape for Josie's family, and now it would serve as Carla's final resting place.

"Did you bring your mom?" Delaney asked.

Josie laughed and held up the box. During the long drive through desert sand and fields of produce in neat rows, she had found peace with the idea of her mom's entire being reduced to ashes.

"We'd always walk this trail," Josie said, leading Summer and

Delaney down a path that eventually wound along a little creek. "Mom would pack us a lunch, and we'd eat at this one spot by the water. Usually Juan wound up soaked. Inevitably, he'd fall in while he was trying to catch crawdads or walk across a log bridge."

"Let's go there," Delaney said. "You can show us."

It was exactly as Josie remembered it: postcard perfect. The huge redwood stump where Mama always laid their picnic blanket still stood off to the side of the trail, close enough to the creek that you could put your feet in while you ate your egg salad sandwich.

The branches of deciduous trees dipped into the water luxuriously, and the surface reflected them back, a wavering mirror image. And the sound. Josie had never forgotten it and hearing it again felt like the perfect medicine.

Birds chirped overhead, the creek gurgled and a breeze rustled the leaves. The air smelled earthy with the spicy edge of redwood bark, and Josie found herself breathing slowly and deeply as if to drink it all in. Summer and Delaney now stood on either side of her, Summer holding her hand and Delaney's arm around Josie's waist.

"Is this the spot?" Summer asked.

Josie nodded. For once in recent history she didn't feel like crying. A new sense of calm washed over her.

"Do you want to say something before you spread the ashes?"

Josie nodded again, and her friends tightened their respective grips.

"Mama," she said. "I miss you so much. Words cannot even express just how much. For a long time, I was so angry that you were taken from me so soon. I'll never get to introduce you to my husband, and you'll never get to meet my children. That thought still hurts me. But I know you'll always be watching over me, over all of us."

"And you were right, Mama. It's better to marry for practicality. Although, a little romance is good to have in the mix, too. You'd like Paul. He's perfect for me. And I know you'll be so proud of my children when I have them. I chose to lay you to rest in this spot because it represents so many things I love about you. It represents practicality. Egg salad sandwiches are nothing if not practical. And a picnic lunch is a perfectly practical way to turn an everyday lunch into something special. It represents romance. You wanted romance when you met my dad, and even though it turned out to be too much romance, this spot was romantic for me. Magical. *You* were magical to me, Mama. And although I've come here to lay you to rest, and to say good-bye to you, it's not good-bye forever. You'll always be in my heart, I know that now. And I know we'll meet again. I love you."

Josie opened the cardboard box and pulled out the bag that held the ashes. She unsealed it and walked forward to the creek's edge. In less than a minute, she had emptied the contents into the sparkling water. Some of the ashes dissolved immediately, while others floated down the creek and out of sight.

Josie, Summer and Delaney stayed overnight in a small cottage in the woods. The owner, a grandmotherly painter with a self-proclaimed penchant for finding the perfect blueberry muffin recipe and a knack for making strong, delicious coffee, welcomed them Saturday evening with citrus-flavored ice water and a basket of cheeses and fancy crackers. Kara McCormick bought the cottage to run as a bed and breakfast when her husband Bud (short for William) died ten years before.

"It was always our shared dream to live in a cottage in the woods," she said, nodding toward the window at the front of the house and the flower garden and trees beyond it. "But we waited. We were always waiting for the right time. He died before that time ever came. One of the greatest regrets of my life. Anyway. Reminiscing. Sorry, girls. You came here for a girls' weekend. You don't need to listen to an old lady blabber. Let me show you to the Quail Room. C'mon then."

All three of them changed into pajamas and flopped onto the bed the moment Kara closed the door behind her.

"I'm so tired," Delaney said. "I guess I'm getting old!"

"You're not old, Dee," Summer said. "You're pregnant. You're growing an actual human in your body right now. It takes a lot of energy."

Delaney didn't answer. She was already snoring.

"So how are you feeling?" Summer asked Josie.

Josie sighed. "I feel content. Like I got closure today. Closure I really needed. And I have you guys to thank for that."

Summer reached across the bed and grabbed Josie's hand. "You're welcome," she said.

Within seconds, she, too, was fast asleep.

Alone and feeling wide awake at the same time as she felt calm and centered, Josie decided to go for a walk. The moon hung high in the sky, casting a silvery glow on the forest surrounding the cottage. She took the first path she came to, one that led into the woods, to a little chapel nearby.

"I'm ready to let go, Mama," Josie said as she walked.

The forest was quiet, but not silent. Creatures scurried along the ground, which was padded with fallen redwood leaves. Somewhere nearby, a stream bubbled.

"It's been so hard, but I'm finally ready. I know now that letting go doesn't mean you're not with me. It doesn't mean I have to forget about you. It just means I'm at peace with you being gone."

THE NEXT MORNING, the girls ate a huge pyramid of Kara McCormick's famous blueberry muffins and Josie relished most of a huge pot of her coffee. They hit the road at seven on the nose, armed with peanut-butter-filled pretzels and black licorice.

Most of the morning passed in silence punctuated by Summer pointing out every train, plane, helicopter or farm animal they saw. "Sorry," she said so many times. "Habit. Kids. You know."

Suddenly, she burst into tears, sobbing loudly. Delaney pulled off the highway and the car jerked to a stop, tall weeds scraping its undercarriage. She and Josie turned around in the front seats to look at Summer, who went from crying to laughing in a split second.

"You guys. Your faces are so comical. I'm fine." She sniffed. "No, really. I am. I'm just so overwhelmed."

With that declaration came a fresh round of tears. Josie and Delaney exchanged panicked glances.

"Oh, stop worrying," Summer said.

Delaney looked around. "I think I see a milkshake place at the next exit. Should we stop?"

They pulled back onto the highway, exited and then drove through a fast food restaurant. Back on the road, Delaney said, "So fill us in. What's going on?"

"It's the band," Summer said.

Josie looked at Delaney, but Delaney's eyes were glued to the road. Would anything band-related cause Summer to act the way she'd been acting lately? There had to be more to this story. *Is she lying?*

"The band, like The Sweets?" Josie said.

Summer nodded. "It's just that ever since we played at The Blue and the rodeo dance, the girls want to play even more gigs. But I just can't. I really want to, but I just can't. It's all too much."

She broke down into a full-out wail. Josie wished she had Summer's knack for always knowing what to say.

"Could you just play some of the gigs?" Delaney asked.

"That's a good idea," Josie said. "I mean, you don't have to go to every single one of them. The band is supposed to be something fun for you, right?"

"It is," Summer said. "And no, I can't do just some of the gigs. I mean, they need a full-time lead singer. Kind of important, you know?"

"Maybe you could take a break?" Josie said, hoping her voice sounded gentle. With her luck she'd send Summer over the edge, straight to a full-out breakdown.

Summer nodded and her expression remained serious. "I know, you're right."

"But of course you're sad," Josie said. "I would be too."

No one spoke for a little while, but Josie's mind was going a million miles an hour. Summer rarely broke down. And if she did, it wasn't about something as trivial as the band. There had to be something else going on. *It's her secret to keep*, Josie reminded herself. Her thoughts wandered to Paul, then, and to the kiss with Scott, and by the time the girls made their second pit stop in just four hours, Josie had had plenty of time to think.

"I've really messed up with Paul," she said as they pulled away from the seedy gas station where they'd each used about a gallon of hand sanitizer after going to the bathroom.

Neither Summer nor Delaney answered, and Josie took their silence as affirmation.

"I need to fix things," she went on, "but I have no idea how. I already apologized. I've given him his space. But I want him back and I don't know what to do."

Out the car window, golden hills rolled by, dotted with black and brown cows and lined with apple orchards.

"You guys don't know what to say either?" Josie said.

"You did mess up," Delaney said quietly.

Normally, Josie would respond with a sarcasm-infused, "Thanks, Delaney," but this time she waited. Summer was nodding, but still, she didn't speak.

"I could use some help, here," she said after another several miles. Amber waves of grain and all that, she thought.

Finally, Summer spoke. "You messed up," she said. "You really did. Delaney and I can't tell you how to fix it. We don't have to tell you that you never should have kept the Scott Smith secret from Paul, and that you really, really never should have kissed him in your house. The house you share with Paul. Your husband."

Just like a teenager caught coming in drunk after curfew, Josie felt ashamed. If they'd been standing in a room, she would have made her eyes downcast, staring at her toes, shrugging her shoulders. But for now, they were in the car, so she focused on the road and kept her hands in her lap.

Summer continued. "But because you have messed up, and so royally, too, you've got to fix this, Not us. So go with your bad self, woman. Fix that shit up. Just know we can't save you on this one."

It wasn't what she wanted to hear. But Summer's advice was spot-on.

"You're right," Josie said. "I made the mistakes and now I have to set things right."

The next several hours gave her plenty of time to think, and by the time they pulled up at her house, she had formed a pretty decent plan.

CHAPTER THIRTY-ONE

Scott Smith lived in a Craftsman-Style bungalow on Cottonwood Avenue, set back away from the street. A huge Sycamore tree stood in the center of the velvety lawn, and a flower bed lined the path from the driveway to the house. Scott Smith constantly professed his love for "putting my hands in the dirt," but Josie knew he actually despised gardening and hired someone to keep the place looking nice. Another secret, Josie thought as she walked toward his front door the day after returning from her trip with Summer and Delaney.

When they first met, Josie daydreamed about living in this adorable house, quaint and sophisticated. She imagined turning the tidy flower bed into a wild English garden. She imagined hanging Halloween decorations from the branches of the Sycamore. She planned out the light-up Christmas scene she would design on the lawn.

Scott came out the door before Josie had the chance to knock. It was spring break, and he wore gray sweatpants and a maroon t-shirt instead of the slacks and button-up shirt his Mondays typically called for. His socks, as always, were pristine. Thick and white as if he'd just taken them out of the package. Josie's mind flashed to an image of Paul's socks: holey and off-white from wear.

For about the millionth time in three days, her entire body

flooded with a deep affection for Paul, for all the little quirks that set him apart. The socks, yes, and the obsession with garlic ice cream. The need to have his shoulders covered and his feet bare when he slept. She hoped with all of her being that she could fix their marriage, bring him back.

His smile wary, Scott motioned for Josie to follow him inside.

"We can talk out here," she said.

They sat down on the wicker chairs on the small front porch.

"Josie—" he said at the same time as she said, "Scott—" and they both stopped and laughed awkwardly.

"I'm really sorry about—" he said at the same time as she said, "I need to talk—" and they both laughed again.

That was another thing about Scott: he had difficulty just letting her speak. "Let me go first," Josie said.

When he nodded, she said, "I need to talk to you."

"About the other day?"

"Kind of. About … everything. Between us. About how you're always there, complimenting my wardrobe or laughing at my jokes. About how I'm always walking past your office, checking to see if you're noticing me. We had a good run, but it's time to end things. For good. No more talking, no more flirting, no more secretive smiles."

"Josie, I—"

"Let me finish." She held up a hand, like she'd do if one of her students interrupted her. "They say everyone comes into your life for a reason, and I believe you were there to help me cope with my mom's death. At the same time, I never really found closure with it. So I think our relationship became kind of a stand-in. If I still had you, I still had her. But I've dealt with it now. And I'm ready to say good-bye to both of you."

Scott nodded, finally leaving some open space in the air. In the span of time that followed, Josie was surprised she didn't feel sad or nostalgic. She didn't secretly wish for him to reach out and touch her face or ask her in for a night cap which really meant come in and have sex.

Finally, he said, "I understand. It hurts. You've been such a big part of my life for so long."

Another lie. This time, to himself.

"I haven't, really," she said. "I mean, we've known each other. But we're essentially co-workers, and have been since I got married."

He nodded thoughtfully. "I guess you've occupied a big part of my mental space."

Normally, she would make some quip, like, "It's only natural," but today, she said, "It's time to move on, Scott. I need to focus on my marriage and you need to find a woman who can love you back. I think you and I both know who that might be."

She saw him watching her as she drove away, and felt an almost giddy sense of relief. Just before she turned off his street, he lifted a hand in a half-wave. She couldn't help but notice he looked a bit defeated.

JOSIE'S NEXT MISSION: to find a bridal gown for Delaney.

She returned to Froth, where Debra Mills greeted her with a cup of tea instead of a glass of champagne.

"I'm not the one who's knocked up," Josie said, and when Debra only smiled, Josie took a demure sip of her tea and followed her to the back room.

"So we need something for a pregnant bride, huh?" Debra said. She pulled several books off shelves and put them on the table, expertly flipping them open to reveal a dozen dresses with empire waists.

"I managed to find a location for the wedding in just a few weeks," Josie said. "So she won't be, you know, like, *big* or anything."

Debra raised her eyebrows.

"I didn't mean it that way. But these," she said, motioning to the dresses, "will fit her better than the ones she tried on last time. *Way* better."

This time, Debra laughed. "You're a straight shooter, you know that?"

"Not as much as you'd think."

"What do you mean?"

Josie surprised herself by going full disclosure on Debra. She explained everything that transpired recently with Paul and Scott.

"I still remember your wedding," Debra said. "I remember how you and Paul looked at each other. It was so obvious you were deeply in love. Forget that cliché about him not taking his eyes off you. He'd gaze at you, and then he'd look at everyone else, like he was asking them, 'Can you believe my luck?' It was heartwarming. I always tell people about that."

For some reason, the description surprised Josie. "You noticed that?"

"Of course," Debra said. "Everyone did. You'd be a fool to miss it."

Josie remembered looking at Paul that day. She remembered feeling as if she was seeing him for the first time, viewing him through that soft lens soap operas use, with those strong beams of heavenly light that shoot down from between thick clouds.

Every time they made eye contact, they beamed at each other, like, "Can you believe our luck?"

"I knew from the moment I saw you, that was a match made to last," Debra said.

NO MATTER how long they'd been married, Josie sometimes felt surprised when she saw Paul out of context. He was so good-looking, like a model for athletic clothes. The cheekbones, the profile, the muscles. He sat at a table inside Umbrella Coffee, and Josie noted with satisfaction that he'd ordered her an iced latte and had set it in what would be her spot when she arrived. She stood just inside the door, admiring him, praying it wouldn't be the last time she had this opportunity.

When an older couple opened the door with a little too much gusto, Josie made an involuntary sound and Paul looked up. She walked to the table quickly, pretending she'd just gotten there.

"Thank you for meeting with me," she said.

"Sure," Paul said. "Any time."

Josie sat down, feeling uncomfortable. "Thanks for the coffee."

"Of course."

"How are you?" she asked, then immediately felt stupid. Of course he was fine. He looked fine. He looked great. He looked edible.

"I'm okay," he said. "Work's going well."

She waited for him to ask how she was doing, but he didn't. Instead, he looked at her expectantly. Seconds ticked by.

"So. I've been doing some thinking," she said.

He inclined his head, inviting her to elaborate.

"I got a visit the other day from some deputies."

Paul nodded. Of course, he already knew. Josie took a deep breath.

"I don't want a divorce, Paul. I want to fix things." He stared at her, and she went on. "I think I figured out why I felt so, um. So attached, I guess? To Scott."

Paul raised his eyebrows. It was an expression he made whenever they got into a debate, whenever she made a comment he found questionable. She had to suppress the urge to giggle, only because she felt self-conscious and uneasy. After taking a long sip of her latte, she told him about the revelation she'd had about her mom. About romance versus practicality. About Scott representing the former, and Paul representing the latter.

"I'm afraid I've been terribly unfair to you," she said. "I boxed you in. I put you firmly in the practicality column, neglecting the romantic aspects of your personality. And I'm so sorry for that. I did the same to Scott. But it was all for the sake of having that conversation with Mom."

Still, he didn't speak. So she continued. "So I'm sorry. Okay? I've made my peace with Mom's death, finally. I didn't even realize that was missing. But I've done it. I've moved on. I've told Scott—with no kissing—that we aren't anything more than professional acquaintances. And I feel so much better. So. I wanted to ask if you'd be willing to give things another try. To throw those (here she struggled to actually use the D-word) papers out and try again."

Paul nodded, a slow, thoughtful nod.

"So?" she said.

"It sounds like you've done some thinking," he said. "And now I've got to do some, too."

It was better than a straight "No," but worse than a "Yes," which she had really hoped for.

Better not to rush him.

Although she did her best to play it cool, Josie felt her heart rate increasing. Her hands shook slightly as she reached for her coffee again.

"All right," she said. "That makes sense."

CHAPTER THIRTY-TWO

It was Delaney's wedding day, and Josie felt as jittery as a bride because she felt like Paul's choice about whether to attend would signify whether their marriage would continue or not. Clouds like wisps of cotton streaked a sky so brilliantly blue it made Josie's eyes hurt to look at it. Flowering apricot trees surrounded the gazebo, their shiny green leaves and fragile white blossoms showing off the best of spring.

"Stunning," Summer said to Delaney. "You look radiant."

She did. Pregnancy suited her, made her skin clear and luminescent, her eyes bright. And the gown Josie had selected showed off her tiny baby bump and her otherwise athletic figure.

"You look like Mother Nature, herself," Josie said.

"Thanks, you guys," Delaney said, hugging them both. "I just can't believe this is happening."

Hannah, too small to carry flowers, sat with Derek in the audience. Sarah stood with Luke and Nate, a protective arm around Luke, just in front of Delaney, ready to precede the bride down the aisle.

"She's been so sweet with him since we found out—" Summer said.

Josie waited for her to continue, to say what they'd found out, but Summer abruptly changed course. "I'm sure that protective arm is actually her way of keeping him quiet. She's probably whispering in his ear right now. 'You mess this up, Luke, and I'll take you down.'"

Now that Summer mentioned it, Josie thought, Luke did look a little like he had an itch in the middle of his back he couldn't scratch. Sarah looked so stern and grown-up Josie chuckled.

Guests began arriving and Josie nudged Delaney further behind the little screen they'd set up to keep anyone from seeing her.

"You're like the bridal police," Delaney said, laughing. "I'm going to have to make you my nanny, you know. Structure, discipline, and just the right amount of love."

All three of them giggled.

"Speaking of police," Delaney said, but stopped cold when Summer elbowed her. "What?" she said.

"Hey, look at that!" Summer said to Delaney. "It's Jake's sister, Jenny. Remember when you thought he was cheating on you with her?"

They all looked at the tall, sleek blonde who walked down the aisle to find her seat, already dabbing at her eyes with a tissue.

"Nice distraction, Summer," Josie said. "But it's okay. Dee, I'm not sure if Paul's coming today. I'm sorry. I mean, when we first planned the wedding, I obviously put him down as my guest. He loves you almost as much as I do. But with everything that's going on, I just don't know whether he'll come. But let's not talk about that. This is your day, and I don't want my own personal storm clouds rolling in to rain on this fantastic parade."

Just then, the harpist began playing her final song. When she finished, the kids would walk down the aisle, then the guys, then Summer and Josie. Finally, the DJ would play the bridal march. Delaney grabbed her best friends' hands, and they all squeezed.

The song ended and the guests quieted, shifting in their seats with anticipation. A few moments later, Jake stood at the altar, and there was a collective intake of breath.

"This is it," Josie whispered. She kissed Delaney on the cheek and walked down the aisle to wait. Summer followed her. Delaney really was stunning, and Josie looked quickly at Jake, whose face looked just as radiant as Delaney's. Once the minister began to speak, Josie scanned the audience.

Paul wasn't there.

. . .

UNDER A SHOWER of birdseed and opalescent bubbles, to a symphony of cheers and cowbells, Mr. and Mrs. Jake and Delaney Rhoades left for their honeymoon, a week at a small but modern cabin in the White Mountains of northern Arizona.

Josie was officially through with her bridesmaid duties, except for taking Delaney's dress to be cleaned and packaged the following week. Summer rushed home, her four kids in tow and up way past their bedtimes, and when Josie climbed into her car, she let her primary bridesmaid duty, the most difficult one—cheerfulness—go.

She put her forehead on the steering wheel. An intense feeling of sadness, desolation actually, made her limbs go limp. Of course she was happy for Delaney and Jake. At the same time, Paul hadn't come to the wedding. His absence was symbolic. Obviously so. The signal was clear: he didn't want to be with her. Their marriage was over, officially. What could she do but go home?

She started the car, took a deep breath, and began driving. As she made her way through Juniper, she forced herself to think reasonably. Of course Paul didn't want to be with her. After spending the past several months being infatuated with another man, she'd kissed that man in the doorway of the home she shared with Paul. It wasn't the steering wheel's fault, but she whacked her palm against it anyway.

I'll just have to come to terms with this. My life as a single woman. With a dog. My personal ad can say something like, "Single woman with large puppy seeks new man after cheating on husband."

Delilah would be waiting at home for her, and would welcome her with all the squirming and licking Josie could stand. That was enough, wasn't it?

CHAPTER THIRTY-THREE

THE POLICE CRUISER PARKED DIRECTLY IN FRONT OF THE ENTRANCE TO Josie's house. Her heart leapt into her throat, pounding as if it wanted to come out her mouth. *What now?*

She slammed the car into Park, jumped out and ran to the front door. Her hands were shaking so much she couldn't unlock it. The knob turned and the door swung inward. The first thing she saw was a blue uniform. The belt, the gun, the handcuff pouch. The buttons traveling neatly up the torso. The badge. Finally, she saw the name plate: COMSTOCK. And then the face.

"Paul!"

Her vision was black at the edges, and blurry.

"Are you okay?" he asked, gripping her upper arms.

"I think I'm going to pass out." As Josie had just envisioned, Delilah danced around her feet, her tail going a million miles per hour. Paul led Josie to the couch, where he sat her down and put her head between her knees. "Why are you driving that patrol car? When I saw it, I had, like, déjà vu from that time you were in an accident. I thought they were coming to tell me you'd been shot or killed. It didn't even register that they weren't in the car. I thought you were dead. I feel like I'm seeing your ghost."

"You're pale," he said, rubbing her back.

"You're not, for a ghost."

Delilah was apparently delighted to have Josie's face at her level, and she licked her cheeks over and over, darting closer and farther away. Josie laughed and sat up, wiping her face.

She'd normally demand, "What are you doing here?" but she caught herself and said instead, "I wasn't expecting you. Why are you in uniform?"

Now she took a moment to look at him, to really look at him. "You look horrible," she said before he could answer.

He barked out a laugh.

"I'm really sorry I missed Delaney's wedding," he began.

Whether she didn't want to hear his excuse or she felt irrationally compelled to tell him how his absence affected her, she interrupted him even though she could tell he had more to say. "I thought you not coming meant you didn't want to be married anymore. I thought it was your final decision."

Paul's body deflated next to hers.

"I'm so sorry," he said again. "That's not the case at all. You wouldn't believe what happened today."

"Try me."

"My shift was nearly over—"

"Wait. Your shift? Why do you have a shift?" The realization dawned on her. "You went back on patrol?"

He nodded. "Last week. I knew it would be better for our marriage, but I didn't want to tell you until I was sure they'd have a spot for me."

Josie's mouth dropped open.

"Anyway," he said, impatient to finish his story, "I was heading home to change. To get ready for the wedding. Just as I turned off the highway, I get this call from dispatch, about a head-on collision on Willow Branch Road. I'm the closest, so I say I'll take it."

Josie nodded. That's just what good cops did. Delilah turned in several circles, and flopped down onto the floor, half her body on one of Josie's feet and the other half on one of Paul's.

By the time he arrived, Paul explained, it was too late. A man coming off a double shift at the cement plant fell asleep at the wheel and crossed the center line. His truck hit a sedan head-on, immediately killing both occupants—a husband and wife, both in their eighties.

To Josie's surprise, Paul started to sob. "I don't even know how long they were married, but in my mind they were married for fifty years. They were long-time sweethearts. They ate Chinese takeout every Valentine's Day, they had three boys and two girls and seven grandchildren. They bought an RV when they retired, and now they drive around the country every summer."

"Why are you crying? You've seen so many accidents and I don't remember you crying over any of them."

"Remember when I got into that car accident a while back, and I had this moment of clarity?"

Of course I remember.

She nodded. A sense of foreboding took root. At that time, Paul's accident made him realize he was unhappy and wanted to move out. Oh, no. Had the car accident made that clarity even more clear? It took everything she had to stop herself from covering her ears. Instead, she flopped back on the couch. It was over. But then Paul said something that surprised her. Something romantic.

"I want that with you, Josie. I love you. I want to be married for fifty years. I want to eat pizza every anniversary. I want to take you all over the country in an RV. I want to have kids. Grandkids."

Josie sat up again and put a hand on his leg. He continued, "Shit, I want to pick up your laundry off the floor of our bedroom for the next fifty years. I would really like to move back in. I would really like to have a go at the next five decades. Are you okay with that?"

"Okay?" she said. She launched herself into his arms, startling Delilah, who jumped up onto the couch.

"I would really love that," she said. "Can we start now?"

"I was hoping we could," Paul said, kissing her. "And I know just how to celebrate a new beginning."

EPILOGUE

RACE DAY DAWNED AT A BRISK FIFTY-TWO DEGREES. JOSIE STOOD AT THE start line. She rubbed her hands together and did jumping jacks to keep herself warm. Summer and Delaney stood on the other side of the fence shivering and clutching paper cups of hot herbal tea.

"Remember," Delaney said. "Wine on the other side."

"And chocolate," Summer said. "Wine and chocolate. It'll be worth every mile."

The announcer began the one-minute countdown and Josie handed her sweatshirt over the fence to Summer. Butterflies swarmed in her stomach.

"You can do this," Delaney said. "You've been practicing."

Josie's hands shook as she put her earphones in.

"Thirty more seconds, runners!" the announcer called.

Next to her, a group of girls cheered.

A couple more quad stretches, some arm circles, and Josie heard, "Five, four, three, two, one."

The starting gun sounded. Delaney and Summer gave Josie high-fives. She began to run.

For the first mile, she thought she might die. But then she settled into a rhythm, concentrating on her music. She surprised herself by waving to some of the spectators, who held signs (*Run Now, Wine Later* and *You said run? I thought you said rum!*) and hollered kudos as the runners passed.

At mile three, Josie surprised herself by picking up the pace—just slightly. The second half of the race didn't exactly fly by, but Josie felt strong as she rounded the final curve. She didn't feel smug because she was entering the final straightaway. She felt smug because there, on her left, was her new building, bearing a temporary sign Summer had designed: The Carla M. Garcia Community Center.

And just beyond it, standing along the fence a few yards past the finish line, stood Paul. He saw Josie before she saw him, and when he called her name, her eyes locked in on him. He raised his arm raised in a cheer, and she raised hers, too, as she finished the race. A volunteer handed her a medal and a water bottle, and she fought back tears as she looked for her husband.

Paul jogged over to meet her. He took her medal from her and put it over her head.

"Congratulations, baby," he said. "I'm so proud of you."

As she enjoyed the feeling of being wrapped in his arms, she let the tears fall. Finishing the race—at the location of the project she'd been dreaming of—felt like so much more than the completion of six-point-two miles. It felt like a new beginning. Josie looked over Paul's shoulder and saw her two best friends approaching.

Before she knew it, she was wrapped in a giant group hug, surrounded by her favorite people in the world. And she was happy.

THE END

TURN **the page for a sneak peak of Book Three in the Intervention Series,** *The Motherhood Intervention.*

PREVIEW: THE MOTHERHOOD INTERVENTION

BOOK 3 IN THE INTERVENTION SERIES

Chapter One

Summer Carson's mother left her in the grocery store when she was ten years old, standing in the produce section next to a perfect pyramid of cantaloupes. As they approached the fresh herbs, Willow stopped and flung a hand into the air, dramatic, Scarlett O'Hara style.

"I forgot my coupons," she said, a touch too loudly and with a fake Southern lilt. "Left them in the car. I'll just run back and get them."

Summer thought to herself, *this is normal, right?* But her memory replayed scenes from earlier that morning, each one of them featuring a glass of honey-colored bourbon.

"You just wait right here, honey," Willow said, patting Summer's hand where it rested on the grocery cart handle. "I'll be right back. Pick out a cantaloupe, would you?"

Because she was an obedient child, Summer lifted melons to her face, one at a time, choosing one that smelled so much like it had already been cut open that her mouth watered. She set it carefully in the basket. Then she waited. And waited. After quite some time had passed, the produce man approached and asked if she was all right.

"Just waiting for my mom," she said.

She applauded herself for sounding calm, when inside, doubt had begun to creep its way into the spotlight. Yes, her mother should be back by now. No, it shouldn't take more than a minute to run out to the car and come back in. Maybe she should just check and make sure the car was still there. It wasn't. A quick glance outside revealed their beat up little hatchback was gone. Maybe Willow got out to the parking lot and realized she left the coupons at home. She just ran home to get them. *Or to get another glass of bourbon*, a little voice whispered.

Rather than subjecting herself to further questioning, Summer decided, she would get the shopping done. She walked slowly through the store, adding the usual items to the basket: orange juice, organic eggs, whole wheat bread.

She completed a full circle and then walked back to the produce section. Still, Willow wasn't there. Distant alarm bells began to sound in Summer's brain, and she forced herself to swallow, loosening the feeling of panic that lodged in her throat. Music played on the speakers, and Summer mouthed the words to "Sixteen Candles," which she knew by heart. She and her mother used to sing it over and over while washing dishes, mopping the floor or folding laundry.

The grocery store doors whooshed open and a police officer walked in. He scanned the produce department in half a second, and his eyes landed on Summer. He walked towards her.

A million thoughts ran through her mind. An unpleasant swirling sensation took over her stomach.

Was her mother dead?

Had she driven drunk, again, and finally crashed?

Had she killed someone? Someone else's mother?

Was the policeman here to arrest her, Summer, for letting her mom leave the store parking lot after taking a few slugs from her flask?

Was he here to take Summer to the hospital to say her final goodbyes?

"Hi, there," the police officer said.

Summer took a deep breath.

"Hi."

Twenty-four years had passed since the day Willow Carson drove off and left her daughter standing next to the cantaloupe, and Summer —now Summer Gray, thirty-four and married with her fifth child on the way—remembered it as crisply as if it were yesterday. Fifteen years had passed since Summer had even spoken to her mother. So why did the grocery store memory still cause her heart to race with panic?

She stood in the cluttered kitchen of her adult life, putting away groceries. The clandestine cantaloupe that had triggered the flashback rolled toward the edge of the counter. She caught it and set it behind the knife block in the corner.

"Don't forget about that melon until it's moldy and smelling up the kitchen," Summer said.

"Talking to yourself again, Mom?"

She laughed. "Yes, Sarah. And I've heard you doing the same. At eleven."

"I got it from you."

"You did. And my good looks, too, you lucky girl."

Summer's sons, Luke and Nate, barreled through the kitchen door as Sarah began putting groceries in the pantry. "You left Hannah in the car, Mom," Nate said.

"I did it on purpose," Summer lied. "So she wouldn't run into the street while we were unloading groceries."

Actually, she'd forgotten Hannah, whose little face would be crimson with rage when Summer eventually released her from her car seat.

She saw Sarah give her a skeptical look out of the corner of her eye, her eleven-year-old expression a bit too adult (and perceptive) for Summer's taste.

"What?" Summer said. "I did."

"Well, we've got all the groceries inside now, Mom," Luke said. "I used my super-secret ninja powers to carry them in. Didn't even touch 'em with my hands."

Someone made what Summer assumed was a super-secret ninja powers sound, and Summer laughed. "Can you guys please use those ninja powers to put the rest of the groceries away while I get Hannah out of the car?"

The boys threw their arms out at the pile of bags on the kitchen floor, shrugged when nothing happened, and disappeared into some distant galaxy. For a moment, Summer felt a prickle of guilt at having forgotten Hannah, but she quickly brushed it away. She wasn't her own mother, after all. Mistakes happened. And as long as those mistakes didn't happen on a ninety-degree day, everyone turned out fine.

She was just distracted, exhausted and eight months' pregnant. And so what if she secretly longed to get into a semi-major car accident or experience a semi-major illness so she could get a few days' vacation in a hospital bed? The thought gave her a strange sense of being pampered: nurses checking on her every couple of hours, someone delivering her food and taking the empty dishes away, no one expecting her to clean or drive or remember any appointments, field trip forms, lunch money or special projects. So what if she imagined driving the van right into the light pole in the middle of the grocery store parking lot so she could be whisked away in an ambulance? Not as sleek as a limo, but still. A hospital holiday. It could be a new thing. But she'd never really do it.

No, she wasn't her mother. When it had come time for Summer to create her own family, she had followed one rule: Whatever Willow had done, Summer would do the complete opposite.

So instead of having just one child, she was intent on having five.

Instead of the numerous flighty romances Willow ignited and squelched in rapid succession, Summer chose a husband who was dependable, reliable, and a good provider.

Instead of leaving her children at the grocery store, she left them in the car on a hot July day.

"Ugh," she found herself saying out loud as she pulled the van door open to Hannah's chants of "Out! Out! Out!"

Hannah had learned to walk earlier than all the other kids had, so now, at fifteen months old, Summer could simply set her down on the driveway and herd her into the house.

She smiled as Hannah toddled through the doorway, her pigtails sticking up on either side of her head. The moment was fleeting, though. Summer heard her phone ring just as Hannah walked directly into the doorjamb and started screaming.

An emotion she couldn't quite pinpoint began to rise up in her stomach as she scooped up the baby and carried her into the kitchen. Was it stress? Urgency? Frustration? The phone kept ringing, and although she knew it wasn't possible, Summer thought it sounded increasingly insistent.

While she could have sworn she put her phone on the counter, she couldn't find it among the bills, school papers, grocery bags and groceries. Hannah continued to scream and only then did Summer notice she had a huge goose egg just above her right eyebrow. Pushing a pile of papers out of the way, Summer set Hannah on the counter. The movement unearthed the phone. Summer answered it, grabbed a bag of peas out of the freezer and pressed it to Hannah's face, which, naturally, produced a fresh round of shrieks.

"Hold on, please," Summer said into the phone.

She moved Hannah into her high chair, tore open the bag of peas and dumped some on the tray. Then she locked herself in the bathroom.

"Hi, Summer, it's Amy from Dr. Thibedeau's office."

Dr. Thibedeau, the kids' pediatrician, let the kids call him Dr. Tippy Toes. They loved it.

"Hey. Did I miss an appointment or something?"

Normally, Amy would laugh, but when she didn't, Summer felt that feeling intensify. Stress. Anxiety. She wasn't sure.

"No," Amy said. "It's Luke's results from the scan. Dr. Thibedau wants you to meet with the heart specialist. I've already put the referral through, and they should be contacting you, um, pretty much right away to make an appointment."

They hung up and Summer sat down on the edge of the bathtub. An appointment with the heart specialist meant Luke's scan hadn't come back normal. From everything Dr. Thibedeau had said, an abnormal result meant surgery.

The police officer must have noticed ten-year-old Summer's panic, because he put a hand on her shoulder, knelt down so they were eye to eye, and said, "Don't worry. You're not in trouble."

"Is my mom okay?"

"That's why I'm here. The store employees called us because they noticed you've been in the store by yourself for a pretty long time. Do you know where your mom is?"

That tight feeling in her throat again. She tried not to cry, but her voice shook when she answered. Her eyes stung and she blinked, hard. "She said she had to go back to the car to get her coupons. But she was taking so long that I went to look for her and the car was gone.

I was thinking maybe she realized she left the coupons at home, and went to get them. So I did the shopping. But she hasn't come back."

The policeman nodded. Summer noticed his dark eyes taking in everything about her, from the messy ponytail and the too-tight jeans to the too-short shirt and the white Reeboks with the hole in one toe.

"We'll find her. Why don't you come with me?"

When she hesitated, he stuck out his hand for a handshake and said, "I'm sorry. I haven't introduced myself. I'm officer Andy Telluride with the Juniper Police Department."

He bought her a box of Cheez-Its and a soda, which would have sent her mom into a tizzy. He let Summer sit in the passenger seat of his patrol car while he used the radio to give someone else her address. While they waited (for what, Summer wasn't sure), he asked her lots of questions about her life. Which school did she go to? What was her favorite subject? What was her favorite book? He had a daughter about Summer's age, he told her, and she was reading "The Chronicles of Narnia."

A while later, the radio squawked and Summer heard another man's voice: "We found the subject. She's passed out on the couch at home. Says she came home to get coupons and fell asleep. Drunk as a skunk, this one."

Officer Telluride jumped, startled, and tried to turn the radio down, but Summer had heard enough. The drinking had gotten progressively worse during the past several months and people they encountered often whispered things like, "Wow, she's plastered," or, "Three sheets to the wind."

It almost *had* to come to this, didn't it?

Officer Telluride drove Summer home and asked her to wait in the car while he talked to her mother. She nodded, but when he went inside, she crept up to the front door and pressed her ear hard against its hot pink surface. Willow had insisted they paint it a gaudy coral to symbolize love and beauty. "We'll have both here, won't we, Summer?" she said at the time.

Not at the moment. Officer Telluride spoke calmly, but even through the front door Summer could hear the anger in his voice. He told Willow how scared Summer was, how hungry she was and how she had wandered the store for hours, alone. He explained that there are very bad people in the world, and one of them could have come along and snatched Summer right up.

While Summer felt a tiny bit defensive, she also felt more than a little angry at her mother. Because everything the policeman said was true. And because Willow didn't seem to register any of it. Summer could hear her saying over and over like a mantra, "I thought it was just for a minute."

When Officer Telluride came out the door, the energy radiating off his body in waves, he nearly stumbled over Summer.

"Sorry," she said.

Again, he knelt down so he could look straight at her. "I'm going to give you my card," he said. "If anything like this ever happens again, I mean *ever*, you call me. Do you understand?"

She nodded, grasped the card in her hand, and hugged Officer Telluride around the waist. He put one arm around her shoulders and squeezed back.

That was the first time Willow Carson disappointed her daughter, but it wasn't the last.

Chapter Two

Most Thursdays, Summer looked forward to her Happy Hour meetings with her two best friends. In her ongoing quest to be reliable, unlike her mother, Summer had become the sounding board and the steadfast support for Delaney Collins (who was now Delaney Rhoades) and Josie Garcia. Not that they didn't support her, too, Summer thought as she approached the swinging doors of Rowdy's Saloon.

But over the course of the past twenty years, Summer had become the proverbial lighthouse. Her role was to provide guidance, find the silver lining, say the right thing. She could meditate her way through anything. Until recently. Life had become increasingly complicated.

Several months ago, her husband, Derek, had lost his job. Her freelance graphic design income wasn't quite enough to support a family of six. Then the Grays turned into a *growing* family, with Gray Baby Number Five on the way. Derek got a new job, but the hours were long, which meant Summer was home with the kids and their puppy, Chuck (the littermate of Josie's Marriage-Intervention-era puppy, Delilah), pretty much around the clock.

And now Luke. Her perfect little boy. He'd always had a heart murmur, and his pediatrician had recently become "concerned" about it. He'd ordered a million tests and then referred them to a heart specialist. The heart specialist hadn't called to make an appointment yet, and not knowing what was wrong or how the doctors planned to fix it set Summer's nerves on a razor-thin edge.

Happy Hour always provided some solace, because it gave her the chance to focus on Delaney and Josie and their lives. She looked forward to the weekly meetings like one of her children looked forward to a birthday party. Not that she'd had many birthday parties when she was a child, but she understood the excitement.

Summer could hear the twang of country music before she pushed the doors open. As she entered the saloon, Delaney waved in greeting. Summer took a deep breath, squared her shoulders and smiled.

"Your drink's on the way," Josie said with a smug, teasing smile.

Summer rolled her eyes. "Thanks. I love lemon water."

They giggled, and Summer slid onto her stool and pointed at Delaney. "You love lemon water too, don't you?"

Benjamin, Rowdy's long-time bartender, sauntered over with a tray. He set glasses of water in front of Summer and Delaney, and a vodka cranberry in front of Josie. Then, with a flourish, he set a bowl of green olives between Summer and Delaney.

"She just smirked," Delaney said, gesturing at Josie with her water glass.

"I did not!"

"You did, too! You smirked because you get a vodka cran and we get waters."

"Now, now, ladies," Benjamin said. "Don't argue. It's not good for the babies."

He tipped his black cowboy hat and walked away, and a beat of silence ensued.

"Actually, Delaney," Josie said, "I smirked because I was thinking about the first time you ate a green olive during Happy Hour. Your eyes rolled back in your head and you were like, 'This is so good.' That's how we knew you were pregnant."

Summer nodded. "Yep. You'd been making fun of my green olive obsession for months. And now you have one, too."

Delaney laughed. "Too true."

"So how are you feeling, Dee?" Josie asked. "You're officially into the second trimester."

"I mean, being pregnant is miraculous and everything," Delaney said, "but it's so uncomfortable. Why didn't you warn me, Summer?"

"You've seen me through four pregnancies. And eight-ninths of another." She gestured at the bulge that was her stomach. "I thought you knew."

"You're always so stoic, though," Josie said.

Isn't that the truth?

"How are you feeling?" she asked Summer.

"I'm okay," Summer said. "I mean, we're down to the last few weeks. So I'm uncomfortable. And big. And exhausted. But other than that…"

She saw Delaney and Josie exchange a look, but didn't call them on it. She was allowed to complain once in a while, wasn't she?

All of a sudden, Summer was back in the trailer she and Willow called home during Summer's sophomore year of high school. It was spring break. Josie had signed up for a professional-track teaching course at Juniper City College and Delaney was off on some exotic vacation with her parents. Temperatures skyrocketed, which was awesome when you lived by the beach, but not so much when you lived in the desert in a crappy single-wide trailer with no air conditioning.

To combat the dry, windy heat, Willow took to drinking more than usual. She spent most of her time on the couch, in front of an electric fan, pressing her sweating glass of bourbon against the side of her face between sips. Summer was hot and bored and cranky. One morning, she came out of her bedroom and sat next to Willow on the couch. If she had known her mother was inebriated, she never would have talked to her, much less said anything about the heat. But it was seven a.m.—way too early for a person to be drunk.

"It's hot this morning," Summer said, her tone conversational.

Willow's head turned slowly, her eyes half-closed. She looked at Summer from under heavy lids. Summer thought her mother was being silly, pretending to suffer from heat exhaustion. So she did what any teenager would do: she laughed.

"Don't you laugh, young lady," Willow barked. "I work hard to put a roof over our heads. Don't you complain about the heat, do you hear me? With the amount you eat, we can't afford air conditioning. If I hear you bellyache again, I'll take a wooden spoon to your backside."

Of course she rarely actually hit Summer, but she seemed to get some kind of wicked satisfaction out of threatening her. Willow muttered under her breath about what an ungrateful slug her daughter was, and for the next few days, she challenged Summer to complain every time they interacted.

"Have anything to say about this dinner?" she sneered when she plunked a bowl of chili on the table. "Want to share your opinion on your shoes?"

Spring break of her sophomore year was the worst week of Summer's life. She vowed never to complain again, and she always kept her promises. Especially the ones she made to herself.

"Earth to Summer," Josie was saying as Summer brought herself back to Happy Hour at Rowdy's. At the bar, the Thursday night college crowd talked and laughed over colorful drinks and cheap beers.

Summer forced a smile.

"Sorry. Reminiscing," she said.

"Liar. You were on a whole different planet," Delaney said.

"I was," Summer said. "But I'm back."

"Oh, good," Delaney said. "Where were you?"

With my lunatic mother in a flamingo-pink trailer with no air conditioning.

"Just thinking about my mom."

Summer felt like crying. She blamed the pregnancy hormones. The multi-colored lights strung around Rowdy's blurred and she blinked rapidly a few times to bring the whole scene back into focus.

"What's going on?" Josie said. "You've been acting weird since you got here."

"I have not," Summer said.

"Yes, you have," Delaney said.

"I haven't even had a chance to act weird," Summer said. She could hear the defensive tone in her voice, and took a deep breath. "I just got here."

"You haven't eaten a single olive," Josie pointed out. "You weren't even listening when Delaney said she's having twins."

Summer's attention snapped over to Delaney. "What? Really?"

"No," Delaney said, laughing. Josie laughed too, and said, "But you practically just admitted you're distracted."

Summer sighed.

"Plus," Delaney said, her expression becoming serious, "you never talk about your mom. I mean, like, ever. So it's weird that you were thinking about her."

Well, that just slipped out.

"I know. I think it's because I'm about to give birth."

"Lies," Josie said. "You've never mentioned her before when you're about to give birth. What's really going on?"

"It's nothing."

"Lies!" Josie said again.

"Stop sounding so gleeful," Summer said. "I'm just stressed, okay?"

Tears threatened again, rising pressure against a closed door.

Delaney gripped Josie's arm. "She's upset. She's going to cry," she whispered.

It was as if someone had turned the doorknob and flung that door open. Summer couldn't contain the tears, and she found herself wailing, her forehead on the table.

"It'll be okay," Delaney said, over and over, while Josie rubbed Summer's back.

Even though she was steeped in emotion, Summer didn't miss the silent conversation going on between her friends. They were worried—understandably so. She knew they meant well, but neither of them had the mental space to take care of her right now. She had to take care of herself, just as she had always done.

Summer cried all the way home after Happy Hour, purging herself before the kids attacked her as she walked through the door. She would walk in, and Derek would be there, dueling with the boys, swords slashing through the air and Hannah strapped to Derek's back like a little Yoda. Sarah would be sitting on the couch with a book, undoubtedly rolling her eyes at the shenanigans, acting as the formal timekeeper as bath time approached.

Derek had become Summer's buoy during junior year of high school, when they were seventeen. As Willow's alcohol threatened to drown Summer, Summer clung to Derek, the nerdy leader of the chess club, with the kind of desperation (disguised as devotion) that would have made even Josie blush.

Not that he minded.

They met on the second Monday of that school year. Summer, seeking an excuse to stay at school rather than going home to Willow, decided to join the chess club. She didn't know how to play, but she could learn. Eyes downcast and feet shuffling, she made her way into the activities room and sat at the table closest to the door.

Derek approached her cautiously, like a person would approach a rattlesnake. He introduced himself.

"I don't know how to play chess," she blurted out, and he laughed.

"No offense, but I didn't peg you for a chess player. Why are you here, then?"

"Just wanted something to do," she said, but what she was really thinking was that she wanted to stay away from home for as long as possible.

"Okay," he said slowly, and then he smiled. "I'll—I mean, we'll—teach you."

His grin, toothy and spontaneous, had her smiling back. Just like that, they became friends.

The memory of their first encounter bolstered Summer's mood as she arrived home after Happy Hour. When she opened the front door, the scene was pretty close to how she'd imagined it, only Hannah was running around from one brother to the other with a makeshift sword (was that a broken stick, or a piece of PVC pipe?), shouting, "Take that!" on repeat.

Derek was on the couch next to Sarah, engrossed in his own book. He looked up at her and smiled.

"How was it?"

She wanted to say so many things to him, in that moment. She wanted to say that Happy Hour was okay, but she'd really wanted to be home with him. She wanted to say that he was the one person she loved more than anything, and together they could get through Luke's illness. She wanted to say that she was scared, scared to lose her perfect little boy.

But instead of saying any of those things, she just smiled back.

"It was good," she said. "I'm glad to be home."

Sometimes she felt like he could read her mind. He didn't question her, but he stood up, took her hand, and pulled her close so they were standing side by side. He kissed the side of her head.

"I'm glad you're home, too," he said.

She leaned against him, feeling his stubble against the side of her forehead, inhaling his aftershave, absorbing his warmth. Sarah broke the spell when she said to her brothers, "It's bath time, you inferior beings."

To a chorus of groans, Summer herded the kids around for their nightly clean-up. Nate didn't make it more than a few seconds before putting a pair of underwear on his head. Luke, of course, stopped to play with a remote control car someone had left out.

Sarah directed Hannah in cleaning up her blocks, and Derek sang some cleaning song he'd made up. Summer secretly wished he'd stop singing, but bit her lip to keep from saying so. The doorbell rang, and with all the other noise, Summer almost didn't register the sound.

"Expecting someone?" Derek said. When she shook her head, he said, "Probably a salesman. Let's have the kids answer the door."

Chuckling, the two of them walked to the door together. Summer pulled it open, and the world tilted when she saw who stood on the other side.

"Hello, Summer. You look exhausted."

Her mother. Willow. Standing on her doorstep after more than a decade and a half of silence. No warning bells, no tingly sixth sense, nothing. Summer felt completely caught off guard, totally unprepared for this interruption in her life. How did the woman even fathom she'd be welcome here?

By now, the kids had stopped what they were doing, and, happily distracted from their clean-up, they crowded around in the hallway behind her.

So the first reaction that came to mind—slamming the door in Willow's face—probably was not the best choice.

"Hello, Willow. What a surprise."

Willow managed to force a hurt expression onto her face. "You're not going to call me Mom?"

Derek looked back and forth between the two women, his expression so quizzical Summer almost wanted to laugh. Instead, she inhaled loudly. He grabbed her upper arm. Having kept quiet for their maximum of one minute, the kids began pelting their parents with questions.

"Who is it?" Nate wanted to know.

"Is it a Bible thumper?" Luke yelled.

"Thumper, thumper, thumper," Hannah sang.

Sarah had come up behind them. "From the looks of it," she said, "I'd say this is—"

"Kids, this is Willow," Summer said.

Willow arched a painted-on eyebrow at her, and added: "Your grandmother."

ACKNOWLEDGMENTS

As always, I owe a huge debt of gratitude to my husband for never complaining about my relationship with my computer as I write and edit and rewrite and re-edit early each morning and late each evening, and for not getting annoyed when I have to ask (countless times) what just happened on our favorite TV show because I'm working while watching.

And a big thank you to the eagle-eyed people who read and helped with this story: Mom, Desirae and Vanessa, and to Donna Rich, proofreader extraordinaire.

Also, huge thanks to Andrew and Rebecca at Design for Writers for bringing my vision to life with the brilliant cover design.

ABOUT THE AUTHOR

Hilary Dartt loves great adventures, whether she's writing, reading, or living them. The author of nine women's fiction novels, Hilary lives in Arizona's high desert with her husband, their three children, her Weimaraner and running partner, Leia, a failed barn cat, and a flock of chickens. She loves camping, exploring in the Jeep, and dance parties with her kids. Learn more at www.hilarydartt.com

www.ingramcontent.com/pod-product-compliance
Lightning Source LLC
Chambersburg PA
CBHW050338190726
48284CB00007BB/2059